Only a Kiss

"My lord," May whispered as he leaned forward, closing the gap between them. The pure scent of him left her senses reeling.

Radford peeled off a glove. The rough pad of his thumb caressed her lower lip. She gasped, unable to catch her breath. Her mind could barely form a protest before his head dipped down and his lips captured hers.

At first, shock paralyzed her. She couldn't have pulled away even if she had wanted to. Then a deep heat rose up from low in her belly, melting her resolve . . . washing away any warring thoughts. She pressed her hand against his chest, thrilling in the raw sensations a kiss—naught but a simple kiss—could conjure in her.

The Marriage List

Dorothy McFalls

A SIGNET BOOK

SIGNET
Published by New American Library, a division of
Penguin Group (USA) Inc., 375 Hudson Street,
New York, New York 10014, USA
Penguin Group (Canada), 10 Alcorn Avenue, Toronto,
Ontario M4V 3B2, Canada (a division of Pearson Penguin Canada Inc.)
Penguin Books Ltd., 80 Strand, London WC2R 0RL, England
Penguin Ireland, 25 St. Stephen's Green, Dublin 2,
Ireland (a division of Penguin Books Ltd.)
Penguin Group (Australia), 250 Camberwell Road, Camberwell, Victoria 3124,
Australia (a division of Pearson Australia Group Pty. Ltd.)
Penguin Books India Pvt. Ltd., 11 Community Centre, Panchsheel Park,
New Delhi - 110, 017, India
Penguin Group (NZ), cnr Airborne and Rosedale Roads, Albany,
Auckland 1310, New Zealand (a division of Pearson New Zealand Ltd.)
Penguin Books (South Africa) (Pty.) Ltd., 24 Sturdee Avenue,
Rosebank, Johannesburg 2196, South Africa

Penguin Books Ltd., Registered Offices:
80 Strand, London WC2R 0RL, England

First published by Signet, an imprint of New American Library,
a division of Penguin Group (USA) Inc.

First Printing, May 2005
10 9 8 7 6 5 4 3 2 1

Printed in the United States of America

Chapter One

Bath, England, 1813

Radford, the fourth Viscount Evers, dismissed Bannor, his irritatingly efficient man-of-affairs, and eased his aching foot onto his study's massive tiger maple desktop. The wretched appendage throbbed like the devil all the way to the tips of his toes whenever the weather turned soggy. Which meant in dreary, sodden England his foot pained him nearly all the time. And the unrelenting patter of rain against the windowpane promised nothing but misery for the next several hours.

A year, three months, and twenty-five days had passed since his foot, his leg, and part of his chest had been crushed under the weight of his horse on the Peninsula. The days ticked by like the second hand on his father's weighty pocket watch he'd begun to twirl between his fingers.

"Taking this man-of-leisure lifestyle a little far, eh, Evers?" Lord Nathan Wynter intruded on Radford's self-loathing without the decency of an invitation. In fact, Wynter, Radford's fair-haired boyhood friend, the second son of the esteemed Marquess of Portfry, had burst into the study without even giving the Longbranch House's stoic butler the opportunity to deny him entrance.

Having awakened in a particularly aggravated mood,

Radford had given his butler very specific instructions to turn all visitors away . . . especially Wynter.

For the past several days he'd shied away from prolonged visits with his friends. Wynter's presence served as an agonizing reminder of the healthy man he was before that cursed Frog murdered his horse out from under him in the middle of that miserable Battle of Salamanca. Not a day passed when he didn't long to turn back time and live as he once had—to savor the kind of reckless living Wynter freely enjoyed.

Days like today he felt as if he was nothing more than his injuries. Trapped.

His friend laughed, with ruddy cheeks brightening as he turned a deaf ear to Radford's vile curses and most ungrateful attempts to turn him away. There was no hope for it. Radford's foul mood only evoked a cheerier Wynter.

"Missed you at the Pump Room this morning." Wynter dropped into a heavily cushioned chair near the fireplace and plucked at the finely laced doilies covering the seat's wide arms.

A flare of anger surged in Radford's chest. "I've no interest in parading my lame leg around in public anymore. And those foul waters aren't doing a bloody thing." He folded his arms like a disobedient child and lifted his gaze to the ceiling. The blasted plaster needed repair.

"That tedious ritual of taking the waters is supposed to speed your recovery, Evers. But I had thought there might be another allure. A certain Lady Lillian Newbury noticed your absence. Her sunny smile faded to a petulant pout when she saw I was making the rounds alone." Wynter shivered dramatically. "Damaged my ego, she did."

Radford grimaced. Lady Lillian paid far too much interest in his recovery. Lovely as a spring flower, she followed him around the Bath events with the most piteous look clouding her crystal blue eyes.

He had no use for pity, especially not from a mere slip of a woman. Of course he'd no option in light of his recent revelation but to play the grateful courtier to her demure interests.

He'd do well to remember that damaged specimens such as himself weren't the choicest morsels on the marriage block.

Wynter didn't seem to mind Radford's brooding silence. His lips twitched while a wry look of amusement danced in his eyes. An outsider might say Wynter was on the verge of laughing at his friend. If he dared, Radford would boot him out on his ear. But he knew Wynter well enough to banish the thought. He trusted his friend as fiercely as Wynter trusted him.

"Since you seem to have planted yourself in my study, you might as well make yourself useful." Radford dashed a glance toward the liquor cabinet.

That was all the encouragement Wynter needed. He wasted no time in pouring two glasses of Radford's finest claret.

"Now tell me, Evers, what the devil has gotten into you today? You're a hundred score ruder than usual." Wynter sipped his claret and that look of amusement spread from his eyes to fill a good-natured grin. Only a longtime friend would know Wynter planned to stand his ground and twist a confession from Radford's lips.

Radford steepled his fingers and frowned. He'd learned on the Peninsula the hard way that some battles were not worth fighting.

"Mother arrived last night."

"Ah." Wynter leaned back in his chair and lazily propped one leg over the other.

"She's reminded me how close I came to facing my own mortality. Reminded me how I was carried home on a litter, insensible, and how the local vicar had been called upon to perform last rites no less than three times." He loathed the note of bitterness in his voice. Bitterness was below him, below the proud line of heroes he'd been born into.

"I suppose your loving mamma had a reason for dredging up that unhappy time from this past year?"

Radford nodded and then drained his glass. "She's reached the conclusion I myself have refused to face."

"Good Lord." Wynter took a deep sip of his own drink. "This sounds serious."

"It is serious. I have a responsibility to my family and my title that has been long neglected. In short, it is past time I get myself a wife and start producing heirs."

The very thought of tying himself to a flitting, muslin-draped, empty-headed lady for the rest of his days turned his stomach.

"In all my experience," Radford said, "I've never known a woman to tax her silly mind long enough to think of anything beyond fashion, gossip, and the financial security only a man can provide."

"Gad, Evers, marriage can't be as bad as all that. We're talking about finding you a gently trained lady, not some harridan."

Radford sighed. Wynter was right. "I suppose it can't be worse than picking through the nags at Tattersall's to find a truly superior piece of horseflesh."

A blond brow rose. "Finding a wife isn't like purchasing a new mare for your breeding program."

"And why not? It *is* simply a breeding program I am looking to begin, is it not? Besides, what in blazes makes you an expert? You're blissfully unattached . . . with no plans to tie yourself up in the foreseeable future."

"True, true, I do try to avoid the curse of such an attachment," Wynter admitted with a lazy wave. "But a lady, Evers. Their natures are more sensitive than even your highest-strung Arabian. And ten times more unpredictable."

"Bah! I wish to make a list of qualities I should consider—a marriage list, I suppose. Make yourself useful for a change. Play the part of secretary."

"I don't know about this—" Wynter muttered.

"Just fetch a pen and a scrap of foolscap. I feel a burst of inspiration emerging."

"Oh please do stop fidgeting, Iona." The generally fearless May Sheffers thought her rebuke rang hollow even to her own ears. Especially when her heart was thumping in her throat. It took all her resolve not to pull out her lace handkerchief and tug it to bits, her nerves were so overset.

This is truly the only way.

The writ of eviction had arrived in the morning post. Luckily, May had caught sight of the letter and whisked the offensive missive from her ailing Aunt Winnie's frail fingers. The dear woman, who'd nurtured May from her fourth year forward, didn't need to know of the heartless treatment that wiry Mr. Bannor sought to bear upon them. Imagine, being tossed out of their home of the past two years like an unwanted pair of worn boots. She'd do anything to protect Aunt Winnie from having to worry about something as horrid as that.

May had spent the past month trying to solve the problem. She'd petitioned Mr. Bannor on several occasions to plead her case, only to find her explanations and promises of payment falling on ears made of stone. And that, along with the finality the writ of eviction presented, had forced May to take this outrageous course of action.

She had no other choice but appeal to the man who paid Mr. Bannor's salary, the owner of the small cottage she and Aunt Winnie currently rented. That was why she'd borrowed Iona's family carriage and was presently on her way to pay a call on the baffling Viscount Evers.

May could only pray Evers would sympathize with her plight.

"It's not as if we deliberately failed to pay the rent these past three months," May said sharply as the carriage swayed up Sion Hill toward their destination. Working up her ire helped sooth her jumpy nerves. "I never asked for Papa's money to be tied up by the courts. He's not dead! Neither is Mamma! Uncle Sires has gone too far. Trying to declare them dead just because he hadn't heard a word from them for the past seven years, indeed. I remember a time when eight years passed between correspondences. They are busy with their investigations, Iona. Not dead."

"Yes, May," Iona said in her proper tone that always grew more subdued, more silent whenever May lapsed into one of her loud outbursts. "I am certain you are correct. But paying a visit on a gentleman and a bachelor? We don't even have a male escort, May. I wish you had allowed me to let my father handle this matter for you. Surely this action steps far beyond the bounds of—"

"Lady Iona Newbury. Do you or do you not still subscribe to the Mary Wollstonecraft school of thought?"

"I do. But—"

"And where does the indomitable Miss Wollstonecraft endorse handing our problems over to a man simply because we were born women?"

At that very moment, Iona's family carriage pulled to an abrupt stop, sending May's heart into another flutter of nervous activity. She fiddled a moment with her russet curls made impossibly unruly by the drenching weather. Her peacock blue walking dress, last year's muslin and design, was slightly faded, but neatly pressed. Her oilskin cape had a small rip in the shoulder.

May sighed. All and all, she looked her usual shabby self.

The carriage driver opened the door and held a large umbrella for the two women to huddle under as they walked along the flower-lined path up to the imposing Longbranch House entrance.

A pair of growling marble tigers stood guard on each side of the double doors. May swallowed a lump of anxiety before boldly knocking. When no one immediately opened the door, she was ready to breathe a sigh of relief and convince herself that the thoughtless Viscount Evers had fled to London or his country estate.

He hadn't taken the waters that morning. Iona's younger sister, Lady Lillian, had returned from the Pump Room in a sour mood after lingering far longer than either Iona or May in hopes he might appear.

He could have left Bath. Fashionable bachelors seldom

lingered in a city that was turning into a haven for the elderly and the chronically dull.

The door opened a crack just as the women turned to leave.

"Yes?" A long-faced butler drawled. He frowned down his nose at the two ladies while they shivered in the damp air. Despite all that was courteous, he appeared dead set against allowing either woman the opportunity to seek refuge inside.

His cold demeanor didn't dissuade May from her set path. It wasn't as if this was her first time facing down an uppity servant. Three weeks out of every year, May and Aunt Winnie visited her uncle Sires at his estate, Redfield Abbey, in Wiltshire. And for those three dreadful weeks, the entire household of servants seemed to sneer down their noses and sniff in indignation whenever finding themselves in May's service. And never once did their disapproval overset her nerves.

Neither would this impertinent butler blocking the entrance to Viscount Evers' home. She narrowed her gaze and thrust Iona's and her own card into the butler's gloved hand. "I demand to see the viscount." A cruel smile curled her lips when he refused to budge. "I will stand out on this stoop and make a nuisance of myself in front of his neighbors if you dare deny me."

The butler grumbled something about having his head served on a platter before throwing open the doors. He took their cloaks, ushered the two women into a cozy parlor just off the grand pink marble entranceway, and then ambled off, still shaking his head and mumbling.

"The viscount won't agree to see us," Iona said as she flounced into a petite chair. "It wouldn't be proper."

"I believe you are correct." May left the warmth of the dainty parlor and followed the path the butler had taken. Iona, not one to ever be left behind, raised her skirts and ran with a hoyden's charm to catch up.

"Well, send them away," an angry male voice carried through the empty hall.

May couldn't make out the butler's reply, but she could guess he was doing a valiant job pleading her case from the shouted exclamation that followed the short silence.

"Take up residence? That is ridiculous, Jeffers. I told you not to disturb me and here you are disturbing me yet again. Go away."

"He sounds like he's in a temper," Iona whispered.

"Naught but male bluster," May said, praying she was right. She held her breath and pushed open the closed door, having determined that the source of the angry voice resided within. Without waiting for a by-your-leave, she took Iona's hand in her own and marched into the leather-appointed study with her head held high, a solid army front.

"Pardon me for intruding," she said in the haughtiest tone she could muster, "but I must demand a word with you, my lord. It concerns a matter of importance that simply cannot be put off for another day."

Her sharp gaze landed on the viscount, lounging like a man who hadn't a care in the world with his booted foot propped on his lovely desk. He was a handsome devil.

Though they'd never been properly introduced, she'd seen him several times when she accompanied her aunt to the Pump Room. While Winnie leaned heavily on her arm as they took a turn around the room, nodding at familiar faces, May had caught her gaze straying more than once to the raven-haired gentleman with those arresting jade-colored eyes. He rarely stopped to converse with anyone.

She had watched as he'd stubbornly struggled to hide a severe limp and make his way around the Pump Room without the aid of a cane. Lord Nathan Wynter always accompanied the viscount, smiling and nodding to the young ladies while swinging the unused cane.

"Ladies." Lord Nathan leapt to his feet, nearly knocking over the small writing desk beside which he was sitting. He sketched a bow, a deep blush rising to his cheeks. May watched with interest as he hastily pushed a piece of foolscap into his pocket.

She wasn't surprised to find him here in the viscount's study. Bath was awash with gossip and speculation centering on Viscount Evers and how he begrudgingly accepted the support of his loyal friend Lord Nathan. One couldn't sit down in a tearoom without being bombarded with stories of how Evers received his injuries in the heat of a heroic battle and how he'd since become just a shadow of the bright young rogue he used to be.

"Lady Iona Newbury and Miss Margaret Sheffers, my lord," the butler announced in a loud voice, as if he'd orchestrated May and Iona's surprise appearance.

"Indeed," Viscount Evers drawled. His dark brows rose at least an inch. He studied the women several moments before lowering his foot from his desk. His jaw tightened as his foot dropped to the floor, the only hint his movement might have pained him.

May felt only the briefest frisson of guilt.

After all, *he* was responsible for his man-of-affairs, Mr. Bannor. And Bannor was the villain threatening to evict May and her dear aunt Winnie from their home—no doubt with the viscount's blessing.

Evers fastened a hardened gaze on May as he rose from his chair. The pressure of his scrutiny wrecked havoc on her confidence until she noticed the reason for his unbreakable concentration. His hand stayed in contact with the desktop while he walked stiffly out from behind his artificial throne.

This wasn't a fearful force more powerful than the king. He was just a man fashioned, like her, from flesh and blood.

"Ladies." He gave a shallow bow. With a languid sweep of his perfectly manicured hand, he motioned to a small sofa by the fire grate. "Please sit and share this matter of business so urgent it supercedes all rules of propriety."

He smiled, flashing his teeth in a wholly unnecessarily aggressive move. The nerve of him, handing her not only a frosty set-down but also displaying a most egregious snarl. May sucked in a breath and opened her mouth to return sharp words of her own, only her words wouldn't be couched in feigned politeness.

But alas, she needed to charm the man—not prick his nerves. With a sweet smile that was anything but real, May obediently perched on the edge of the sofa he'd indicated. Iona crowded next to her. Like a nervous bird, her friend shivered, which did nothing to bolster her own wearying nerves.

"Please fetch a pot of tea," Viscount Evers said quietly to the butler. Curiously, Wynter responded to the request with a nod and a playful wink.

What in Heaven was going on? Never had May felt more like she'd stumbled into a den of lions. Perhaps the rules of propriety, deeming it unseemly for a woman to visit a bachelor in his home, were based on some very real danger. She felt her smile strain.

"Gentlemen, I sincerely appreciate your taking the time to receive us after we've practically stormed the gates."

"Practically?" The viscount's raven eyebrows jutted up again. The one word nearly exploded with sarcasm.

"Well, yes. I do apologize for my behavior. Lady Iona is only here because I wouldn't allow her to change my mind about seeing you, and she insisted I not make this visit alone." May swallowed her pride and kept her painful grin firmly in place. "I wouldn't have dreamed of disturbing you in this manner if there was any other way. . . ."

His expression glowed with interest. He leaned against his desk and cocked his head. The fabric of his buff-colored superfine suit coat strained across his chest's wide expanse.

Oh my. She really shouldn't notice such things. She could be certain he wasn't noticing anything alluring about her person.

No man ever had.

She was worse than plain. Uncle Sires had judged her an ugly duckling with no hope of ever blooming into a swan. Aunt Winnie had protested the charge, but given May's ruddy hair, olive-tinged complexion, and rather stout shape, the dear woman didn't have much material to work with. *She has a heart of gold,* Winnie had finally concluded.

And no chance for attracting a husband. Uncle Sires' biting words had been spoken six years ago when May was barely eighteen and had excitedly inquired about her come-out. They still held power over her today. A heated blush rose up her neck.

She'd no right to look longingly upon a man as handsome as the Viscount Evers. No right at all. For all she knew, his stomach was churning from being forced to gaze upon a full-grown duck as unappealing as her.

His lightly arched brows furrowed and his glare grew impossibly hard. "If there was any other way . . . ?" he asked.

The question caught May off guard. What was he asking? Any other way, what? A growing blush stung her cheeks as she realized her overlong stare had interrupted her own explanation, midthought. His question must have merely been an attempt to prod her into talking and to bring her to the point.

"My aunt and I rent number twelve Sydney Place," she said.

His expression was as empty as a clear sky.

"You own the property," she prompted.

"Do I?"

For a moment May had a nervous feeling that she'd made a terrible mistake, that she'd intruded into the wrong man's home. "Mr. Bannor is your man-of-affairs, is he not?" she asked with a crisp tone.

"He is. He handles my assortment of properties and investments." Something dark and quite wicked crossed his brows. "Has Bannor offended you in some way, Miss Sheffers?"

May could not describe the relief that surged through her veins. "Indeed he has, my lord."

She peeled the writ of eviction from the silk reticule that matched her gown and held it out for him to take. "He has sent this. Luckily, I opened the letter before my aunt Winnie had a chance to read it. She's in poor health. Her heart. It was her ailing health that brought us to Bath from London, I'll have you know. A shock such as this would only worsen her condition."

"Indeed?" he drawled.

He took a moment then to read Bannor's letter. May held her breath as she counted the slow passage of seconds.

"The writ claims you and your aunt have failed to pay rent for the past three months," he said after more than two minutes of breathless silence. May was convinced she'd turned blue. "Is this true?"

"Yes, but—"

Evers cut her off with a staying hand. "This is a matter for Bannor, miss. I have no interest in squabbles of this sort. I don't interfere with my man-of-affair's occupation." His tone nearly coated the room with frost.

"Perhaps we could but listen to the women, Evers?" Wynter said, his gentle smile powerful enough to sway even the most stubborn of goats. "Surely, the task we were completing could only benefit from the experience?"

The viscount cast his friend a sidelong look. "No." He took several stiff steps, closing the distance between him and May. "We shall change the subject."

The long-nosed butler interrupted then with a tea tray. Steam rose from the finely handpainted blue pot. An intricate scene depicting several maidens crossing an oriental bridge came to life on the porcelain. May couldn't help but wonder at the small fortune the viscount must have paid for the tea service as she silently poured the tea into the cups.

She took a long sip, a bounty of flavors filling her mouth. Her aunt's watery brew tasted like dirty hot water in comparison.

"A change of topics, then?" Wynter prompted after taking a sip of his tea as well. Mischief sparkled in his eyes.

May strangled the teacup's handle with a small measure of alarm. Perhaps the men were planning to make sport of the two foolish maidens like a scene out of a children's fable after all.

"I would rather—" she started.

At that very moment Viscount Evers blurted, "How old are you, Miss Sheffers?" He looked serious, too serious.

"Four-and-twenty. Now if you would please but listen."

"Is that on the shelf?" Evers turned and asked Wynter.

At least Wynter had the honor to drop his mouth open with embarrassment. "I don't believe so," he said, wincing. "Not quite."

"And horses, Miss Sheffers? What are your thoughts on them?"

The question was utter nonsense. Had the viscount's war injuries addled his mind? "I—I don't know, my lord. I've lived my entire life in London and don't know much about the creatures. They are rather *large* . . . imposing, I suppose."

He merely shrugged. "And you, Lady Iona? How old are you?"

Iona, bless her, tilted her chin up like a true lady. "I am one-and-twenty, my lord, and by no means on the shelf. Neither is Miss Sheffers. My own mamma didn't marry until she was five-and-twenty, having to wait for my papa to come to his good senses."

Wynter tossed back his head and laughed boldly. "Very good, my lady."

The behavior of the two men, as if they shared a private jest at hers and Iona's expense, went beyond improper. Their idea of humor was just too much to bear. May felt at a loss. What should she do? Salvaging this confrontation with the viscount was clearly beyond hope. She sprang to her feet. Coming to his home was a mistake. A blot on her normally logical mind.

"My lords"—she swept the room with her most menacing glare—"since you are unwilling to listen to my plight and help a gentlewoman in need, I believe I have no choice but to bring this farce to an end. Good day."

She snatched up Iona by the wrist and bolted from the room.

"It was truly a pleasure," Iona had the grace to call as they rushed out into the drizzly rains without the protection of their cloaks and worse . . . without having accomplished anything beyond making complete and utter fools of themselves.

"A pleasure, you say? Viscount Evers can take his cursed home with all its cursed expensive handpainted fineries and go straight to the devil for all I care!"

Chapter Two

"Did Miss Sheffers just wish you to the devil?"

Wynter's wide gaze and gaping mouth went beyond shocked. The man appeared utterly flabbergasted, a look Radford had never associated with his even-keeled friend.

"I believe she did." A smile creased the corners of Radford's lips. He eased down onto the sofa the women had vacated. Three half-filled round teacups stared up at him from the side table next to him. The fourth little cup in the set, missing. "I believe she also pilfered from my fine china."

Miss Margaret Sheffers.

Before an hour ago, he hadn't the slightest clue that the lady existed, let alone that she resided on one of his properties. She was the kind of woman he generally overlooked. Gently shabby, small, with not one extraordinary feature to attract a man save for a pair of unusually vivid violet eyes—before today he'd guess such a woman would make a fine lady's companion or governess, fading into the draperies. She was of so little import her initial burst into the room had his gaze shifting to the alluring Lady Iona, not her. So just how did such a woman manage to leave him with his heart throbbing in his chest?

"The marriage list we've just completed," Radford said and thrust out his hand. "I believe you stuffed it in your pocket."

Wynter eyed Radford for several moments before pulling the crumpled piece of foolscap from his pants pocket and dropping it into Radford's palm. "What in blazes was that all about, Evers?" The note of anger was unmistakable . . . and completely a surprise.

"What was what?" Radford asked somewhat absently. He struggled to his feet so he could pace like a normal man while he reviewed the list of qualities he'd demand in a wife.

"Your damned behavior, is what. I've never witnessed a ruder display. Is this how you plan to woo a wife? If you do, you had better start preparing for a long bachelorhood."

"I just wished to ascertain their qualifications." No vagaries on his list, nothing left to chance.

"Qualifications, Evers? This isn't Tattersal's, where you can pry open their mouths and peek inside. You have to use your charm. Before you bought that bloody commission, all you had to do was wink and every damned woman in sight would swoon."

"That man no longer exists. For one thing, I am no longer a prime pick. Look at me! I'm a cripple, naught but half a man."

Wynter sighed, long and loud. "It's your acid tongue, not your injury that scares women."

Radford continued to pace, feeling his limp grow more pronounced. The pain in his foot returned with a vengeance.

How was it that for the past half hour he'd been free of the searing pain? Something about pricking the anger of a plain, utterly forgettable faded bloom had completely erased the state of his injured body from his mind.

"Perhaps a wife is exactly what I need."

"Bloody funny way of going about finding one." Wynter helped himself to a second serving of claret. He held up the decanter, offering to pour a glass for Radford.

Still pacing with his jerky movement of half dragging his lame leg, Radford waved Wynter away. "Not now," he grumbled. He needed to think. To plan.

Just as on the Peninsula, everything lived and died by the

force of strategy. No matter what Wynter said about the necessity of charming a woman, Radford knew there was more to this chase for a wife than that. He'd seen the fleeting glances the society ladies sent his way, their sidelong looks literally twitching with a blend of fear and pity.

Miss Sheffers' mystically deep violet eyes had sparked with anger, not pity.

Long gone were the days where every lady he met would stare up at his healthy physique with moon-eyed affection.

She hadn't been moon-eyed, but she'd appeared indifferent to his condition.

"Never mind my offending the woman, Wynter. She didn't meet even one marriageable criteria." Radford shook out the foolscap.

"Didn't she?"

Radford began to read from the list. "Number one, age. She needs to be young enough to be pliable, readily molded into my image of the perfect wife and viscountess for my estate. No younger than eighteen—I have absolutely no wish to bed a child—no older than one-and-twenty. Need I go on?"

"I see no problem as of yet," Wynter said with a shrug.

"Number two, appearance. She should be fair of complexion, like an angel smiling down from Heaven—I believe the poet in you added that last part. Her body should be sturdy, full enough to fill a man's hands, and possess wide hips—"

"Within reason," Wynter interjected.

"—to safely produce a brood of sons." Miss Sheffers' compact body, like a coiled spring, no doubt fit the second part of the description. The muslin gown hinted at the curves hidden underneath. But, alas, her unusual olive skin tone, angular features, and bright violet eyes gave her the look of part elf, part gypsy. A combination well suited for fairy tales and fantasies, but not the refined position of viscountess. "Again, need I continue?"

"I don't see why not." Wynter made himself comfortable

in the overstuffed chair by the fire, enjoying the claret as well as the dissection of this woman's shortcomings a little too much. Radford ground his jaw.

"Number three, disposition." His voice rose along with his aggravation. "Above all things, she should possess a gentle disposition. Behave properly. Be agreeable in all things."

"To be fair, Evers, circumstances forced her to act as she had. I'd say she handled herself very well, considering . . ." The reproach deepening the blue of Wynter's eyes didn't go unnoticed.

"Very well, we'll skip that one for now. Not that it matters." Radford drew a steadying breath. "Number four, family. Born to a respectable family of suitable rank and possessing a sizable dowry." He cast a pointed look across the room, daring Wynter to argue in support of Miss Sheffers' family, convinced her family name passed his friend's ears as meaninglessly as it had his own.

Wynter shrugged. "As for the dowry, I don't dare speculate. One can never assume the financial stability of another when so many live high on credit. But her family name stands on its own merit."

"Exactly." Radford stopped his pacing, uncertain. What did his friend mean, *stands on its own merit*? No matter. The last qualification was perhaps the most crucial, the one point he would never bend. "Number five, horses. She must"—the word underlined, twice—"possess a full knowledge and genuine affection of horses. I am planning to continue my breeding program whether or not I am able to ride again."

His doctors all agreed. They'd been blunt. He'd never be able to properly seat a horse or ride for prolonged periods. The heartless men might as well have taken up a knife and carved out his heart. Never ride again, his love, his life torn away as easily as that?

"My wife will share my love of horses. I will not give up my stables. I simply will not." He looked at the second piece of foolscap in his hand. He'd completely forgotten he still possessed it—Miss Sheffers' writ of eviction. Feeling nearly unhinged, Radford shouted his next words. "So you must agree. Miss Sheffers admitted it herself, if not in words in tone. She's deathly afraid of the beasts!"

Wynter started with a sudden jolt of confusion. "Miss Sheffers? I thought we were discussing the very eligible Lady Iona."

May avoided her aunt Winnie and made a straight path up the stairs to her chamber to smooth her unruly hair and change out of her damp gown. Her shivering hands, not from the rainy chill but from the fury still boiling inside her, drew her attention to the thin teacup still lodged between her fingers. Bright blue parasols and flowers danced around the outside of the perfectly rounded cup.

His teacup. In her rush to escape before angry words poured from her lips and shamed her, she made the horrible mistake of taking the teacup with her.

Your father's gypsy blood ruins you, makes you unruly, makes you as wild and impossible as him. Those bitter words, her uncle's, rang loudly in her head. He tried to beat the willfulness from her, ruling her with a heavy hand those three weeks out of the year when she was forced to endure living with him.

You're just a passionate child. Aunt Winnie, always trying everything she could to fill the void only the return of her mother or father could truly repair, would coddle May in her arms, humming a sweet tune while a much younger, painfully innocent May wept. *There is nothing wrong with passion.*

Yet there was. May learned under the heat of disapproving *tonnish* glares, wielded by some of the most imposing society matrons, to dampen her spirit, to fade—like her gowns—into something colorless, nearly transparent. She carried the crime of her father's birth with her everywhere. Not until her entrance into society did she understand the weight of the burden or the discouragement her uncle Sires felt when he looked upon her. Only after she came of age did her dreams of marrying a man who could love her as passionately as her father loved her mother disappear.

Her birth, her looks, her lack of fortune, and her very manner frightened eligible men away. Gradually, she and her aunt exchanged positions and May became the caretaker, a lady's companion. An honorable profession for a woman destined for spinsterhood.

In time, May grew accustomed to her role. She took pride in providing for Aunt Winnie in the same loving manner she'd been raised. There was no room in her life for a husband, not with the full-time responsibility of caring for her aunt, running the small household, and accompanying her to an exhausting string of teas, balls, exhibitions, and dinners.

As for a family—what woman didn't long for children? But her heart was full. She had the love of her aunt and of her friend, Iona. And that was enough. It would be greedy to ask for more.

The only need in her life was time. She fingered Viscount Evers' teacup, recalling just how he'd humiliated her. *I have no interest in squabbles of this sort,* he'd said, belittling the amount of pride May had had to swallow in order to enter his home like a beggar. He'd refused out-of-hand to hear how she'd already forced down a whole pantry full of pride when she'd petitioned her uncle for funds after the fretful Mr. Thomas, the local banker, explained how the courts had seized her parents' money.

Two and a half months had already passed, and still no word or reply from her uncle.

If it were just May's fate in question, she'd understand his disinterest. But Aunt Winnie was Uncle Sires' eldest sister. He always appeared in awe of Winnie and, even, faintly wary of her opinion. Absent siblings of her own, May had nothing to compare it with. Yet she assumed his behavior a form of brotherly affection.

So why turn his back on Winnie now, when she needed him most?

She and her aunt were caught between the indifference of

two men—that's why. May chewed her bottom lip, uncomfortable with the feeling of being beholden to any man. She carefully placed the viscount's stray teacup on her dressing table next to her brush.

That silly teacup. What the viscount must think of her! She crossed the room to the velvet cord, thinking to call the housekeeper and ask her to return the cup posthaste. Her hand had just touched the cord when she heard a clamor rise below and the rumble of horses.

She peered out the tall floor-to-ceiling windows that looked out into the small front garden, the street, and the fashionable Sydney Gardens. A carriage, bearing an intricate golden crest emblazoned on the door, swayed as it stopped in front of their humble cottage.

May reached for her throat, uncertain of what to do.

What could it mean for *him* to come here? This was most unexpected. She rushed a brush through her hair, despairing at the stray curls already pulling free from the pins, a regular condition only worsened by the rainy weather.

There'd be no time to change her damp gown. Aunt Winnie would need assistance preparing for company.

May glanced out the window one last time and watched a liveried footman with a dark umbrella in hand open the carriage door with measured purpose. She stiffened her spine—this would just have to be endured—and set off downstairs in search of her aunt.

Chapter Three

The rains had died away, and the heavy clouds parted just enough to allow a sparkling ray of sunlight to pass through to the city. That moment, the first break in a storm, usually calmed May's heart. It was in that magical instant she felt closest to the mother and father who were as illusive as the sunlight.

Today, May could only spare a wistful glance to the sky from the parlor window. The storm, it seemed, hadn't truly passed but only moved inside.

Their guest paced the length of the parlor. Dressed in gray breeches with a long black coat fashioned from broadcloth, his heavy body filled the room. He hadn't arrived alone, either.

Uncle Sires, the eighth Earl of Redfield, had brought with him a stranger. Mr. Tumblestone, a finely dressed gentleman as portly as Aunt Winnie's lazy tomcat and nearly as old as her uncle, smiled fondly on May while he was presented to her. He took her hand in his and pressed his rather large set of lips to her gloved knuckles.

With introductions out of the way, family members inquired after, and tea sent for, Uncle Sires took to strolling about the parlor again while Mr. Tumblestone settled into a tapestry-covered seat. Aunt Winnie, panting from too much excitement, allowed May to assist her to her favorite chair near the fire.

Her uncle's sharp gaze missed nothing. His frown lengthened as he took notice of Winnie's weakened condition. Nothing appeared to please him, in fact. He paused to inspect a silver four-stemmed candleholder set on the mantel. He lifted the piece, turning it in his hand. The expensive wax candles had been burned down all the way to their nubs. Though the silver was polished, the cheaply made candleholder was dented from years of use in a string of households. He wiggled a stem. May held her breath, praying the brittle metal wouldn't snap under the force of his hand.

He sniffed—a haughty sound—and set the candleholder down. His roaming gaze surveyed the women while Portia, the housekeeper, carried in a tea tray piled with an assortment of sweetmeats, cookies, and toast.

"Thank you," May said with a kind smile. The unexpected guests had sent Portia into a flurry of activity in the kitchen. Uncle Sires' arrival, so near to the approaching dinner hour, made one wonder not only if he expected to be fed, but also if he expected to be housed for the night. And not just him.

There was that stranger, Mr. Tumblestone, with him.

"So this is the cottage you wrote to me about," Uncle Sires said, raking the room with his gaze.

The parlor had always felt cozy to May. Today, under the cloud of her uncle's glower, it merely felt impossibly small, inadequate.

"You wrote to your uncle?" Aunt Winnie inclined her head toward May. She sounded genuinely baffled. "Whyever didn't you tell me?" Winnie's surprise wasn't unfounded. May never wrote her uncle without her aunt's prodding.

"I didn't wish to worry you, Aunt Winnie," May said and then hesitated. Mr. Tumblestone had leaned forward in his chair—a chair conveniently positioned next to May's—and appeared far too keen on listening to what promised to be a painfully private family matter.

For once Uncle Sires seemed to approve of her reluctance. "I see my niece is quite the gardener. If I recall properly, she does have an uncommon flare with roses." He pointed to a small plot just outside the parlor window.

May had tried to encourage a collection of roses to climb an arbor in their tiny garden, allowing bushes of pale pink cabbage roses to intermingle with the white and pale yellow Albas. Her efforts created a tangle of vines heavy with blooms. The flowers were suitable for flower arrangements. They were not, not by any stretch of the imagination, a garden showpiece.

"Perhaps you would like to take a closer look." In typical Uncle Sires form, the request was presented like a royal command.

Mr. Tumblestone fidgeted nervously for a moment. Drawing his wide lips into a closemouthed smile, he directed the strange expression at May and then upon Aunt Winnie. "I think I would enjoy inspecting the blooms." His smile returned to May, and his watery gaze lingered on her body for several uncomfortable moments. "I am a great lover of beauty."

He stood then, gave Uncle Sires a knowing nod, and excused himself to go wander outside. May breathed a sigh of relief when the parlor door closed behind him. Something about his manner, like a man starving for sustenance, put her nerves on edge.

"Someone will explain," Aunt Winnie demanded. Though her heart might be growing weak, her resolve was as strong as ever. "Why would you have correspondences with Sires without my knowledge? And why, Sires, did you bring this man into my house?"

May rushed to her aunt's side. She crouched down beside the chair, positioning herself between her uncle and Winnie with the hopes of shielding her aunt from hearing anything too upsetting. Winnie placed her hand in May's. Her aging skin felt thinner than the finest muslin.

"I only meant to protect you," May said when Uncle Sires opened his mouth to speak. "You must understand that." May could not imagine a world without Aunt Winnie. She'd do anything to protect the sole person whose love persisted as a sunny constant in her life.

She turned to her uncle. His scowl deepened when their

eyes met. "There was no need for you to come all this way over a trifling," she said.

"Hush, May." Aunt Winnie's gentle voice belied the rebuke. She intended to be included in the discussion. The only clues of her aunt's budding exasperation were the light blotches of color appearing low on her throat. "Sires, you may speak."

"The child wrote to me asking for money." Very rarely did Uncle Sires use May's name. To him, regardless of her age she was forever *the child*, spoken with a healthy dose of sulfur.

"Is this true?" Aunt Winnie asked of May. "Did something happen to your parents' funds?"

"The child's parents are dead," Uncle Sires announced before May could think of how to explain the situation without worrying her aunt.

Winnie gasped at the horrible news and clutched May's hand.

"They are not dead," May said. Her voice sounded shrill like a petulant youth's. She cleared her throat. "They may not have written for many years, Uncle. Beyond that, there is no evidence that anything is amiss."

"The child understandably refuses to accept the truth. They were last seen entering a dangerous jungle in South America seven years and five months ago. In light of that and the painful fact no one since saw them leave, I petitioned the courts to dispense with the legal matter of declaring them dead."

Her aunt squeezed May's hand, pinching it—a subtle reminder for May to hold her temper.

"I do not understand, Sires," Winnie said. Her weary gaze hardened. "What does this have to do with May's request for money? Her parents' funds should still provide her with a sufficient income."

"Uncle Sires had the courts seize control of the money, Aunt." May could not keep the anger from her voice.

Nor could Winnie. "What is the meaning of this?"

"As you know the child's mother—"

"Our youngest sister, Viola," Winnie corrected.

"Yes, yes. Our grandmother's inheritance went solely into Viola's name. Absent a will, there are questions surrounding the inheritance. I have asked the courts to take control of the funds until the questions are resolved."

"And who, besides May, do you believe is entitled to Viola's fortune?"

"I am, of course. As head of this family, it is only right that I should control the purse strings. A romantic fool, our grandmother, to bestow a fortune to an errant granddaughter. Viola besmirched the family name by marrying that gypsy bastard against my wishes. What assurances do I have that this child won't act in the same manner? With the promise of a fortune, there is many a blackguard who'd woo the child into some scandalous marriage with false proclamations of love."

"May would never fall for such trickery." Aunt Winnie freed her hand from May's and rose. "She has a level head on her shoulders. She economizes with that money and has never sought to spend frivolously, unless for my benefit." She closed the distance between Sires and herself, approaching like an ancient dragon. Her careful steps lent her a rare grace. Winnie normally leaned heavily on a cane or May's arm. May knew well how it took all her aunt's concentration to walk unassisted.

She feared the exertion would prove too great a strain on Winnie's heart.

"Now, Winnie." Sires retreated a step. "I only have the family's best interests at heart—even the child's."

"Do you? And what did you intend her to do without access to her parents' money? Will you have her grovel for crumbs? She's a proud woman. She shouldn't have to beg."

"No, no. I would never allow that." Sires retreated another step.

"And what of me? What did you expect would happen to me without May's care? I have never possessed a fortune of my own. Will I too be forced to beg?"

Sires stepped back again only to find he'd reached a wall.

He sighed deeply and held his hands out in front of him, as if trying to hold Winnie back. "Listen, you know I would never hurt you. I miss you, in fact. I want you to come back to Redfield Abbey with me." His gaze traversed the room. "And I want you to move into my home here in Bath—with me tonight."

He had a house here in Bath? The bounder! They'd made no secret of the necessity to move from their London town house to Bath. Aunt Winnie had been more than forthcoming with him regarding her failing health. He knew and yet never offered to open up the family home to them?

May pinched her lips together and prayed for calm. Uncle Sires denied his own sister the luxury of his property out of hatred for May—and the sins of her father's bastard birth. A thousand times a bounder, he was.

"Please, Winnie. Let me see to your care." His voice slid as smooth as honey off his deceitful tongue. He lowered his hands, no longer trying to hold his sister back but lure her closer.

"But what is to become of May?" Aunt Winnie asked. She gave a nervous glance over her shoulder to where May stood, still half in shock.

"Why, she'll marry, of course."

"Marry? But she has no prospects, no suitors. She's not had the opportunity to pursue that avenue." Tears appeared in Aunt Winnie's eyes. Her button nose and round cheeks bloomed a bright red. "She's spent nearly every waking hour taking care of me. You worry she'll make a hasty marriage, and then you ask her to do just that?"

"But she must marry," he said as if May wasn't in the room or, possibly, too brainless to understand. "Look at her. She's nearly on the shelf. Before our foolish sister ran off with that crazed gypsy and abandoned her child into our care, she dreamed of the day her babe would marry. Besides, the child's too headstrong to sink gracefully into the background as you have done, dear Winnie. She needs a man with an iron will to care for her."

He gave a meaningful glance out the parlor window to where the graying Mr. Tumblestone was making a show of admiring May's vibrant yellow and pale pink roses.

May could see it in her uncle's eyes then. The man truly believed he was doing her a great kindness. He smiled as he spoke. "In fact, I have already taken it upon myself to select a suitable gentleman for precisely that task."

"He means to marry you off to a decrepit old man?" Lady Iona's ice blue eyes couldn't possibly open any wider.

"I don't believe he is decrepit." Though his skin appeared as fragile as Aunt Winnie's and twice as mottled with unusually shaped liver-colored moles, he moved with the energy of a man half his age.

May swallowed hard, remembering the intimate way Mr. Tumblestone leered at her upon his departure, his hungry gaze not reaching her eyes, his cod-shaped lips moistening. "He is most certainly old," May whispered.

Iona linked arms with May as they continued to promenade around the interior of the Pump Room, tilting their heads in greeting to acquaintances. Aunt Winnie sat on a cushioned bench near the grand fountain that circulated the sulfur waters prescribed by doctors as a curative for just about every ailment.

The water smelled sour, not much different than eggs left sitting in the sun for too long. Despite her aunt's constant persuasions, May refused to taste a sip.

Their morning schedule rarely varied. They'd arrive at the Pump Room at eight in the morning, early enough to avoid the thickest crowds, yet late enough to mingle with some of the most influential members of society, which included Iona and several of her unmarried sisters. Iona's family, led by the respected Duke of Newbury, were all the rage this season, being the highest ranking family to choose Bath over the more popular summer destinations of Brighton or Scotland.

Before anything else, May would first help her aunt to a comfortable bench and then fetch three glasses of the water, the generally prescribed number to drink a day. Winnie took her time sipping the foul liquid while speaking with friends from her youth. When she had drained the glasses, May would offer her arm as support and the two women would take a turn through the marble interior of the Pump Room, spending more time visiting with members of the *ton* than getting any sort of vigorous exercise.

This morning, when May offered her arm, Aunt Winnie had declined. She claimed she wished to save her energies for the evening's fancy ball at the Upper Rooms. May believed otherwise. Her uncle's surprise appearance had upset Winnie. She appeared paler than usual, her eyes hazy.

It was Aunt Winnie who'd suggested May stroll with Lady Iona in her stead. May accepted the suggestion gratefully, desperate for a private moment with her closest friend.

She related the whole story to Iona, including how she'd been too shocked to object, too shocked to do anything but promise to accompany her uncle and Mr. Tumblestone to chapel that afternoon and then stroll along Pulteney Street.

"You cannot agree to this marriage. It is barbaric." Iona's hold on May's arm tightened. Whenever matters became sticky, Iona would cling to the nearest female object. May rather appreciated the close contact.

"I don't have many options. Uncle Sires has made quite certain of that by taking my parents' money away. He did relent and agree to pay the past three months' rent to the viscount, claiming it was the only proper thing to do."

May had lain awake in bed the night before, trying to think of another course of action. Although overdue rents would be paid, Uncle Sires had been most adamant about not paying any future bills. A woman without a shilling to her name didn't have many options.

"I could seek a position as a lady's companion or governess if I can convince Aunt Winnie to go against her brother's wishes and provide me with a reference."

"Oh no, you mustn't do that!" Iona squeezed May's arm so tightly May's fingers turned numb. "You mustn't take a position or marry or do anything rash that will take you away from me! Perhaps Papa—"

A burgundy-smooth voice interrupted. "I beg your pardon, ladies."

Iona was the first to turn to greet the speaker. "My lord." A graceful smile froze on her lips. A deep red blush spread all the way up to the roots of her hair.

Disquieted by her friend's reaction, May turned around. "My lord," she gasped.

Viscount Evers looked as fierce as the devil, dressed in a high-collared black cut-away shortcoat. His cream vest wasn't fully buttoned, a common style among the wildest rakes. His tan trousers were loose-fitted, casual. His sharp features and jade-colored gaze bore down on her in a most oppressive manner. Why ever would he address her—here—in public? Would he call her out for yesterday's shocking behavior?

May took a step back, as if retreat could stave off trouble. It wasn't so much herself she was worried about. Her life was nothing—meaningless. Iona, dear precious, always proper Iona, would be in a world of trouble if her father, the duke, ever learned about their most improper unescorted visit to the viscount's home. "Please, my lord," May said, lowering her voice. She was prepared to play the part of withering female and eat a king's portion of humble pie to safeguard her friend's reputation.

She didn't get the chance.

As if trying to prove her uncle's belief that there was something innately unacceptable about her, her foot slipped. A small puddle of water spilt by some careless drinker made the marble floor under May's feet slick. Her foot shot out from under her and before she could catch herself, the toe of her slipper became entangled within the folds of her gown's long skirt. May pitched forward and fully expected to humiliate herself in front of the utterly grim Viscount Evers.

Time slowed. She watched as he stepped forward and spread his arms like a lover greeting some long-lost key to his heart. He caught her, his gloved hands curling delightfully around her shoulders in an attempt to save her.

He teetered, his fingers digging into her skin as he struggled to gain his faltering balance. His injured leg could barely support his own weight much less hold up against a clumsy cow such as herself. How nobly stupid of him to rush to her rescue.

Not until that moment did May realize he wasn't very tall. He was much taller than most women, yes. But he didn't tower over her like some men, which at the moment was probably a very good thing. Many a time her aunt had swayed, just as the viscount swayed now—a fall imminent. She had never allowed her aunt to fall, and since the viscount was so doggedly determined to save her, May planted her feet and used her strength to help steady him.

"Bloody hell." His jade gaze simmered with anger once they had both found a solid footing. He released her arms and took a hasty step backward. His jaw tightened as he gritted his teeth and fought gravity's pull on his injured leg.

May refused to be shocked by the foul language he'd muttered only loudly enough for her hearing. Her aunt had been known to spew far worse after such a close call. Infirmities had to be terribly humbling.

That's not to say she didn't feel a slight burning in her cheeks. She had so much to be embarrassed about—the near public stumble brought the room's gazes upon her. A man's cursing couldn't possibly aggravate her already mortified state.

"I say." Lord Nathan Wynter advanced, white-faced, from where he had stood chatting with Lady Lillian, Iona's very fair, very beautiful younger sister, and her doting mamma. He darted a distrustful eye in May's direction. "Are you quite well, Evers? Shall I summon a sedan chair to carry you home?" He waved the cane in his hand, trying in a most obvious manner to get Viscount Evers to take the prop.

"Get that away from me, Wynter," the viscount forced from behind clenched teeth.

May stiffened and so did Viscount Evers—visibly so. Lord Nathan's rush to assistance only rubbed salt into a prideful man's wounds.

A crowd was beginning to form. Questions poured out from helpful friends and the merely curious-minded. May's cheeks felt fire-branded, singed beyond repair. She could feel the viscount's humiliation as if it were her own.

This was her fault. Grace and elegance, such important traits for a proper lady, were foreign elements in her limbs. Hadn't her uncle, her governess, and many of the *ton*'s matrons declared it to be so?

May held up her hands to quiet the crowd to a dull murmur. "I must thank you, my lord," she said loudly enough for everyone nearby to hear. "My careless ankles are forever putting me in impossible situations. If not for your quick actions, I believe I would now be sprawled on the floor, hopelessly tangled in yards of muslin. You have my humblest gratitude for saving me from such a horrific fate." She gave him a sweet smile, bowed her head, and curtsied deeply.

The women in the crowd nodded with smug satisfaction. Several of the town tabbies vocally agreed with her assessment. The scene ended as quickly as it had begun with members of the *haut ton* wandering off and returning to their own sphere of concerns.

Only Lady Iona, her younger sister, the very pale, very lovely Lady Lillian, Lord Nathan, and the viscount remained behind, their gazes directed generally toward May. Lady Lillian quickly turned from May and beamed—quite unabashedly—up at Viscount Evers.

He gave the group a cursory glance before capturing May's gloved hand in his own. His brows crinkled as his expression darkened. He pulled her a step closer to him, holding her a hairbreadth away from improperly close.

"Madam," he said, his voice a low scold, "what are you about?"

Chapter Four

"What am I about?" Miss Sheffers tilted her head back till her bonnet hung at a precarious angle, much in danger of falling off. She glared up at Radford with those haunting violet eyes. Her nose wrinkled in concert with her frown.

What was she about? Such a simple question, yet he doubted it was one she could answer.

Madness must have possessed him to wonder about such a fairyland creature. Why else would he have approached Miss Sheffers and Lady Iona Newbury but for a freak onset of madness? He'd been speaking with Lady Lillian, trying his hand at flirting outrageously—a safe undertaking under the watchful eye of the young lady's mamma—when he caught sight of Miss Sheffers. She was wearing another worn dress, faded pink in hue. Her russet hair, a riot of curls, was barely contained under a straw bonnet.

As Lady Lillian spoke softly about a gown she had recently purchased, Radford had found his attention drawn to the rather elfish Miss Sheffers. She'd appeared to be in the middle of a serious tête-à-tête with her friend, Lady Iona. An eerie darkness cast a shadow over her expression.

Miss Sheffers was troubled?

Of course she was. Only a half-wit wouldn't be troubled with a writ of eviction hanging over her head. The lady was in imminent danger of being tossed out on the street. A fey creature such as she might be tempted into taking a foolish action—like forcing her way into a bachelor's home.

With a wave of his hand, he could save her.

He had hobbled over to impulsively do just that when both women turned and gazed upon him as if he were the devil risen from hell with the smell of brimstone still fresh on his clothes. And that was when all hell actually did break loose. . . .

Radford shuddered at the memory. His cursed leg had failed him before he could utter two coherent words to the lady. Though he had tried to save her from falling—she ended up saving him. Humiliation flooded his veins.

What was she about?

She'd added insult to his humiliation by taking the full blame, by making herself look the fool.

"I don't welcome your help or your pity, madam," he said to her, his anger growing as he conjured up the only reason she would have fallen on the sword for him—him, the villain evicting her from her home.

Pity.

She pitied the poor, helpless cripple.

"I am quite capable of taking care of myself. I don't need an insignificant speck of a lady on the brink of disgrace and disaster as a champion."

"Very well." She twisted her wrist, trying to wrench free from his iron hold without drawing attention to herself. She blinked furiously when he refused to break his hold. "Very well," she said again, her voice growing husky. She swallowed hard. "I will never deign to assist you again, my lord. Flames may spew from your head and I would not spare you a drop of water."

He enjoyed far too much the spirited way she fought him. His body heated as he entertained visions of playing the part of a villainous count set on dragging this uncommon fairy princess back to his lair. Then he might slay her with passionate kisses on those satiny lips of hers and perhaps do much more than that. . . .

Good Lord, he *was* mad.

He let his fingers slip away from her delicate wrist.

"I say," Wynter drawled. He inserted himself between the sputtering, yet somehow utterly sensual, Miss Sheffers and Radford, hooking his arm with the latter. "I do beg your pardon, Miss Sheffers, ladies. Evers and I have a morning appointment and we mustn't be late."

They had nothing of the sort. But Radford understood his friend's motives and agreed. Something about Miss Sheffers' manner drew out the rogue in him. Such uncontrolled behavior couldn't be borne.

He had a wife to find, not a mistress.

In light of that, he bowed and gave his excuses, purposefully flattering the flowery young Lady Lillian before taking his leave. For Lady Lillian, not some impoverished wood elf with a questionable heritage, satisfied the qualifications on his marriage list. The lady would prove an unquestionably acceptable viscountess and no doubt produce a brood of unquestionably acceptable children.

Uncle Sires and Mr. Tumblestone arrived at May and Aunt Winnie's little cottage a few minutes before noon to accompany them to afternoon chapel services. The two perfectly matched black carriage horses with white blazes on their foreheads snorted and pawed the cobbled road, anxious to be moving again.

May eyed them carefully. It wasn't in her nature to trust such great beasts, preferring to travel under the power of her own two feet. Though they may not always be reliable, she felt confident that she could keep her own feet from running away in a panic as she'd seen some carriage horses do on the noisy London streets.

If not for Aunt Winnie's health, May might have spoken up and suggested a stroll. For her aunt, she bit her tongue and lent her shoulder to help guide Winnie to her uncle's carriage.

Aunt Winnie wrapped herself in a wool shawl and shivered in the stiff summer breeze.

"Are you certain you shouldn't stay home?" May asked for the third time.

Winnie looked drained. The lines on her face were more deeply etched than ever before, and she leaned on May's arm with nearly all her weight as they made the long walk to the carriage. "I am convinced God would not ask you to risk your health in this manner."

"Poppycock." Winnie bristled. Struggling, she took a few steps before reaching out again for May's assistance. "I may be tired, but I am by no means an invalid."

There was no hope for it. Aunt Winnie would climb out of her deathbed rather than miss afternoon services and have her friends guess the extent of her ailing health. May tried her best, but the old bird had an unbreakable will of her own.

In that, they were kindred spirits.

Only, May's strong spirit was beginning to feel the strain of responsibility. The morning post had brought a letter from her father's solicitor in reply to a desperate plea she'd made over a week earlier. He'd written that despite his disapproval of her uncle's actions to declare her parents dead, he could do nothing legally to put a stop to it. So, unless her parents appeared on the next boat landing in London, May would have to find another source of funds.

All she wanted was to keep Aunt Winnie safe and happy and to hold on to the content, albeit slightly dull, life she led.

She would just have to find a way . . . and be more discreet the next time she decided to act. That rogue, the slightly unhinged Viscount Evers, only compounded her troubles. She was still reeling over the shabby way he'd treated her in the Pump Room before turning to Lady Lillian and lavishing all those pretty compliments on the lady's ears.

He was a scoundrel, a villain. She'd find no help from that quarter.

As always, she would have to rely on her own survival instincts. They got her through a bumpy come-out and through her required visits with her uncle. She was confident her sharp instincts would see her through this current crisis.

Her mind was still working on that very problem as she helped her aunt climb into the carriage. She felt hemmed in within the contraption after her uncle and Mr. Tumblestone climbed in behind her and filled the small dark space.

As the carriage carried them to the small chapel adjacent to The Circus, where Uncle Sires owned a house, the conversation focused on Aunt Winnie's health.

"I have contacted the most respected doctor in London, Winnie. He has agreed to travel here within the week to see you," Uncle Sires said. "I wish to have you settled in my home before he arrives."

Aunt Winnie gave May's hand a squeeze. "I am happy at the cottage. I do not desire to move anywhere."

Uncle Sires flicked a glance toward May and frowned. "I understand your attachment to the child. But you will have to let her go. She has her own life to live, do you not agree?"

"Of course she does, but—"

"You will be happy with me, Winnie. You will want for nothing. I have been remiss, letting you flounder so near poverty with May. But I have made plans to change that. Everything has been decided. You will see. This is for the best."

No one in the carriage could argue the point. Uncle Sires had the wealth of Croesus. No longer would Aunt Winnie need to drink watery tea while nibbling on day-old cakes. She would have everything. *The best.*

Wasn't her uncle's offer also May's fondest wish for her aunt come true?

After church, Uncle Sires directed the carriage to carry Aunt Winnie back to the cottage for a rest while he chaperoned Mr. Tumblestone and May on a walking tour of Bath.

"Give it time. We need to let the relationship bloom," May overheard Uncle Sires telling Aunt Winnie just before the carriage jerked into motion.

Mr. Tumblestone strolled beside May along a stretch of shops on Pulteney Street. Like a man who'd never visited a city as large as Bath, he had expressed a keen interest to walk the famed Pulteney Bridge. May didn't have it in her heart to deny him, even if she were given the chance. Uncle Sires led the way with Mr. Tumblestone and May lagging just a step behind.

All and all, the elderly Mr. Tumblestone acted a complete gentleman, doing nothing to force her attentions. He spoke in docile tones and made an effort to include May in the conversation, asking her opinion and occasionally pausing to admire a dressmaker's elegant gowns or some fine piece of metalwork in a shop window.

Unlike the previous dreary day, the sun hung high in the cloudless sky and a cool breeze eased the summer heat. Everything was perfect, absolutely perfect.

So why did May silently pray for the earth to open up and swallow her whole?

This was every woman's dream—to find a kind man willing to marry her. This could be the beginning of a new adventure and perhaps even her shot at finding her happily-ever-after.

"One has to work to find it," Aunt Winnie once told May. "You cannot sit idle and hope happiness will discover you. It takes courage and a heart filled with faith to find one of life's most precious treasures."

"Why haven't you ever found happiness, Aunt?" the impertinent child May of years ago had baldly asked.

"Haven't I?" Winnie had given May a hug then. But even a child could see the regret reflected in her eyes.

"Remember, dear. It takes a heart filled with faith," her aunt had whispered in May's ear just an hour ago before leaving May to spend the rest of the afternoon with Uncle Sires and Mr. Tumblestone.

Faith. May blinked up at Mr. Tumblestone. His round cheeks did hold a certain merriment. His clothing was the height of fashion. Though he was missing a few teeth, his breath smelled clean. If only he wasn't so old.

"Mr. Tumblestone is a neighbor of mine," Uncle Sires said as they strolled about the Pulteney Bridge.

Cozy homes and apartments had been built upon the wide bridge, lining both sides. The only evidence suggesting they were standing on an arched bridge was the glass-domed pavilions crowning the ends.

"He lives not more than a thirty-minute carriage drive away from Redfield Abbey. You will never be far from Winnie, you see."

Uncle Sires was proud of himself. May could see it in the sparkle of his brown eyes. He was doing his duty as head of the family, taking care of its members to the best of his ability—whether they appreciated it or not.

Oh, how low May felt at that moment. The night before she had cursed her uncle and his scheming ways, convinced his actions were aimed at stealing her parents' small fortune.

She saw now how wrongly she'd judged him.

With a grand sweep of his arm and a wink, Uncle Sires directed May and Mr. Tumblestone into a small shop that sold ices and paid for the cool treats without hesitation. What May considered a fortune had to be naught more than mere pocket change to a man as wealthy as her uncle. She was guilty of doing what so many had done to her, judging without taking the time to look beyond the surface.

May set aside her spoon and smiled up at Mr. Tumblestone. "Please, sir," she said, her dream of one day finding a handsome, young prince fading, "please tell me all about your home."

Chapter Five

That evening lights twinkled high in the street lanterns as crowds dressed in their best finery promenaded toward the fancy ball held in the Upper Assembly Room. May had purchased a season subscription to all the balls and concerts, knowing how such events pleased her aunt. The fancy ball, held every Thursday night during the summer, was Aunt Winnie's favorite and in turn May's.

Uncle Sires and Mr. Tumblestone escorted the two women to the spectacular event. They arrived in her uncle's carriage, making quite an impression with the *ton.* Her uncle's presence was greeted with warmth and genuine enthusiasm. Since titled gentry were scarce in Bath this year—the most fashionable choosing to follow The Prinny to Brighton—even an old bachelor like the Earl of Redfield created quite a stir.

Mr. Tumblestone, by association, was fawned over shamelessly by many of the matrons, who twittered like schoolgirls as they gathered around the two new faces. Mr. Tumblestone's manner shined as he charmed the older women while never failing to keep an attentive eye on May.

Though she felt nothing more than a faint gratitude toward him, May had to admit the aging Tumblestone did cut a handsome mark dressed in a shimmering pale green satin coat trimmed with the softest forest green velvet. He looked younger and slightly thinner draped in such expensive fabrics.

May felt quite the dowd promenading through the Upper Rooms beside such a finely turned-out gentleman. She had donned her second-best gown, a ruby ermine-trimmed pelisse worn over a rather simple white satin gown with matching ruby-colored flounces dancing down the front. The outfit was topped with a Henry the Eighth hat of ruby velvet sporting two white feathers pinned to the front. The hat was an extravagance Aunt Winnie had insisted she purchase. Though the neckline of her gown was modest compared to current fashions, May felt uncomfortable. Her rather embarrassingly full breasts pulled the material tight.

Her unseemly shape must have embarrassed Mr. Tumblestone as well. His watery gaze slipped toward her bosom more than once as they processed through the Octagon Room to enter the long ballroom.

The ballroom never failed to take May's breath away. From the high ceiling hung five glass chandeliers that provided a dazzling light for the room. Adding to the brilliance, two gilt-framed looking glasses at each end of the ballroom redoubled the chandeliers' glow. The whole of the ballroom was lined with Corinthian columns and entablatures resembling statuary marble.

Whenever she came here, May liked to imagine herself stepping back in time to ancient Rome—to a place where no one knew the circumstances of her birth or the abandonment by her parents. She'd spent many an hour reading about fantastic ancient places. Surely this ballroom rivaled any ancient Roman palace in its magnificence.

Yet no matter how comfortable the fantasy of faraway places and nameless heroes, May couldn't allow herself the luxury of such dreams this evening, nor could she fade into the background. Her mission was clear. For her aunt's sake, she had to please Mr. Tumblestone and convince him to agree to marriage with her.

She danced two country-dances with him and two more

with her uncle. All the while her gaze raked the crowd. Her heart beat an unsteady rhythm as she continued searching.

"Whomever are you watching for?" Aunt Winnie asked partway through the evening.

Until that moment, May had not realized that she had been craning her neck to peer through the thick crowd.

Whom indeed was she searching for? Certainly not that despicable Viscount Evers. Why ever would she be interested in him?

"No one, Aunt," she said, forcing her eyes to keep steady on one point. "Why, there are just so many people here dressed in such a splendid array of colors."

"Poppycock!" Aunt Winnie scolded. "Lying is so unbecoming, May. This night is no different than the week before, nor the week before that. In fact, these events are fast becoming quite a bore. Who has turned your head?"

"No one has." May felt her face heat. "No one of import." Definitely not the dashing Lord Evers.

"Mr. Tumblestone appears quite taken with you this evening, does he not?"

May caught herself before giving into the temptation of peering around the crowded room again. Although the viscount often attended, he rarely lingered long in the ballroom. For a rake like Evers, the card room better filled his needs. Certainly she wasn't searching for the viscount, was she?

"Yes, he does," she answered absently.

"And what do you think of him?" her aunt asked. "Do you think he would be able to make you happy?"

"No," May answered thoughtlessly.

Did she spot the viscount's square shoulder through the crowd? No, that gentleman with the stark black coat was Mr. Rankcor, a happily married London banker.

Aunt Winnie's pursed lips and carefully set frown startled May back to reality. Winnie cared as deeply for May's happiness as May cared for Winnie's. And Winnie would willingly move to Redfield Abbey to live in luxury with her brother if she was confident that May was happily settled. If not for concern over May's future, Winnie probably would have already agreed to let Uncle Sires care for her.

May fluttered her hands. "I mean, Aunt, I don't really know Mr. Tumblestone, do I? He seems a very kind man."

"He does." Aunt Winnie sat back on her bench and peered out from half-lidded eyes. May felt as if her aunt's gaze was trying to tease out the truth. "Marriage is an important decision, May. You would be wise to avoid doing anything rash."

How could Aunt Winnie know that despite Mr. Tumblestone's behavior being the model of propriety, May was already wracking her mind with plans to wiggle out of a marriage with him?

"I promise to consider all aspects of marriage before making a decision, Aunt." She would have to marry Mr. Tumblestone . . . if only for Winnie's happiness. No other man had ever offered.

"There is something you must know, dear." Winnie leaned forward and whispered, "Before you make up your mind. You must understand—"

Mr. Tumblestone approached with a confident swagger. Winnie blushed prettily as she looked up and noticed his approach. Whatever May needed to understand must have slipped Winnie's mind as she straightened her skirt and gave May's suitor a welcoming nod.

Tumblestone smiled widely, his gaze lingering again on May's embarrassing chest while he bowed. "The night grows late, ladies. It is nearly eleven o'clock. The last dance begins." He offered Aunt Winnie his arm. "And yet, my dear woman, you have not yet danced a set."

How kind Mr. Tumblestone was. How thoughtful of him to think her aunt in need of rescue. Aunt Winnie, who rarely danced a set since the onset of her illness, fluttered her hands and accepted graciously. She looked decades younger as she batted her lashes while accepting Mr. Tumblestone's hand.

"Please be careful, Aunt," May could not keep herself from warning. Country-dances contained vigorous moves.

Winnie mustn't overexert herself or her heart wouldn't be able to take it.

"Oh, pooh! You worry overmuch. You're no different than an old clucking hen sometimes. I daresay I'm strong enough to survive one mild dance," Winnie said as Mr. Tumblestone led her out to the marble dance floor.

May settled on the wooden bench in the spot Aunt Winnie had vacated. Her gaze continued to search as she watched the last set of the night begin.

No prince appeared from the card room nor from deep within the crowd. Why should she expect him to? He never danced.

May swallowed hard and straightened her spine.

She was a fool, naught but a fool.

There were no magical princes lurking in the shadows . . . at least, none searching for her.

Chapter Six

"Tell me you haven't sunk into a foul mood again," Wynter demanded of Radford when he barged into the drawing room in typical Wynter fashion.

The two had avoided each other for most of the day after parting in anger the previous morning. After the incident in the Pump Room—which still left Radford cringing—Wynter had dressed him up and down, using language colorful enough to make the most hardened rough-and-tumble foot soldier flinch.

"Gentlemen, no matter how arrogant or high-in-the-instep, do not treat women as if they were naught but sotted servants," Wynter had said finally.

Though Radford agreed, he refused to put voice to his holding the same opinion or to promise to change his ways. He merely professed a willingness to court the young Lady Lillian. A confession that sent Wynter into another rage.

"But, Wynter, you must see the benefits," Radford had said with hopes to sooth his friend's ire. He then patiently listed the lady's qualifications. She was young, soft-spoken, fair-haired, born into a respected family, and known throughout England as an accomplished horsewoman.

"What else could a man want in a wife?" he asked.

What else, indeed?

To that question, Wynter simply could not give a coherent answer. And with them at such an impasse, they had parted ways.

Today, they'd plans to meet for drinks before escorting Radford's mother to a private concert the Duke of Newbury was hosting. The lovely Lady Lillian had penned the invitation with her own hand, Radford had been told. All was moving forward smoothly with his plans to woo her properly.

Yet this disagreement with Wynter left Radford feeling slightly askew. He wondered whether his friend would appear as planned or leave him to face the lovely lady and her mother on his own.

But sure as the rains, always dependable Wynter arrived on time. When Radford growled his regular greeting, Wynter, quite uncharacteristically, growled back.

Curse his foul moods. Try as he might, Radford couldn't seem to settle his own flaring temper that evening. Perhaps it was because it wasn't just his mood that pained him.

Radford had hurt more than his pride with his near fall in the Pump Room the day before. His foot throbbed with a devil's vengeance. He'd retreated to the parlor that evening and propped up his foot on the sofa cushions while waiting for Wynter's arrival.

"Once again, I find myself having to ask you to forgive me," Radford said, grateful for the few friends who'd stayed with him despite his infirmities and sour moods. It wasn't good form to snap at Wynter without a worthy cause. "It pleases me to see you willing to put up with a worthless blighter like me."

"That tone is even more pitiful than your growl," Wynter said while tugging on his waistcoat—a sure sign he was on the verge of losing his temper. "If you don't stop feeling sorry for yourself, I will feel compelled to bash your head into the ground."

"Bash his head—?" a missish voice preceded a delicately boned, fair-haired, willowy woman into the parlor. She was dressed in a pale peach silk sheath that hid how much weight she had lost in the past year. "I will allow no such violence in my home, young man."

Wynter bowed his head. So did Radford. His mother was a beguiling force no man could resist.

"Lady Evers," Wynter said. He swept across the room and took up her hand in his, brushing his lips across her knuckles. "May I say your beauty tonight puts the fragrant nosegay you hold to shame?"

"Flatterer," she hissed. A smile creased her thin lips as she batted him away with her silken fan. The stresses of the past year had etched deep lines on her slender features. To lose a husband and watch her only son crippled by war within a span of a few months had taken a harsh toll. Radford thought it a wonder she could find it in her to smile at all.

"Are you certain you are up to the concert tonight, Mother?" Radford asked. He pulled his leg from its soft perch on the sofa and struggled to his feet.

Lady Evers rushed to his assistance, tugging on his arms and fluttering her hands about him. "What have you done with your cane? The doctors say you should use it. Look at you, ready to fall. My word, you will be the death of me."

The fuss she made only pricked at his anger. But he could not turn his temper on her, not after all she had suffered and all the anguish his injuries had caused her so soon after his father's death. So he once again turned his bitter tongue on his long-suffering friend.

"Is there not but mush in your nob, Wynter? Can you not even wipe that grin from your dreadful face long enough to put yourself to use?" Radford roared.

When he chanced a glance of his mother's eyes after such an outburst he was horrified by what he saw. She never hid her feelings. Sorrow spilled over into a light sheen of tears.

"Please, Radford, try not to fuss so. You will surely make yourself ill again." She believed him an invalid, unable to care for himself. Many a time she had complained how his valet was inadequate to see after his care. He needed to hire a nurse, she had told him for the sixth time just that morning at breakfast. The helplessness her loving care provoked only added flames to his fiery temper.

Wynter's grin didn't help either. "Looking to put three sheets to the wind before introducing your mother to the woman you have decided to marry, eh, Evers?"

"Go to the devil," Radford roared, forgetting for a moment his mother's delicate ears.

Lady Evers released Radford immediately. Her cheeks flooded with color. "Is this true?" she whispered the question as if afraid she had heard Wynter wrong.

Radford huffed and tripped his way to the sideboard. He hadn't planned on involving his mother in his courting process, at least not so soon. She would be sorely disappointed if he failed. Thanks to his *friend*—he sent Wynter a killing glance—his mother would undoubtedly put all her energies into seeing the deed done.

"I have not exactly decided to marry her, Mother." It was a hopeless gesture. Her eyes were beaming brighter than the sun. He splashed a bit of brandy into a glass. "She barely knows me, in fact."

"But she will have you," Lady Evers said with determination. "She must. Who is this lady you have selected? I trust she is from a respectable family?"

"Oh yes," Wynter answered before Radford could attempt to dissuade his mother from having him married and off to Scotland for his honeymoon before the evening was out. "Her father is the Duke of Newbury."

"Newbury!" Lady Evers clutched her hands to her heart.

Her sudden look of rapture pleased Radford. He was doing the right thing. This marriage was exactly what his mother needed.

"There could not be a better choice. All of his daughters were raised to be proper ladies. Not an unseemly trait in the lot. I heartily approve of your choice. Heartily."

She threw herself in his arms with such force his glass spilled and his lame leg bowed—reminding him. Lady Lillian might not be interested in marrying half a man.

"She has not accepted me, Mother," he warned. "I have not even formally declared my interests."

Nothing he could say could diminish her enthusiasm or quell her planning. In her mind, the marriage was a certainty.

"You will just have to pay a visit to the duke on the morrow to declare yourself, son."

Wynter snickered and wisely stayed out of punching range. "Shall we depart? I daresay there is a certain Newbury daughter breathlessly awaiting your speedy appearance, Evers."

Radford glowered. The thought of seeing Lady Lillian again and having to woo the pretty young thing made his stomach churn. She might not take to him. She was young and pretty. Surely, such a woman wouldn't feel compelled to settle.

But what was he to do?

He straightened his shoulders and tugged on his dove gray gloves. The deed was done. He would not, no matter what he felt in his heart, disappoint his mother.

The concert dragged at a painfully slow pace. Though the entertainment was first rate and the company friendly, May found maintaining her gracious smile a tiresome chore. Mr. Tumblestone fawned over her, her uncle scowled over her choice of gowns, and the fool Lord Evers flirted shamelessly with Lady Lillian.

She needed to escape . . . just for a moment . . . to catch her breath.

At an intermission, May slipped into the duke's darkened library and swiftly closed the door behind her. She let out the breath she'd been holding and slumped against the door. This evening was intolerable.

"Perhaps I should call a constable, my pretty thief."

From the far side of the room an ember blazed as it floated up the flue from the banked fire. Other than that brief light, darkness blanketed the room. The unmistakably smooth voice seemed to sink even deeper within the library's depths.

Startled, May's hands flew to her mouth. "Whyever for, my lord," she replied, her gaze searching the gloom for the viscount. "I am a guest, not a thief."

"Is that so? Then why is a delicate little cup missing from my china set?"

The blasted teacup! In the chaos of the last couple of days, she had completely forgotten to send her housekeeper around to return it.

"Did you shatter the poor thing into tiny pieces in a fit of rage?"

"Of course I did nothing of the sort." May found no comfort in speaking to a gentleman under the complete cover of night. Especially a rogue . . . an incredibly handsome rogue who had persisted to haunt her unruly thoughts. Her hand curled around the door handle. Not generally a coward, she was more than prepared to flee tonight.

"If not a thief, what are you doing hiding in the darkness?" he asked.

Curiosity kept her hand from turning the doorknob. "What are *you* doing in the darkness?" she asked. "Do not forget, I was the one who found you in here. Not the other way around."

The rustle of material alerted her to his approach. He was mere steps away from her and her thundering heart when a curtain parted and welcomed a beam of moonlight into the room.

"I was trying to find a moment's peace," he said and then sighed deeply. "And you?"

"The same," she admitted.

"Ah." He took a step closer. His sharply defined features were bathed in the ghostly pale light of the moon. "Our hosts would be horrified to learn of the reason for our escape."

"I just needed a moment to collect my thoughts"—she rushed to explain—"not flee from anyone particular."

"No? Not even from that droll Mr. Tumblestone?" His brows rose. He crossed his arms over his chest and presented a languid pose only properly executed by the most notorious of rakes. "He is what? Sixty years old? I shiver at the rumor that you are soon to be his bride."

Was he mocking her?

"I wonder if Lady Lillian is shivering at the thought of you as a husband," she returned cruelly.

A frightening look of pure anger tightened his lazy expression. His lips hardened into a thin line.

"I have struck a chord, have I?" *Good.* She was glad for her tongue's accurate marksmanship. "Perhaps you're only too aware that you're old enough to be her father." May wasn't certain of the fact. She knew that Evers had passed his thirtieth year. For how many years, she could not guess.

"My age?" His grim expression relaxed. "You think my age frightens her as thoroughly as Mr. Tumblestone's frightens you?" He laughed then, a low sound that rumbled in his throat. "You've overlooked one important fact, my pretty thief. I am a man in my prime. A man with lustful needs."

May didn't trust the wolfish gleam that suddenly brightened his eyes or the deepening pitch of his voice. She had read stories about men being transformed into beasts by the sight of a full moon. The situation coupled with an inordinate amount of moonlight pouring through the window was enough to make her wary.

A single woman should never be caught alone with a man, especially in an unlit room. Such an oversight in propriety could leave her reputation in tatters.

"My lord," she whispered as he leaned forward, closing the gap between them. The pure scent of him, a refreshing blend of cheroot and vanilla, left her senses reeling.

He peeled off a glove. The rough pad of his thumb caressed her lower lip. She gasped, unable to catch her breath. Her mind could barely form a protest before his head dipped down and his lips captured hers.

At first, shock paralyzed her. She couldn't have pulled away even if she had wanted to. Then a deep heat rose up from low in her belly, melting her resolve . . . washing away any warring thoughts. She pressed her hand against his chest, thrilling in the raw sensations a kiss—naught but a simple kiss—could conjure in her.

* * *

The caress wasn't much more than a brush of her lips. Radford reined in his desire to run his tongue over her soft lips and tease open the entrance.

She'd tensed at his initial touch. He'd fully expected her to jerk her head away. The sensual sigh she breathed instead emboldened him. She wanted this kiss as much as he. When she pressed her hand against his shoulder, he took the cue and pulled her closer so their bodies could meld together.

Her fairy lips tasted of the sweetest nectar, stirring a mysterious, overpowering sensation in the center of his chest.

Ah, if only he could kiss those full, warm lips all night—but alas, that was not all he would be doing if he did not draw away . . . immediately . . . without a moment's delay.

He tore his lips from hers but kept a firm grip on her shoulders. If the misty look on her shadowed expression was any indication, she was on the verge of a swoon.

"A thousand pardons, Miss Sheffers," he whispered.

Her swollen lips remained pursed, invitingly kissable, as she stared upon him with befuddlement.

He realized then what he should have known right away by the tentative play of her lips against his. This woman . . . this four-and-twenty-year-old sensual woman had just experienced her first romantic kiss. He had awakened her body to the enticing pleasures of the flesh and she'd responded like a woman long starved for affection.

Her passions had stirred timidly at first, but they promised to burn hot enough to make his head spin.

Damnation. *His* passions were stirring as well.

"I should have never," he said with a rush, though it was a lie. He regretted nothing. "I forgot myself. . . ." *And the lovely Lady Lillian he planned to marry.* "I do apologize."

She blinked. A lusty glow softened her strange elflike features. In the pale moonlight she looked otherworldly . . . almost beautiful.

He should have never started something in this darkened, leather-scented library that he could have no hope of continuing. Despite all her earthy allure, Miss Sheffers fell short of the qualifications he'd detailed on his list.

"You do understand?" He wondered if anything he had said had penetrated her foggy head.

She blinked again, this time clearing the innocent bedroom glaze from them. "I did not scream or slap your cheek, my lord, because I dearly wish to avoid a messy scene." Her voice was husky and not without a tremble. "It was most inappropriate for you to have taken advantage of me like that . . . kissing me, indeed! I hope you do not attack other women who might have the misfortune of stumbling into an empty room with you."

Her chin came up, and her features tightened into a prude's scowl.

"My dear Miss Sheffers"—Radford could not help but chuckle—"I believe you did much more than refrain from protesting."

Even in the dim light he could see the color of her tan cheeks deepen.

"I certainly did not—"

He pressed a finger to her mouth and silenced her protests as he indulged in one last pleasure and caressed those apple-sweet lips.

"You certainly did," he whispered. He could feel her skin quiver in response to his touch and the sound of his voice. A hint of milky passion returned to her gaze.

She blinked it away. "Excuse me, my lord. I will be missed."

Miss Sheffers ducked her head away from his gentle strokes and slipped out of the library.

And his life . . .

For never again should he consider such a dalliance. Raised by a father who held honor and chivalry above all things, Radford firmly believed in a man remaining faithful to his wife—or in his case, his future wife, the lovely Lady Lillian.

Chapter Seven

It was only a kiss.

May picked up her pace and tried to ignore the warmth the memory of the previous night's surprising and wonderful encounter in the Newbury library brought to her cheeks. Aunt Winnie, feeling drained and tired after two consecutive nights of excitement, had wanted to spend the morning lounging abed. So they decided to forego their regular visit to the Pump Room.

With the morning free, May set out on a brisk walk up Beechen Cliff, hoping the fresh air and vigorous exercise would do the trick and clear her mind. For a third night, sleep had eluded her while she puzzled over her feelings toward the changes occurring in her life.

Gracious, it was only a *meaningless* kiss.

Men kissed women all the time.

Just not her.

Never her. At least, not before last night.

Not that she had minded being overlooked. Men only seemed to laud women who displayed a meek mind, spirit, and body—a weakness May loathed to feign. She was strong and healthy. Why should she slip into a fit of vapors just to win a man's kiss?

May's cheeks heated anew as the memory of the way the viscount's lips had pressed against hers replayed its pleasing script. That simple brush of lips had made her tingly, alive all the way down to the soles of her feet.

But his magic had not addled her mind!

She'd seen women turn into besotted fools. An educated, independent woman such as herself must resist falling pray to such folly.

Viscount Evers displayed only too clearly his typical male character in the way he'd fawned over the simpering Lady Lillian once he'd rejoined the ball. He spent the rest of the evening laughing at her inane chatter and offering his arm when she appeared near to fainting—as ladies were wont to appear after a long evening in the company of a beau. His catlike grin was smeared with satisfaction as he supported Lady Lillian's weaving pose. The expression told May all she needed to know.

Even though he didn't pursue her company after stealing such a kiss, even though his gaze had never once strayed her way during the long hours that followed—he could have at least taken notice of her standing beside him while she spoke with Lady Lillian. No matter, she would have no interest in such a man, anyhow.

Mary Wollstonecraft had warned in her treatise for women's rights how men who sought a withering woman for a wife made dreadful companions. Men such as those were only too ready to throw the yoke of servitude on the *weaker sex*.

May would never allow herself to fall prey to a man who could not respect her as an intellectual equal. Respect, Mary Wollstonecraft had written, had to come before marriage.

Gracious. Just a week ago, May would have happily considered herself a spinster—a woman well suited to live life alone or in service as a lady's companion. But now her uncle seemed set on seeing her married. And soon . . .

Just last evening he hinted that an announcement might be made by the end of the week. The end of the week!

That was why she'd escaped the party and fled into the darkened library the night before. Everything was moving too fast. She and Winnie had always enjoyed a relatively quiet existence. When in London, suffering the droll company at teas and losing a night's sleep when attending a dinner party or ball were once the worst of her worries. Of course that was all before Winnie had fallen ill.

Much like her parents, Winnie would not always be around.

May shuddered in the early morning breeze that whipped down from the top of Beechen Cliff. The chill passed through her like an unwelcome premonition. Uncle Sires was in the right to want to take Aunt Winnie away with him back to Redfield Abbey. He had the money and connections to see that his sister got the best care.

For May to cling to her beloved aunt would be unfair—as unfair as her uncle declaring her parents dead. There was simply no solid logic to support the decision.

The slope of the hill turned steep. May's thoughts drifted off as her gaze turned to the ground and her concentration on keeping her balance.

"Ho there!" a voice called out as she neared the top.

May cupped her hand over her brow and peered up at the broad silhouette of the Viscount Evers standing on the ridge, his hands on his hips like a conqueror. She was only a few yards below him and could not politely turn around and pretend she hadn't seen or heard his call.

The best she could do was curse quietly under her breath and brace herself for the encounter. A shame, really. She was looking forward to enjoying the sweeping vistas of Bath and a few blessed moments of solitude to straighten out her poor, mixed up head. Seeing the viscount, now, when she needed to forget him, could do nothing good for her nerves.

"Do you require assistance?" he asked.

"I can manage well enough," she said through clenched teeth as her foot slipped on a rock. Her balance wobbled for a heartbeat—much too long for her pride. Belatedly, she added a half-cowed "Thank you."

"I doubt I would be able to rush after you if you were to

trip. You would undoubtedly roll all the way back to Bath," he said. An unmistakable lilt of laughter moved underneath his smooth tone.

"I would never expect you to make such an effort for my sake, my lord." She'd taken a difficult path and was forced to lift her skirts in order to make the last steep step to the top. The bounder didn't have the good graces to avert his gaze.

A fiendish grin spanned the length of his cheeks and he crossed his arms over his chest. "I cannot tell you how glad I am that you refused my helping hand. I would have hated to miss such a view."

"You are a cad, my lord." May lowered her head and made a show of smoothing her skirts in an effort to hide her embarrassment.

"And you, Miss Sheffers, must be a shameless hoyden."

May's head came up with a snap. "A what?"

"A shameless hoyden, Miss Sheffers." Viscount Evers held her gaze prisoner with his peculiar expression, a heady mixture of amusement and attentiveness.

The look stole May's breath. She could only whisper, "I do not know what you could mean, my lord."

An ebony brow rose on the viscount's perfectly serious face as he looked around. "Perhaps you have hidden your companion or outpaced her?" he said. "For only a hoyden would venture so far afield alone, wouldn't you agree?"

Having been raised by a very proper aunt, she naturally agreed. May only took these occasional early morning excursions of hers to places she supposed deserted.

"My aunt is not well enough to take such a hike and our housekeeper is far too busy to be burdened with the responsibility of following me about." It wasn't a strong argument, but it was the best May could utter.

Blast the man. His wicked presence muddied her mind. She was an independent woman, well accustomed to free use of her thoughts. She would not let him do this to her.

"I had hoped for a few moments quiet, my lord. Your presence here intrudes on that." She managed to say in the gentlest tone possible. She did well to keep her passions in check around a rake who could lure her into a kiss with the mere brush of his thumb against her lips.

Viscount Evers lowered himself to sit on the ground, struggling with his stiff leg. "I believe we both are looking for the same thing. Join me." He sat with his legs sprawled out in front of him and patted the ground beside him.

May lifted her chin. "It would not be proper."

"Because your Mr. Tumblestone wouldn't approve?" Evers asked, his tone mocking. "He will soon be your affianced, will he not? Your name and his rose amongst the tittering last night. You should be grateful to have found a willing man, one woman said. She made some vague allusion to your family background." He tilted his head toward her.

May's back stiffened. Her family history was none of his business. Heaven knew she had been taught to keep quiet about it. Uncle Sires used to threaten to lop off her amber curls and make her go around as bald as a smooth marble if she were ever to even breathe her father's name in public.

"You have no right to pry into my private business, my lord," she bit off the words.

"Pry?" A wicked smile played at his lips. May could feel her cheeks heat as she remembered how those lips of his had touched hers. "Why, no, I suppose I don't have a right. I just was wondering who in your life would believe it improper for you to sit here . . . beside me . . . unescorted."

A hungry gleam darkened his eyes. May took a step back.

"Perhaps *I* find it improper, my lord. There are dangers, are there not, in a lady finding herself alone with a gentleman?"

He didn't answer right away and when he did, his tone was laced with regret. "Yes, Miss Sheffers, I believe there must be."

Radford had started out at dawn without a destination. The climb to the top of Beechen Cliff had been an arduous one despite the fact that he'd forged a much gentler slope than the ridiculously steep route Miss Sheffers had taken. The effort had been worth the pains pulling through his leg.

He hadn't lied when he'd told May that his quest was similar to hers. Up here, with the orderly Georgian city below punctuated with the medieval spires of Bath Abbey at its heart, Radford felt removed . . . free almost.

His mother had purred her delight over Lady Lillian all during the carriage ride home last night. The marriage was a fait accompli, to hear her speak.

Instead of relieving his own doubts regarding the decision, her happiness only seemed to shrink the cage he'd been confined to the day his horse had been shot out from under him. He felt trapped—angry. He'd been cursing the birds in the trees when he saw *her.*

He shouldn't have been surprised. Miss Margaret Sheffers, with her unusual wood-sprite features, would naturally be at home up here, under the gently rustling beeches. Without a care for staining her bright yellow-and-white-striped cotton dress she climbed straight up—the most direct route, if not the most difficult.

And now that he and she were up on the hill together, Radford had to fight to keep his thoughts about her from straying from the respectable path.

"You were here first. I will leave you to your thoughts, my lord," she said and turned to make a descent following the same steep path.

"Wait," Radford called.

As much as her company disturbed him and his solitude, he knew her departure would leave him more miserable than before. He struggled to his feet, silently cursing all the while his foolish notion of lounging on the ground like some high-flying Corinthian. Somewhere in the back of his mind, a horridly shameful thought sprang to life. The thought whispered in a singsong voice that if he could find a way to take a tumble in the grass with this fairy creature, his weaknesses and pains would disappear—and become naught but a bad dream brought on by an overindulgence in some rich meal.

Yes, she'd chase his misery away like the sun would extinguish a nightmare. For where else should such dreaded dreams be vanquished but to Avalon, where this creature with her mysterious birth must call home?

"In good conscience, Miss Sheffers," he said, "I simply cannot allow you to continue to traipse through the countryside unescorted. As a gentleman, I'm compelled to protect you from your imprudent actions."

The quelling glance she sent his way could have burned the oriental paper off his parlor walls. He was glad they were in a wide-open space.

"Please, Miss Sheffers," he said with considerably more tact, "I would suffer terribly were I to hear you'd come to harm on the long hike home. Please allow me to escort you."

After an insufferable pause, she gave a short nod. Her lips had thinned to a mere line and resembled nothing of the swollen passionate petals he'd tasted the night before.

The kiss. There were a few things he should say to her in regard to that kiss. But where to start?

"I cannot follow you down such a steep trail," he said instead, even though she had remained motionless, letting him take the lead and set the pace.

They walked in silence for several yards down a well-used path. He sensed her stiffen with each step until she appeared to be strung as tight as a bow ready to spring.

"I may play the part of a rake, Miss Sheffers, but I vow you are as safe with me as you would be with my old toothless sheepdog."

"I know," she agreed far too quickly.

"What I mean to say—" He struggled for the right words. How did he explain without scandalizing her or damaging her virgin's sensibilities? "Although I dearly enjoyed kissing you and long to do so again, I am a man of virtue. I would never force my attentions or put you in a situation that would have your reputation questioned."

"Thank you," she said.

Her two-word replies dug into his gut. She wasn't making the task an easy one. And why should she? He saw how society treated her. She was Lady Winifred's companion, the lowest rank a young lady could hold. Most of the guests at Newbury's party looked through her. She didn't even seem to mind that she was expected to step back from the fashionables and fade like a servant into the wainscoting.

Radford had been about to intervene at the party last night when the bubbly Lady Iona had appeared and taken Miss Sheffers' arm, dragging her into the middle of a crowd of women. In fact, the Newbury family, with the exception of Lady Lillian and her mother, treated Miss Sheffers as one of their own—as part of the family.

As interesting as his meandering thoughts were, they did nothing to solve how he was to address his kissing her. He should offer up some additional explanation . . . but what?

"Why do you refuse the use of a cane?" she asked in the lengthening silence.

The question stopped Radford where he stood. He wasn't ready to speak of this. His injuries were his burden and his alone. To speak of them would only make them more real.

He truly believed that if he pushed himself, ignoring the pain and the weaknesses, he could will the damage away.

Miss Sheffers stopped on the grass path and turned to face him. "My aunt often refuses the aid of a cane. Pride, I believe, keeps her from depending on such a luxury. She leans heavily on my arm, instead."

"That must be quite a burden. Lady Winifred must weigh at least twenty stone."

"It's a burden I gladly bear. My shoulders are strong." She tilted her head up and peered into his eyes from beneath her straw bonnet. "But you don't lean on anyone. Why?"

"I don't need to."

A slow smile, the closest expression to pity he'd seen on her lively features, stuck him in the belly like an icy sword. The last thing he wanted from her was pity.

"You fool yourself, my lord. Bowing to the use of a cane cannot diminish your manhood. Your injuries, no matter how fleeting, are a reality—"

"You know nothing. You cannot begin to imagine what has become of my life," he said bitterly.

"Now my aunt, she will never recover," she said at the very same moment. "She will only weaken."

Radford couldn't miss the raw sorrow he heard in her voice.

"I am sorry," he said. "For your aunt, I mean. She is all you have?"

"I have my parents and my uncle, the Earl of Redfield." The words rang hollow.

"Ah." There was much more to that story. What, he could only guess. "The earl is Lady Winifred's brother, I believe. He is also the one who introduced you to your beloved, Mr. Tumblestone?"

May blinked furiously. He'd obviously touched a sour topic. "There are more important things than love when considering marriage, my lord."

"Of course. So you found yourself a rich man, eh?" he teased. "Perhaps he owns half of England?"

"I do not believe Mr. Tumblestone's state of finance is any of your concern." She forged ahead at a brisk pace.

Radford had a devil of a time catching up to her as she rounded the hill heading down toward Sydney Gardens. His limp grew more pronounced, and his foot felt like it was being torn apart from the inside.

"Please"—sweat broke out on his brow—"slow down."

May took one glance in his direction and drew to a quick halt. "You are in pain?"

"No, damn it! For Heaven's sake, what kind of proper lady marches at a pace rivaling a bloody foot soldier's?"

"You *are* in pain." She took his arm. There was considerable strength hidden in her small limbs. "You will lean on me . . . or would you rather rest?"

A felled tree lay near the path. Although Radford was

more than set on pushing forward and gritting through the pain, May's firm grip guided him toward the rotting log.

"It's such a beautiful day," she said as she arranged her skirts and lowered herself onto the dirty log without a thought to the stains she must be causing. "I think I would prefer nothing more than to take a moment to enjoy the sunshine before returning to the cottage."

Her smile was as bright as the sun. Radford could not help but stare and wonder. She lied so prettily to save his pride. She sat, not bothering with him, not pressuring him to join her and take the weight off his leg. She gazed off into the distance, looking over the city glittering in the morning's glory and completely ignored him, in fact.

Since it would have been ungallant to disregard her efforts to protect his pride, Radford eased down beside her on the log and stretched his stiff leg out in front of him. The comfortable silence spanned several minutes.

He was the one to finally break the gentle spell.

"I intend to tell my man-of-affairs, Bannor, to rescind the writ of eviction," he said. "Your uncle has paid the back rent, you must know."

Miss Sheffers kept her head turned away and her thoughts to herself.

"I understand you are short of funds. But since I would rather like to call you my friend, I would be loath to force you from your home. Please know you may continue to live at Sydney Place for as long as you require."

"It would be improper to accept, my lord. I will not live as a kept woman." Her biting tone surprised him. How could she not see he was doing her a kindness?

"Good Lord, you misunderstand me! I am not asking you to be a kept woman." He could delay no longer. They would have to speak further of the kiss. "What happened last night was an apparition—a startling whim never to be repeated. . . ." *Which would be a great sacrifice indeed.*

His body ached for another taste of her sweet nectar.

Miss Sheffers shook her head. "Whether you expect payment for your kindness or not, it does not matter. All that matters is what society would believe. I will not risk my reputation in that way. You do not need to concern yourself with my affairs. I will manage."

"Manage by marrying a man who is old enough to be your grandfather?" He recognized immediately that it was wrong for him to press the issue. Mr. Tumblestone's attentions clearly troubled her. Even though she did nothing publicly to spurn him, he'd seen only too clearly the disheartened way her brows furrowed whenever she smiled upon the old gentleman.

"Forgive me, Miss Sheffers. That remark was unworthy of you," he said quickly. "I truly would like you to consider me a friend. I will not pry further into your affairs."

Her bonnet bounced as she made some vague gesture.

"I do wish to be friends," he said. There was nothing in the world, besides his health, that he wished for more. Being with her, tripping over his words and acting the worst sort of clumsy gentleman, was the most fun he'd experienced since he returned from the Peninsula more dead than alive.

He actually looked forward to waking up in the morning for the first time in months.

"Take off your boot," she said suddenly, her tone as crisp as a general's. Her sudden change in manner and the fact that his throbbing foot felt like it was ready to break the boot's stitches had Radford scrambling to comply.

The tiny Miss Sheffers knelt down on the ground and cradled his injured foot in her lap. "It is swollen," she murmured after gently massaging the pulling muscles. Her deft touch relieved the worst of the pain and sent heat spiraling throughout his body. Ah, move those magic fingers of hers any higher up his thigh, and he doubted he'd be able to be responsible for his actions.

She turned her head to gaze up at him then. Was it her soothing touch or the sharp intelligence glowing in her violet gaze that eased the biting pain the most? A question formed on her lips like a delicate O.

Good Lord, he had to get control over his unruly body before he frightened the poor gel by trying to kiss her again. Radford tried out an indulgent smile.

"Yes, Miss Sheffers?"

"You walked here all the way from Sion Hill? All the way across the city and up this hill?" she asked. Before he could answer, her words marched on. "You are a foolish man, my lord. A foolish, foolish man."

"Am I?" No one, other than Wynter, had ever dared call him a fool. And she didn't just say it once, but three times. Three times she called him a fool. The charge didn't sit well in his spleen.

"Only a fool would abuse his body so," she said.

"Is that so?" How dared she? Perhaps he'd been wrong. Perhaps Miss Sheffers could not be considered a friend. Oh yes, her mere presence helped him forget his aches. Yet, at the same time she constantly pricked his anger to the point of making him dangerous.

Radford grabbed his boot, jammed it back on his swollen foot, and pushed up to his feet.

"I will escort you home now," he said.

If he lingered, letting her scold him while she rubbed his foot with those elfin fingers of hers, he would soon feel compelled to shake her or kiss her. And that brand of foolishness just couldn't be allowed to happen . . . not while he was set on making Lady Lillian his wife.

Chapter Eight

Aunt Winnie stood at the cottage door, one hand on her hip and the other propped against the doorjamb. May took one look at Lord Evers. She suddenly felt as naughty as a child caught stealing candy from the kitchens.

"Lady Winifred." Lord Evers approached Winnie and offered her a quaint bow. "I gladly leave your young companion in your safe care." He smiled like a cat that had just tipped over the flour jar. With a flick of the wrist he tilted his hat with the skill of a man well practiced at the fine art of seduction. His head bowed low, he gave May a nod filled with promises and wickedness, before taking his leave.

Aunt Winnie's gaze narrowed as she watched him limp away. May's dear aunt hadn't invited the viscount in for refreshments, hadn't asked if he needed to rest his weary leg.

Her ire was unquestionably piqued.

"Now, Aunt—" May began only to be cut off by a quelling glance.

"Go sit in the parlor, child."

May obeyed without argument. This late in the morning, the parlor with its black and gold curtains and matching tapestry chairs was swathed by deep shadows. It appeared so dreary and dark compared to the bright morning sky she'd just shared with the viscount.

She should have never allowed herself to get so carried away. She should have never agreed to let the viscount escort her home. But their conversation had been quite lively. He knew of Mary Wollstonecraft's writings and even agreed with a few of the woman's edicts. They'd good-heartedly debated philosophies until the little cottage she shared with her aunt came into view. Then, as if by mutual agreement, they had walked up to the cottage in silence. What folly to believe the morning adventure had been a safe one.

With a deep sigh, May chose a chair near the window and waited for Aunt Winnie to begin her lecture.

Oh, she dearly deserved one, too. She'd called Lord Evers a fool—what a lark! She was a greater fool, believing the shameless rogue might try to kiss her . . . longing for him to press his lips to hers again.

She needed a chaperone to protect her from herself. Never had such a fool walked the world before her.

"I promise I will never—" Again, her aunt's quelling glance kept her from finishing her vow to never venture out into the wilderness without a companion.

Aunt Winnie remained on her feet. She huffed several times before speaking, her large torso heaving with the effort.

"Viscount Evers," she said at last with a haughty tenor that closely resembled her brother's. "How well are you acquainted with the poor devil?"

Surely Aunt Winnie couldn't believe she'd sneaked away for a lovers' assignation. Mortification bloomed anew. May's cheeks heated with an unrestrained vigor. For the first time she was glad for her unfashionable dark coloring. Her olive complexion hid all but the deepest changes in tone.

"He—he is naught but a friend, Aunt. I vow it. I took a stroll up to Beechen Cliff when I happened upon him. He insisted he escort me home."

Aunt Winnie studied May for several long minutes, seemingly gauging whether to believe her errant niece or not. Luckily, May had always been a horrid liar. As a child she could never talk her way out of mischief without breaking out into a fit of tears and confessing all.

"I swear it, Aunt. The meeting was all in innocence," May said with a steady tone.

Aunt Winnie finally relented with a long sigh of relief. She settled in her favorite chair near the fire.

"I pray in the future you will act with greater prudence, especially considering your potential connection to the very proper Mr. Tumblestone." Winnie did not have to raise her voice or speak harsh commands to press her point. The strength of the punishment came from her eyes. The cross look left May quaking in her kid boots. It had always been this way. Aunt Winnie carried herself with a certain grace that brooked no disobedience.

May lowered her head. "I will, Aunt."

"You do wish to marry Mr. Tumblestone, do you not?"

The question was not one May could easily answer. She raised her head and noticed how the hair peeking out from below Winnie's frilly cap appeared grayer and how Winnie's complexion had turned bilious over the past couple of days.

"I want you to be happy," May answered while fingering the thick threads decorating her chair. "I want you to get the best care and not worry about me."

A sheen of tears threatened in her aunt's weary eyes. "Not worry about you? I raised you, May. I love you. I will always worry about you. It is in my blood."

The declaration made May only more determined to do what was right for Winnie.

"I believe I would enjoy having a family," May admitted. "And Mr. Tumblestone, though not ideal, seems a stable sort of gentleman. I feel lucky he finds me an attractive choice."

Winnie harrumphed at that last statement. "And Lord Evers. What are your feelings toward him?"

Knowing it fruitless to lie, May tried to deflect the question. "My feelings for him are of no great import. He is determined to take Lady Lillian to wife."

Winnie's brows creased and she seemed to be concentrating deeply for several long moments. "I didn't suppose him to be that big a lobcock," she said after a while. "Perhaps he needs to be made aware of his options."

"It wouldn't matter, Aunt," May rushed to say.

If her future truly lay with the elderly Mr. Tumblestone, her heart would not be able to survive even the barest of hope that there could be a man out there in the world who could love and cherish and thrill her all at the same time.

"What I mean to say is that even if he were to find me attractive, his rank is still too high for the likes of me to aspire to. Such a match would surely cause a scandal."

"Nonsense, May. You would do well to remember—"

Aunt Winnie did not get the chance to tell May what she needed to remember because at that very moment there was a loud knock on the door, followed by a tittering of laughter.

"We will speak on this later," Winnie promised and shifted in her chair while they waited for Portia, their poor overworked housekeeper, to direct their guests into the parlor.

Lady Iona charged into the room, her apprehensive gaze darting from May to Aunt Winnie. "Why weren't you present at the Pump Room this morning?" she cried. "You worried me ever so much. Please do tell me nothing is amiss—not after Mamma and Papa's party last night. It would break their heart to think the festivities caused you any undue harm, Lady Winifred."

May rose from her chair, rushed across the room, and clasped her hands with Iona's to reassure her. "Aunt Winnie was just weary after the late party. So was I, I must admit. The excitement of the past several days is wearing heavily on the both of us."

"I should say," Lady Lillian said as she swept into the room behind her sister. Her thin snowy-white arm was linked with Lord Nathan Wynter's. The quiet voice she often used lured May to lean in closer and give Lillian her rapt attention.

An elegant pink gown swished around Lillian's ankles as she glided across the room toward May. She moved like an angel, like a beautiful, spectral spirit fallen from the heavens.

"You must be out of your head with excitement at the thought of accepting a marriage proposal."

"There has been no proposal," Iona was quick to point out. "There will be none, if I have any say."

"Well, you don't," Lillian said with a briskness rarely heard outside the Newbury family home.

Lord Nathan twisted free from Lillian's alluring clutches and stepped between the two sisters. His superfine navy blue coat matched his flashing blue eyes, and his crisply tailored pants fit like a second skin.

Iona blinked up at him and swayed, a reaction May found only too interesting.

"Ladies, please. I have not even had the opportunity to greet our long-suffering hosts."

In the hushed moment he'd created, Lord Nathan reverently greeted Aunt Winnie, sketching a bow suitable for a queen. Winnie appeared quite taken by Lord Nathan's cheery smile and square, masculine features. Iona sighed, making May wonder whether her friend could be even more charmed by his flowery praises of Winnie than Winnie herself.

"I hope we won't be forced to linger long," the only too perfect Lillian said not nearly loud enough for anyone but May to hear. Lillian and May had never rubbed along well. From their first meeting Lillian had made it abundantly clear how she, like most of society, disapproved of May's pedigree. Lillian did have the training and manners of a lady, though. She paid her warmest respects to Aunt Winnie.

The chit even went as far as to sit beside Winnie and begin a long discourse on how she had convinced her father to purchase the extravagant bonnet sitting askew on the top of her head. Three bright pink ostrich feathers bobbed as she prattled on about how she couldn't do without the feathered bonnet now that she was being actively courted.

"You see," Lillian said in that mild voice of hers, making her sound ever so harmless, "the Viscount Evers has set his cap for me."

A sharp prick of jealousy turned in May's chest as she felt drawn to listen.

"Mamma says I am well suited to be a wife for a man of his social standing. Just think of the balls and teas I will host in his London town house. Mamma says I will get along well and become the rage of London. Ladies of the highest rank will be panting for an invitation. But do not fear. I will of course invite you, Lady Winifred, to every single event. You may bring your silly companion along as well."

"That is very kind of you, dear," Winnie said coolly while Lord Nathan choked on a short fit of laughter.

He winked at Iona, who immediately returned the gesture.

Such curious behavior. Something devious was definitely in the works between the two. May prayed she would soon have the free time to be included in whatever mischief they were plotting. Perhaps they were planning to teach Lady Lillian a lesson in humility.

Curse the sky, May scolded herself. She had no right to wish ill on Lady Lillian. The viscount deserved all that was beautiful and perfect, including Lillian.

Jealousy was an emotion better suited for a lady with the status and social acceptance to compete with such lovely perfection. May had nothing to offer the viscount besides a fouled family name and an empty purse.

Besides, she didn't have the time or energy to waste on impossible dreams. Everything in her life was so topsy-turvy at the moment, she doubted she'd have time to read the latest gothic novel, much less try and indulge in a little mischief with her best friend.

Still, her unruly curiosity was again peaked when Lord Nathan and Iona slyly maneuvered themselves toward the parlor door and chatted privately while May and Aunt Winnie listened politely as Lillian prattled on and on about her plans for Lord Evers' future.

"We will naturally live in London most of the year. But we will wish to follow The Prinny to Brighton in the summer, don't you agree? Bath has its benefits—I have never seen Mamma's stomach so calm—but the social life can be so tiresome with the lower classes putting on airs just because they have a few shillings to spend. I hear Brighton is not at all the same."

Winnie nodded and smiled fondly at the young woman, patting her wrist occasionally. A trembling hand rose to her lips as she stifled a yawn. May guessed her aunt had long stopped listening and was fast growing exhausted.

"Shall I ring for tea?" May asked when Lillian paused for breath. Sending for tea was the proper thing to do, but that was not why May had suggested it. Lillian would never willingly come visiting here. Iona must have veered them away from their true destination to inquire after May's and Aunt Winnie's health. The fastest way to get them moving again—not that May cared to rush anyone but Lillian away—was to offer to start the process of heating tea.

Lillian reacted exactly as May had predicted. She leapt up from the chair as if fire had struck her. "Tea? Oh, no. We couldn't. We really couldn't. I must apologize, but Lord Nathan is escorting me to call on Lord Evers, you see. All above board, of course, with such a large crowd of us and with Lord Evers' mother in residence."

My, Lillian's tongue ran unfettered. May nodded, her feigned smile beginning to pain her.

"Evers has purchased a new horse. A young filly," Wynter calmly explained on the heels of Lillian's excuse to leave. "His own prized stallion served as stud. You can understand how he is naturally excited about the horse's arrival today and is intent on showing off his newest acquisition to Lady Lillian."

"Oh, yes." Lillian's cheeks glowed. "He is having the filly delivered here, to Bath, instead of to his stables in Northhamptonshire, at a great cost just to view her. We really must be going. I would hate to be late."

"You are welcome to join us, Miss Sheffers. Evers does enjoy showing off his ability to pick the finest horseflesh." Wynter shared a merry look with Iona.

Despite her suspicions about her best friend's motives, May's heart jumped at the temptation to accept. Silly, really, to want to spend time with a man who was destined to wound her heart. She'd be wise to keep her thoughts focused on the rational, the logical.

That is precisely what Mary Wollstonecraft would have done.

"Thank you for the kind invitation, but I must refuse." May took a step toward Aunt Winnie as if searching for support in that quarter. "I am ever so busy, you see. And my aunt is not at all feeling up to snuff. I should worry something terrible if I were to leave her."

"But, May, you simply must come." Iona tugged on her arm. "I will be unforgivably sore with you if you refuse."

May cast a silent plea in Aunt Winnie's direction. The older woman yawned into her hand and mumbled something about wanting to nap all day.

Lord Nathan even joined in the persuasions with a tempting offer to treat all the women to chocolates on the way.

Only the willowy Lady Lillian supported May's reasonable decision. "La, let her stay, Iona. It is her occupation to care for Lady Winifred, is it not? We should not pretend she is something other than what she is."

"And what is that?" Iona was quick to inquire, though there had been no need. May had recognized early on how most society ladies treated her no differently than a servant.

Aunt Winnie rose from her chair and quieted the room with a single clap of her hands. "May, you spend too much time with ladies and gentlemen far older than yourself. It is unhealthy. A young gel needs the companionship of fellow youngsters. You will go."

Not even Lady Lillian dared object to such a royally presented command. She turned up her nose before latching onto Lord Nathan's arm again.

"You weren't teasing, my lord, were you?" she cooed after saying her farewells to Aunt Winnie. "You will treat us to chocolates?"

Lord Nathan murmured some placating words and let himself be led from the room.

May kissed her aunt on the cheek and promised not to stay away long while Iona hurried May out of the parlor in pursuit of Lord Nathan and Lillian.

Since the decision had been taken out of her hands, and it would have been rude to disagree with her aunt, May decided to enjoy the afternoon outing . . . even if it meant risking her untested heart.

Chapter Nine

Radford eyed the cane sitting on his tiger maple desk in the study and brooded while waiting for Bannor to arrive. He had so many reasons to feel anxious. His stable manager was due to arrive within the hour so Radford could see firsthand the young filly he'd purchased from the Duke of Grafton, for one thing. The filly would only stay in Bath for a few days before the stable manager returned home to his stables in Northhamptonshire.

Ever since the accident, Radford had avoided his horses. He even left the sole care of the pair of playful and perfectly matched grays he used for his carriage to the able hands of the young groom he'd brought with him to Bath. So today his eagerness to finally meet this new horse, bred from one of his own stallions, was tinged with bittersweet anticipation. How would it feel to see her and know he would never be the one to ride her? He would never again learn a horse's personality firsthand in the vast fields and woods of his estate.

Such concerns were reason enough to brood. Why then did he insist on blaming the stubborn Miss Sheffers for the bulk of his nerves?

On the way down Beechen Cliff, she had insisted he use her as a prop. Her, a dainty woman, no less! He'd been humiliated. Mortified. Never should a man be so betrayed by his body that he'd be compelled to depend on a woman.

Ah . . . but her assistance had lessened the sharp pains

worrying his calf and foot. That couldn't possibly be the reason he'd spent the past fifteen minutes studying his cane, could it?

"You wouldn't push a horse with a lame leg," he grumbled to himself. A horse needed time and a goodly amount of pampering to heal. He spared no expense to coddle his horses to keep them healthy. So if he knew what it took to heal an injury, why should a woman's scolding be necessary?

That stubborn and utterly forgettable elflike creature had called him foolish. She'd gone beyond that and proved his foolishness by insisting he lean on her arm.

He was no horse, but he was flesh and blood just the same. May was right. If he wanted to heal he'd need to take the expense and pamper himself for a while.

Damnation! He must be a fool . . . for he wanted nothing more than to send for her and lavish poetic sentiments of gratitude on her dainty head. Worse, he dearly wished to have her standing by his side to feed him her courage when he went out to see this new horse of his.

And to kiss her . . . oh yes, kiss her. He had been greatly tempted to cover her lips with his when she dared call him a fool. The temptation hadn't diminished. He still wanted to kiss her and, Lord help him, perhaps do a little more.

"My lord?" Bannor stood in the doorway, his expression a gaping depiction of bald embarrassment. "I had knocked," he quietly explained.

Radford realized suddenly that he'd picked up his accursed cane and had been beating it against the floor while silently berating himself. He'd no right for feeling those damnable soft feelings for an ordinary bird like Miss Sheffers. She was not at all suitable for marriage to him—the blasted list had already proved that. His time would be better spent contemplating how best to please his Lady Lillian or reviewing business matters with his man-of-affairs.

With a quick toss, the cane clattered to the floor. He cleared his throat. "Before we begin going over the books," he said, "I have some matter of business to ask you about."

Bannor nodded as if seeing his employer in a royal rage were a common occurrence. He pushed his wire-rimmed glasses up his nose and took his regular seat opposite Radford's desk. His nimble fingers plucked a quill pen from its stand and blotted it very precisely.

Bannor did everything with precision. Radford's father wouldn't have hired this man to serve as his estate's man-of-affairs if he had been anything but the model of perfection.

"What is this matter of business, my lord?" he asked once he finished his lengthy ritual of setting up his papers at the desk.

"That young lady renting number twelve Sydney Place." Radford kept his tone purposefully neutral.

"Number twelve?" Bannor fiddled with his papers. "Ah, yes, Miss Margaret Sheffers. Although the back rent has been paid, there is no sign that she or her elderly aunt will be able to produce any future payments. They should be out by the end of the month."

"Yes." Radford negligently waved his hand. "About that. Don't evict them. If they wish to leave on their own accord, we naturally cannot stop them. But I will not have you push them out."

Bannor dropped his pen. Ink splattered on his ledger. "But, my lord, we are not a *charity*."

"Nor will this be a regular practice. Tell me, what do you know about the lady?" Although he had promised her he wouldn't pry into her affairs, Radford could not curb a nagging feeling that he was duty-bound as a gentleman to take some action. She was considering marriage to an old codger, for Heaven's sake. Miss Sheffers had to be at the end of her rope.

"I spoke with her banker. He told me her account had been seized by the courts. I do not know the reason."

"And her family? I suppose she is related to the Earl of Redfield?"

"That is her uncle," Bannor supplied, though Radford already knew as much. "Her mother, I believe, was the earl's youngest sibling. Miss Sheffers cares for her aunt, who is the earl's eldest sibling. I sense a strained relationship between the earl and his sister, however. I imagine that is one reason why the pair of hens were allowed to flounder for so long."

"Very good." This told Radford nothing new. "Find out whatever you can about the two women as soon as possible. I want deep, dark secrets if there are any to be had. Understood?"

Bannor swallowed hard and adjusted his glasses. "You—you aren't planning to coerce the young lady in some disgraceful manner, are you?" He whispered the question.

"On the contrary, Bannor. By gathering this information I hope to keep someone else from doing just that."

Bannor breathed a long sigh of relief.

"And, Bannor? That was an impertinent question. In the future, be advised I will not tolerate such questions against my character. If it happens again, you may find yourself needing to search for employment elsewhere."

Bannor nodded furiously and colored a bright crimson. "You must forgive me, my lord. I meant no insult. Truly, I didn't."

"Shall we review the books?" Radford said, hoping to move past the awkward moment as soon as possible. He had a day crammed with awkward moments to look forward to and no desire to dwell on any of them.

Try as she might, May could not keep her stomach from fluttering nervously as the viscount's butler, the long-faced Jeffers, slowly opened the heavy door. He gave a start when he found himself staring down upon her and the smiling Lady Iona.

Lord Nathan grunted at the shocked pause, not taking notice of either the speechless Jeffers or the mortified May. He brushed past the butler and led the group into the parlor. With shocking brashness he announced himself and the ladies to the frail-looking woman lounging on a velvet sofa.

The woman sat up slightly and, smiling all the while,

scolded Lord Nathan for his unconventional behavior. Her hand rose in the air for him to kiss. She was dressed in layers of the most diaphanous fabrics and her silky brown hair was peppered with gray.

So this was Lady Evers, the viscount's mother, May thought after the introductions were completed. Lady Evers rose with great care, as if fearing her thin bones might snap. May worried for a moment that Lady Evers' weakened legs wouldn't be able to hold her weight. But the lady surprised May when she managed to cross the room and embrace Lady Lillian with great enthusiasm.

She cupped the young woman's face in her hands. "Every time I see you I think, my, this girl is as lovely as a jewel. Just look at you," she said. Her gaze tripped over May and held steady for a moment on Iona. "And your sister. I do pronounce you both diamonds of the first water."

May's natural smile tightened into something quite forced. There was no reason to feel slighted. Lady Evers' reaction to her had been no different the night before, nor was it any different than many of the *ton*'s. But here, under the viscount's roof, Lady Evers' expectation that May meekly fade into the background stung worse than the most thinly veiled insult Lady Lillian could ever utter.

Lillian and Iona naturally drank up the praise and lapsed into comfortable conversation with the viscount's mother. It was only right that Lillian should make friends with Lady Evers. The woman would very likely become her mother-in-law, after all.

Just once, May thought. Her smile strained till her jaw ached. *Just once, I would like to be the pretty one—the one everyone is dying to love*. But that would never happen. Not even her parents—the very two people who should love her no matter how ugly a duck she turned out to be—they didn't even love her enough to stay by her side.

She stepped back toward the window seat, as was her habit, and allowed herself be forgotten. An interloper, perhaps . . . but she did have her pride.

A lifetime of minutes passed before Lord Evers entered the parlor. Cane in hand, he was blessedly giving his injured foot a well-deserved rest. Despite May's discomfort at being the forgotten guest, her smile relaxed at the sight of him using that cane. Her words that morning must have made an impact. He was letting his finely polished wooden cane with a golden cap take the weight off his damaged leg . . . and looking more dashing than ever for it.

His gaze swept the room. A brief hesitancy darkened his expression as his eyes flicked from Lady Lillian's lovely pout to his cane and back to Lillian again. The gel played the part of coquette to perfection.

Lillian turned her head and whispered in Lord Nathan's ear, twittering lightly. The viscount remained standing at the threshold, looking adorably cross. May saw right away what he'd missed. Since he hadn't immediately plied Lillian with flowering praises or complimented her ridiculous ostrich-feathered bonnet, Lillian had chosen to punish him by flirting shamelessly with his friend.

Fortunately his mother seemed to know the rules of the game Lillian had chosen to play. She came immediately to his rescue.

"Radford," she cried. "Come tell your Lady Lillian how beautiful she looks. Haven't you noticed her lovely new bonnet and how it complements her rosy complexion?" She took Lillian's arm then. "You must forgive my son. Just like his father, Radford can be blind to such delicate matters. He appreciates the final result without taking adequate notice of the details that make our beauty a success."

Radford?

His given name fit his straight, proud stature. The name literally tripped off May's tongue as she whispered it. No matter how hard she tried she could not seem to wrench her gaze away from him.

He'd changed his clothes. His buff pants were tight, probably too tight for his injured leg. His coat was also tight, accentuating his broad shoulders. An intricately pressed cravat cascaded from his neck. All in all he looked very well turned out. His style could rival the most fashionable London dandies. Were they in London, he would doubtlessly win a nod from Beau Brummell, society's arbiter of taste and fashion.

May watched Radford with fascination, realizing with a short gasp of horror that she was a little more than half in love with him. He fawned over Lillian, kissing her hand and gazing intently into her blue eyes. She, in turn, swatted his shoulder and made him promise to never overlook her lovely bonnets again.

"I wouldn't dream of it, my lady. You have the loveliest taste in clothing," he said in the same honeyed tone he'd used in the moments before he'd gifted May with her very first kiss. "I bow to your genius on all matters of fashion. You are a goddess in that respect. A beautiful, talented goddess."

That first kiss he'd given her had meant the world to May.

A knife twisted in her gut. The green-eyed monster, jealousy, stabbed her but good. That very same kiss had been nothing more than an empty diversion to Radford.

May fervently prayed that love was indeed a fleeting emotion, as Mary Wollstonecraft had suggested. How would she be able to bear the ripping pangs in her heart otherwise? How could she live the rest of her life while such aches burrowed deep into her soul?

There was no one, save her aunt, who had ever found her worthy of being loved. The realization threatened to pull tears to her eyes. May blinked them back furiously. She was a woman grown, not some besotted child who still believed in fairy tales and romantic endings. Such things only lived in novels.

Happy endings were certainly vacant from her quiet life.

Radford hadn't even noticed her presence. It was as if she'd actually melted into the wainscoting. Without wishing to till at windmills, May shifted deeper into the window seat, half-hidden behind the heavy curtains, dearly wishing she could disappear altogether.

Radford encouraged his mother and *his* Lillian to join him on a long sofa. He motioned to a cozier velvet sofa, inviting Lord Nathan and Iona to also make themselves comfortable.

Lord Nathan cast a wary glance in May's direction and refused the offer to sit. Iona followed suit.

"I would prefer to stand, my lord," Iona said in that low, proper tone of hers that always sounded like a rebuke to May's ears.

Her refusal left Radford in an awkward position. He was stuck between the polite need to sit with his mother and intended fiancée or remain standing with Iona. His eyebrows arched slightly and he flashed a quick snarl toward his friend.

"Very well," he said. "I am anxious to inspect my filly. Word came around not ten minutes ago of my stable manager's arrival. Perhaps we should—"

His gaze met May's at that moment and he froze.

He was angry. She could sense anger in the air, and she was convinced it came from him. He didn't want her in his parlor, in his house, or in his life. Agreeing to Lord Nathan's silly notion that she would be welcomed was a fool's folly May deeply regretted. But she could not change her course now. She swallowed hard and rose.

"My lord," she said crisply and curtsied.

He blinked.

"My sister insisted *she* come along," Lillian said in the ensuing silence. Neither Lord Nathan nor Iona moved a muscle to come to May's aid. Instead, they stepped back and smiled at each other in a knowing sort of way. "Iona likes to bring her along on our outings. Perhaps it is *charity.*"

Charity? May was far too proud to accept charity.

"Lady Iona and I are friends, my lord." Since no one else was going to defend her, May determined she would simply defend herself. "Lord Nathan had suggested I join the group, explaining how you are so very adept at judging horseflesh. He wished I be impressed by your great knowledge, I suppose."

The corner of Radford's mouth twitched. Whatever was

going on in his head couldn't be good. He dipped an exaggerated bow. "A thousand pardons, ma'am," he said. "Please forgive me for overlooking you. I suppose I am doomed to fall prey to all sorts of humiliations today."

With that said, Radford strolled from the room, leading the way to a large empty field beside his house. May lagged behind, hoping to remain in the parlor, until she noticed his mother also planned to remain there. Lady Evers stretched out like a treacherous tiger on the velvet sofa.

"Don't be anxious." Iona took May's arm and pushed her outside.

"But horses are such large animals . . ." May said.

"You are frightened?" Radford asked. He lazily leaned against one of the portico's Ionic columns while Iona and May emerged.

May's heart skipped a beat. She fought a fresh attack of embarrassment, realizing he had overheard her put voice to her silly fears. She was the only lady she knew who didn't have a rudimentary knowledge of riding or horses. Having been raised in London with an aunt who shared May's unhealthy fear of the beasts, May hadn't been given much of an opportunity to learn how to even approach a horse—much less sit atop one.

"I have no experience, my lord," she said somewhat stiffly. "I don't know what to do with them."

He chuckled. "I will hold your hand, Miss Sheffers, and guide you so you can pet her velvet nose." He took May's arm from Iona's then and walked between the women out to the field. A man in a tweed cap and baggy breeches stood holding the reins to a very tall cream-colored horse with a brown dappled rump. The filly tossed her dark brown mane and danced sideways as they approached.

May would much have preferred to try and pet Lady Evers' perfect nose than tempt one's fate with the foul-tempered beast looming in front of her. What could Radford be thinking suggesting she dare touch such a wild thing?

"Ooooo," Lady Lillian sighed. The filly danced sideways

again. "She is ever so lovely, is she not? May I ride her? She must glide like the wind. Does she, Lord Evers?" She pushed her sister out of the way and latched onto the arm Radford had used to hold his cane, tugging on him as if he were a child's wooden pull toy. "Does she ride like the wind?"

Radford stiffened. May felt the very air about him grow still. How thoughtless of Lillian to ask such a question. His injuries had obviously kept him from riding. A condition that surely created deep wounds in his pride.

"She will go well enough," he said after a lengthy pause. He shrugged away the tension and his eyes lit up as he studied his beast. "She is a beauty, Lyles. Her legs look strong. Perhaps we should enter her in the races."

"Aye, m'lord, I believe so. She has the frame for speed," Radford's stable manager drawled. He smiled, a wide grin showing a line of missing teeth. "She's a beaut, m'lord, jus' like her pa."

The filly tossed her head as if agreeing.

"She wants to run," Radford said.

"Aye, my gig's horse trotted far too slowly for Princess' liking."

"Princess? Is that her name?" Lillian asked, her soft voice growing ever more mild. Her expression sparkled as she gazed up at Radford. "How delightful. Oh, how I would love to own such a horse."

May fully expected him to promise Lillian the filly as a wedding present, or at least hint that he might do something so foolishly romantic. He shocked May when he ignored the comment.

Instead, his gaze turned sharply away from Lillian and toward *her*. "Princess will be part of my foundation stock. I may race her, but she will principally be a breeding mare."

"Lord Evers, you are scandalous. You make me blush," Lillian said and batted his arm.

May found herself blushing as well because Radford had begun to trace tiny circles on the inside of her wrist with his forefinger. He probably didn't realize he was doing so, but there was a hint of heat in his gaze that made her suddenly suspicious.

No, she was being foolish again. He had baldly told her that there could never be anything between them. That he wouldn't even ask her to be his mistress.

By the time May pulled herself out of her thoughts, Radford had released her arm and returned his attentions to Lillian. He fawned over the young lady in a way no one, not even May's aunt, had ever done with her. She needed to be careful. There was nothing but pain waiting for her if she allowed her fantasies to run away with her again.

No man wanted her.

Well, Mr. Tumblestone did—but May still couldn't figure out why.

Lord Nathan, Iona, and Lillian were all speaking at once, praising the horse, while standing far closer to the beast than what May thought could possibly be safe. The filly stomped her heavy foot as if angered by their presence and kicked up a spray of mud that splattered on May's cotton dress. No one noticed the stain or May's growing distress.

She retrieved a handkerchief from her sleeve and patted at the mud. It was hopeless, she knew. She would be mud-splattered until she could change out of the gown.

Radford didn't spare her a passing glance once he'd pried his arm from Lillian's clutches and stepped away from his friends' praises to speak with his stable manager.

Lillian didn't seem to notice him missing. She chattered on as if he were still standing between herself and May. "Papa will absolutely be thrilled to hear how skilled you are at judging horseflesh, Lord Evers. The last two horses he purchased came up lame within a month. He has no eye for such things, you must know. I will tell him first thing. . . ."

One of the ostrich plumes on Lillian's bonnet dipped forward and teased the filly's nose as she continued to explain how she dearly wished her father could see Princess. Her head bobbed with her words, and the feather continued to strike the young horse. May watched as the skittish filly's eyes began to roll.

Something bad was going to happen. May could feel it in the way her heart began to pound. The filly was going to bolt and stamp them all to death. Poor, poor Radford. He would never forgive himself if his prize horse were to injure his beloved Lillian.

Princess whinnied and ducked her head, as if trying to escape the brightly dyed feather. She stomped her foot and whinnied again when the troublesome feather seemed to follow her.

"She's a spirited one, she is, m'lord," the stable manager drawled and pulled the leading rein tighter.

"She is a pretty horse," Iona said. "Just look at the unusual coloring."

"You've done good this time, Evers," Lord Nathan said. "All your hard work at the stables is beginning to pay off."

No one other than May sensed even a whiff of danger. Lillian's feathered bonnet continued to bob and torment the horse, her speech continuing without pause.

Such a great beast, May couldn't help but think. *She shall kill us.*

She fought the urge to escape to a safe distance away. But she was never one to cower. If the others weren't afraid, she wouldn't show her budding terror . . . even if it meant risking her neck in order to protect her pride.

Oh what a foolish sin, pride. May had noticed more than ever how such a stubborn emotion could be the cause of some quite unnecessary troubles.

The filly snorted after the feather danced in her nostril. She tossed back her head, reared up, and made a horrid sound.

Everyone froze. Even Lillian closed her mouth long enough to send the filly a wary glance.

"I say, my lord," she then said rather shrilly, "I have never seen—"

Whatever Lillian hadn't seen, no one would know.

Princess landed with a thud and nipped the bonnet right off Lillian's head. Lillian shrieked and tossed herself into Lord Nathan's arms. Both Radford and the stable manager struggled with the reins, trying to calm the great beast. As she strained forward, her large, square teeth showing, she looked as if she was going to nip off a hunk of Lillian's thick blond locks.

Without much thought for her own safety, May snatched the offending bonnet from the ground and leapt between Lillian and Princess. "Here is your enemy," she said in a firm voice and pushed the bright bonnet into the filly's mouth. It was the hat, not Lillian, that had offended.

Princess took the bonnet and shook it to bits while the stable manager used sheer strength to drag her a goodly distance away.

May stood frozen, her eyes tightly sealed now that the immediate danger had passed, and listened to the commotion all around her. Lillian whimpered while Lord Nathan and Iona tried in vain to soothe her.

"There now, that was a damned brave thing," Radford said.

May's heart skipped at the sound of his voice. He'd come to praise her for her quick thinking. She peeled open one eye and then the other.

The breadth of her gaze was empty.

Radford had bypassed her completely and taken the trembling Lillian into his arms. "I should expect any gentle lady to be frightened out of her wits after such an experience. Horses are so large, are they not? Their grand size must be off-putting to women, especially those as dainty as yourself. You were so very brave, my lovely Lillian."

Lillian clutched Radford's coat and sobbed into his cravat.

"You seem shaken yourself, Miss Sheffers." At least Lord Nathan had the decency to remember her valiant effort to save Lillian's precious hair. "If you desire, you too may sob into my cravat and ruin it." The smile he flashed was contagious.

"No, thank you, my lord." She gave a mock curtsy. "I believe I will endure." Though his joking settled her discordant nerves, it did nothing to relieve the jealousy bubbling through her veins. It literally pained her to see Radford petting Lillian's undamaged hair.

The emotional twit was unworthy of him. He should have set his cap for Iona, a much finer cut of womanhood. Surely May wouldn't be plagued with a jealous heart if she were watching him seduce her friend, instead.

You are such a liar.

No one, not even her closest friend, could prove suitable for Radford. Budding romantic affection was turning out to be an illogical affliction. May hated the loss of control.

"My, Miss Sheffers, who has trampled on your grave?" Lord Nathan asked. "You look as angry as Princess did just moments ago. I won't need to guard my hat from your gnashing teeth, will I?"

May smiled weakly and wandered off to sit on a bench set out under a smooth-barked beech tree. Watching from a distance did help a little.

Radford was still petting and cooing over Lillian. Despite May's efforts to close her mind, she could still hear everything said. Every word etched itself into her memory.

"Did you see what she did to my bonnet?" Lillian wailed. "That horrid, horrid girl fed my bonnet to your evil-tempered horse. Her jealousy of me has always caused problems. And now she nearly got me killed."

"I don't think Princess' behavior was May's fault," Lord Nathan drawled lazily. He looked oddly pleased with himself.

"You must have startled her, sweet," Radford said in a voice smooth enough to soothe a colicky baby. He rubbed his hand up and down the length of Lillian's arched back. May shivered from just witnessing such an intimate gesture. If his gentle hands were touching her back in that very same manner and if those words had been for her, she would be melting into a puddle of bliss.

Lillian didn't melt. She twisted free, her cheeks blooming a bright red.

"You think *I* startled her?"

Radford tried to enfold her into his arms again. "Let me carry you inside. You can rest on the sofa and sip some warm tea while you compose yourself."

Lillian punched his shoulders until he released her. "I want to go home," Lillian shouted. Tears streamed down her pretty pink cheeks. "Just look what that evil-tempered beast did to my new bonnet. Just look!" The straw bonnet lay scattered in shreds on the muddy ground. "How dare you blame me! I shall never forgive the monster. You will just have to sell her, my lord, or I shall never forgive you!"

She was fast becoming hysterical, her voice growing ever more shrill. Both Iona and May knew the warning signs only too well. The last time they had witnessed such a scene was three years ago after the duke had purchased several yards of shimmering exotic silks for Iona's eldest sister and had refused to buy Lillian an equally expensive bolt.

"I think we should get her home," Iona said quietly. "Thank you for your assistance, Lord Evers."

He gave a curt nod and wrung his hands. "Of course."

"I will walk the ladies Lillian and Iona home." Lord Nathan gave a meaningful glance in May's direction. "Perhaps you might wish to soothe Miss Sheffers? She, too, suffered a fright."

One of Radford's raven brows quirked up. "Indeed?" he asked and turned her way. "Have you suffered terribly, Miss Sheffers?" he called.

May rose from the bench, made as graceful a path as possible through the tall grasses, and rejoined the group. Her pride interfered with what her heart wanted to say. Interfered with her longing to bury herself in his soiled cravat and enjoy his closeness. "Of course not, my lord," she said, her chin jutting in the air. "Lord Nathan is jesting at my expense."

"Then you shall stay with the viscount and pet the filly's nose?" Iona asked.

"And I will hold your hand," Radford said before May could protest.

"What about me?" Lillian wailed.

Iona took her sister in her arm and led her to the bench May had been using. "You need to stop your sniffling. I will not walk through Bath with you in such a state. Tongues would wag for weeks."

"She is in a temper," Radford said as he assessed his new filly with a frown. The beast was still stomping the ground with her hoof and pulling on the reins. "I can't imagine why. Perhaps we should keep our distance for now."

May released a healthy sigh and thanked Heaven for the reprieve. "Another time, then?"

"Yes, another time."

There would never be another time, of course. May and Radford could never be close, could never be friends. Not when her heart ached just from standing near him.

He touched her hand. The simple act stole her breath.

Five minutes later, May, Iona, and Lord Nathan led a much calmer Lillian from the field. May gave Radford a wave farewell that went unreturned. His attentions were on his horse, a frown shadowing his aristocratic features.

They were partway down Sion Hill when a great shout went out. A clamor of hooves beat a path adjacent to the road. May was the first to see her. The filly, pretty as her royal namesake, ran toward them, her reins fluttering unattended behind her. There was a primal beauty in her movement.

May stood transfixed as the powerful animal leapt over a wooden fence and landed not a yard away from her. Lillian screeched. Iona called a warning. The great horse seemed madly intent on getting at May, and she could have no hope of outrunning such an agile creature.

All she could do was hold her ground, close her eyes, and hope for the best as the thunder of hooves grew ever louder.

She had no great desire to die but could see no opportunity for escape. May kept her eyes tightly sealed and waited to be trampled to death.

A great velvety nose nudged her brow. May forced open her eyes and peered into Princess' long face. The horse's hot breath swirled all around her.

"You're not going to hurt me?" May said with a bravado that had to be dredged up from her deepest depths. She spoke in the same quiet, refined manner Iona took whenever she grew agitated. The ploy worked. Princess nudged May's shoulder and whinnied softly.

The leather reins hung at May's feet. It was a simple task of taking them up and walking back up the road toward Radford's Longbranch House. Princess followed like a motherless pup. It was a rather endearing experience.

The stable manager ran down the hill, followed by Radford, his lame leg practically dragging behind him. May winced at the pain he must be feeling. But he didn't let the injury slow him. He passed the manager and stopped, breathing heavily, a few feet from May.

"Are you harmed? As soon as you went out of view, she bolted. I was terrified . . . she was running after Lady Lillian, perhaps. Thank goodness you stopped her," he said while still trying to catch his breath. He looked pale, ill.

"Lady Lillian is unharmed, my lord," May assured him. She worried at his wan complexion. He had overexerted himself, but she knew better than to inquire after his health.

His pride rivaled her own.

"She is half in love with Miss Sheffers, Evers," Lord Nathan said. He had to pry Lillian off his arm to take a step toward them. "The filly ran straight to her and gave her a friendly nudge."

Radford gave May a queer look then. He frowned and tilted his head, staring at her as if he were seeing her for the first time. May looked back, her insides trembling. Though she didn't fully understand why, that timeless moment between them was yards more sensual than their first kiss.

A smile came naturally to her lips as she handed over the leading reins to him. "Good day, my lord." Her voice sounded soft and husky. "I thank you for a lovely afternoon."

Radford captured her hand before she could slip away and raised her knuckles to his lips. "My pleasure."

A wealth of fantasies sprang into May's fertile mind in reaction to those two simple words. *My pleasure.*

She prayed for a long, uninterrupted night of sleep.

Oh la, the dreams she planned to have . . .

My pleasure, he'd said.

Chapter Ten

"You will simply have to sell the beast." Lady Evers had risen from her lounge and strolled across the room. Her gown's fabric billowed around her, reminding Radford of a feather helplessly caught in the hot summer wind. "I shiver at the thought of your Lady Lillian suffering such a fright. You must make immediate amends. Send her a household full of flowers. Purchase a lovely bonnet to replace the one your horse ruined. Pay her a visit to assure her of your concern . . . but first, get rid of the beast!"

Get rid of the beast? Princess was a horse he had worked years to acquire. Before leaving for the Peninsula, Radford had scoured the countryside for the perfect mare. The list of qualifications had covered three pages. The mare had to be a sturdy match for his powerful male, strong in areas where his best stallion was weak. The joining of two such animals should produce a horse worthy to be considered for the foundation of his stable.

Once such a horse had been located, Lyles, his stable manager, had worked for over a year to close the deal with the Duke of Grafton in Radford's absence and arrange for his stallion to breed with the mare. The first horse born had been a male. A second breeding was required, since his stable needed a filly.

After six years of hard work, he had finally gotten to

touch the results of his labor. She was a beautiful, lively young thing, too.

He would not give her up.

"It was just a silly bonnet, Mother," Radford said. "Lady Lillian overreacted. Surprising really, she is supposedly a renowned horsewoman. A spirited filly shouldn't have frightened her." He thought of May then. She had been terrified to stand so close to the young horse. Her hand had shivered in his. Yet, *she* didn't shrivel into a quivering mess when Princess attacked Lady Lillian's bright ostrich-feathered hat.

Despite her fears, May had foolishly stepped between the startled horse and the hysterical Lady Lillian and prevented a true disaster. Amazing, really.

He'd seen her in a new light. A common lady dressed in a drab cotton gown and wearing a wide rimmed, straw bonnet with no ornamentation save for a single pale peach silk ribbon—she was by no means a raving beauty. But when he saw her leading his horse up the lane, he felt a sense of calm only the return to his Castlemain Hall and his vast fields of horses had ever given him. She was as earthy and natural as the spirited filly. He felt a strong sense of tenderness for Miss Sheffers. The silent attraction pulled him like none other.

"Radford!" His mother clapped her hands to recapture his attention. "Attend me. You aren't taking this matter seriously enough. A young lady has delicate feelings. You must tread carefully."

"Yes, Mother," he said docilely. He'd agreed to marry, after all. And he had found Lady Lillian, the woman who best matched his requirements. "I will send for flowers straight away."

"And you will sell your new mare." His mother would not let the point pass without a firm commitment . . . one which Radford was unprepared to give.

"I will look into the matter."

"You will sell the beast."

"Not until I understand what happened. And I will not discuss this further." He stole from the room with his mother's gasp haunting his ears.

She had suffered as much as he had. She deserved to be pampered and surrounded by happy grandchildren. He would give that to her, even if he had to sacrifice a little to do so. He would go as far as marriage to a silly emotional young woman like Lady Lillian.

He would not, however, give up his dream of developing one of the best stables in England.

"I will not let you crush her dreams like you did with mine, Sires."

May was approaching the upstairs drawing room, which also served as the library, with the thought of seeking out the horridly romantic novel *Udolpho* to lose herself in when she heard her aunt's raised voice. She'd been home only long enough to change out of her mud-splattered gown and tame her unruly curls. She had no idea her uncle had made a surprise visit.

What he must think of her! She'd abandoned her aunt all afternoon to pursue some frivolities of her own. And to what gain? Her heart had only slipped farther down the bottomless void of love while she bruised her pride, ruined her dress, and unsettled her mind by a fearsome beast with heavy hooves.

"Crush them?" Uncle Sires said in an even tone. May nearly had to press her ear to the drawing room door to hear him. "Is that what you believe? I am not a heartless monster, Winnie. I have her best interests in mind when I make these decisions . . . just as I had yours so many years ago."

"She will never be happy with him. He is too old. Admit it, Sires. You only paraded him here to hurt me."

"To hurt you, dear sister?" What he said after that was lost in the heavy wood door separating May from the interior of the drawing room. Besides, eavesdropping was beneath her. She should be in the room at her aunt's side.

May hesitated for just a moment before pushing the door

open, beaming a smile toward her aunt, and then providing her uncle with an obedient curtsy. "I hope I didn't stray from home too long, Aunt," she said softly and pretended she had not heard a word of their strained conversation.

"This is why I worry after you," Uncle Sires said with a grand wave in May's direction. "She is wild, unreliable. She should be here with you, not traipsing through town like some hoyden."

"She is young," Winnie said. "She needs to spend time with ladies and gentlemen nearer her age, not be cooped up with some weakened old biddy like me."

"She's not that young. Four-and-twenty. Some would claim the child is already well set on the shelf."

"You are not an old biddy," May said over Uncle Sires. It was rude to speak out of turn and interrupt the head of the family. But she felt she needed to explain how she had never tired of her aunt's company. "You are a delightful companion and always full of clever conversation."

"Please"—Uncle Sires turned on May—"don't spout falsehoods to cover for your shortcomings. We all know you cannot bear to remain under a roof for long stretches of time. You are your father's spawn . . . naught but a gypsy dressed in fashionable rags."

His insults rarely pained May. Over the years she'd come to expect them from him. But for a worrying minute, his charge troubled her. She was discovering that she did indeed prefer a romp outdoors to a quiet read in the drawing room's window seat. Did that mean there was something innately wrong with her?

Radford had teased her earlier that morning. He'd called her a shameless hoyden. Had he truly believed that of her?

"I love Aunt Winnie. I have never regretted a moment spent with her," May said slowly with what her uncle called her unfettered gypsy tongue. "You must know that, Aunt."

Winnie gave a short nod. "You will cease this foolishness,

Sires. I will not listen to your opinion. You do not know May as I do. I daresay you never will."

"But you must agree, sister. Tumblestone's farm will give May ample opportunity to live a life free from high society's constraints. No one in the village will hold the circumstances of her birth against her. No one will snarl if she spends the afternoon under the blazing sun. She will be happy."

Happy? Somehow May could not see it. How could she be happy married to a man she didn't know? A man older than her own father. How could she be happy with Mr. Tumblestone when another filled her heart?

No matter how she felt or the heated way Radford looked at her, she was no naïve girl fresh from the schoolroom. She knew there could never be anything between them. Winnie had taught May to guard herself.

"She will not be happy," Winnie proclaimed as she rose from the cushioned chair. "She will not be happy with him."

"Be reasonable—" Uncle Sires began only to clamp his mouth closed when Winnie shot him a sour look. She struggled without the aid of a cane or May's arm to gracefully leave the room with an air of hauteur lingering in her wake. The effort must have been great. Aunt Winnie was as gray as a ghost by the time she reached the stairs outside the door.

May charged after her, thinking to lend a hand, when Uncle Sires stepped in her path and blocked the door.

"My sister's emotional outbreak has nothing to do with you, child." He spoke down to her with broad, round tones that could still frighten May all the way to the tips of her toes. His cold, brown eyes remained fixed on her as he gathered up his cloak, hat, and gloves. "Walk with me."

May lowered her head and batted down a flaring desire to disobey him. "Yes, my lord," she said, suitably cowed.

Sires smiled, his lips thinning with the joyless expression. "Mr. Tumblestone is a fine gentleman, do you not agree?" he asked as they walked side by side down the narrow stairs. May was pressed up against the wall.

"I do not know him well enough to judge, my lord." She had no great desire to learn more about Mr. Tumblestone, either. And now, with her aunt less than pleased with the match, May found her interests in Mr. Tumblestone fading fast. "He is old."

"His age is of no great consequence, child. What with the rigors of the childbed, husbands naturally live much longer than their wives."

That thought sobered May. "Has he buried many wives then?" she asked once they reached the front door.

"No, none. He has never been married, you see."

"Never?" May found that hard to believe. He appeared to be a man of consequence, though meager when compared to her uncle's standards, and he owned property. Such a man should have married to secure his future long before reaching an advanced age. "Why?"

"The reason is not important. He is willing to marry now. He is willing to marry you."

The thought that a man, a consummate bachelor at that, should agree to marry a woman he had never met made May wary. "He was willing to take me as his wife before he met me. Why?"

"Why? To gain entrance into our family, of course." He answered as if bucks and beaus should be banging down the door to offer their hand in marriage just to align their families with hers. Gracious, that was so far from the truth that May had to swallow a bubbling giggle that threatened to burst from her mouth.

"Do you have any more questions about him?" he asked. "I want you to feel comfortable when you accept his proposal next week."

Accept his proposal next week? *Sires must be mad.*

"I—I don't know him yet!" May shouted. "I can't do it!"

His grim smile did not waver. "I will arrange for you to spend more time with him, then. There is no need for all this womanly emotion. I am giving you a full week to become accustomed to the idea, for Heaven's sake."

"You are giving me?" May sputtered, her anger now fully unleashed. "You—you are a pompous ass, my lord. You have no say in my life. None at all. I am only bowing to you and considering your wishes in deference to Aunt Winnie. If I choose to marry, it will be to the man of my picking . . . a man I can dearly love with all my heart. Something you surely know nothing about!"

Sires caught her chin in his thick hand and pinched it between his fingers. "You, child, will school your temper or else I will take a whip to you." His voice was a harsh whisper. "I am still the head of this family and like it or not, you are part of my responsibility by my younger sister's blood. Do you understand me?"

"Yes, my lord." The answer came automatically.

His hand tightened on her chin. "You need to be beaten, child. This willfulness of yours is a bane to our entire family. Before you make any further rash decisions, consider your aunt's health. Consider what your willful disobedience will do to her."

He released her sore chin and looked as if he were contemplating abusing her right then and there. For several tense minutes the only sound in the hall came from a ticking grandfather clock. May held her ground and maintained eye contact with him the entire time.

"Consider your aunt," he said as if May needed to be reminded. "I will bring Mr. Tumblestone by tomorrow morning." Then he stormed from the house.

She would meet with Mr. Tumblestone in the morning, all right. Such a meeting would be most welcome for she planned to tell him exactly what she thought about her uncle's heavy-handed attempt to marry her off to the first man he could find who would have her.

After returning from their regular visit to the Pump Room the next morning, May donned a shortsleeved spotted muslin walking dress. Aunt Winnie had purchased the gown as a gift at the beginning of summer. May wasn't particularly fond of the material. The rosy spots made her too noticeable. She much preferred the dull, faded colors filling her wardrobe. The gowns were worn and comfortable. Above all they allowed her to disappear into any social background, which pleased nearly everyone concerned.

However, since May had no plans to go visiting, she had chosen the dress to please her aunt. She didn't mind sticking out in her own home. Let Mr. Tumblestone, who was due to arrive with her uncle within the hour, take notice of her. She wanted his complete attention when spurning his marriage offer.

Mr. Tumblestone was a kind man. She supposed he must be a good man. But, with Aunt Winnie's blessing, May was determined not to become any man's wife. If Uncle Sires persisted in holding her parents' money ransom, she would simply seek employment as a lady's companion.

With the details settled—at least in her mind—May waited anxiously for the men's arrival. She looked forward to shocking her uncle while gently refusing the kindly old Tumblestone's proposal.

The morning was bright and warm. Birds chirped pretty songs from high in the trees. Aunt Winnie was smiling again. Everything felt right.

The clock was striking the hour when Uncle Sires' carriage rambled to a stop in front of the cottage. Portia put the kettle on the fire while May offered Winnie her arm and helped her settle into her favorite chair in the parlor.

"Be brave," Winnie whispered a moment before the housekeeper led Sires and Tumblestone into the room. "As long as you are following your heart, you are doing the right thing."

As the men crowded into the room, Winnie remained seated. She harrumphed a less than polite greeting. May, on the other hand, curtsied and murmured her welcomes. "The tea will be here presently," she then told the men.

Mr. Tumblestone, his gray hair poking out from beneath

his polished hat, smiled broadly at May. He took her hand and pressed his lips to her knuckles.

"I have been told that you and your uncle came to an agreement yesterday. Our future is forged. I am very happy."

"So am I," May said. She pried her hand from his bony grasp. "But you must allow me to speak, Mr. Tumblestone. No one can be certain of the future, do you not agree?"

"What nonsense are you spouting, child?" Uncle Sires approached, his round belly bounced with agitation. "I will permit no puzzling speech today. The banns have already been prepared. They are to be published this weekend. You will not confound us because your weak mind is suffering from a case of nerves."

May tilted her head to one side and hazarded a glance toward her aunt. She sat serenely with her fingers steepled in front of her pursed lips. No one was going to come to her defense, May knew. She would have to do this on her own.

Her aunt's presence in the room was support enough, she supposed. She didn't want anyone fighting this battle for her. As a woman prepared to forge a new path in the world, she had to continue to think and act alone.

"I will strive to make my meaning as plain as possible, Uncle." She smiled then and took the time to enjoy the tense calm. The silence would be short-lived. "Mr. Tumblestone, you have treated me with the greatest courtesy these past few days. For that, I am grateful."

"You have a gentle manner, Miss Sheffers," Tumblestone said. He produced a small box from an interior pocket of his coat. "We will rub well together. You will see."

The lid of the box had been removed. A dazzling blue sapphire ring lay in a nest of pink silk.

The sight of the polished gold and glittering stone flustered May. She didn't want his proposal. He wasn't giving her time to explain.

"Please." She took a step away from him. He was a very tall man and she had to crane her neck to peer into his eyes. "Please, put that away, sir."

He took the ring from the box and followed her retreat. "I would rather slip it on your finger, Miss Sheffers."

This was not going the way May had planned. They were supposed to listen to her well-scripted speech—not interrupt. Panic welled inside her. No matter how far they pushed her into a corner, she would not give into her fiery gypsy passions and shout her rejection.

Last night she'd lost her temper with Uncle Sires. She would not do it now.

So instead of shouting how uncomfortable Mr. Tumblestone was making her feel, she lifted her chin just an inch and tightened her jaw. "Sir, I thank you for your interests." Her tone was so devoid of emotion it sounded utterly flat. "But to be brutally honest, I am feeling trapped. I do not know you at all well enough to accept your proposal. To quote my uncle, I am well on the shelf and have grown comfortable with the freedom such a position provides."

"You stupid, stupid child. You have no freedoms!" Uncle Sires shouted. Perhaps he had a few drops of hot gypsy blood pumping in his own veins. "You have no money, no prospects, no choices. What do you plan to do, beggar yourself to your relatives?"

"I would never dream of it, my lord." May dearly wished Iona could witness her grand performance. Such theatrics were wasted on so small an audience. "I plan to seek employment and pay my own way in this world."

"Winnie"—Sires whirled around, the floorboards creaking—"you schooled her to stage this rebellion?"

Winnie glared at him over her steepled fingers. "I support her decision."

"And what of your health? Will you continue to refuse my offer to let me care for you?" Uncle Sires shouted loudly enough to make the porcelain figurines on the mantel rattle.

"I have no desire to live with an old despot," Winnie declared. "I will make do on my own."

What in blazes was her aunt saying? May couldn't trust her hearing. Surely Winnie wasn't refusing what promised to be a brighter future. Sires could provide for Winnie. He had more money and connections to the best medical practitioners.

"What is this?" May asked, feeling shocked . . . truly shocked. "What will you do, Aunt?"

"I will manage." She continued to glare at her brother. "As I have often managed, alone."

No. This could not be. They didn't have the funds to afford their home, their food, or her aunt's medical care. Winnie had to accept Sires' help. There was no other way.

Before May could launch a protest, Mr. Tumblestone raised his hands and stepped forward. Thankfully, he had tucked the ring back into his coat pocket. "Miss Sheffers, will you stroll in the garden with me?"

"I do not believe this is the best time." Even if it were, she had no desire to lead him on a merry chase. No matter what, she would not consider his suit.

Unfortunately, he wasn't easily dissuaded. He captured her hand and gave her a little tug. "Please—I believe we should discuss our future."

After May failed to twist her hand from the trap of his grasp, she relented. "Very well, sir. I shall stroll with you for but a moment."

There was a bench out back under a spindly oak. Tumblestone led her there and pulled out a handkerchief. Always thoughtful, he laid the linen on the bench's seat and invited May to sit upon it. He crossed his arms and waited for her to get settled.

"I do not know you," he said bluntly. "I do not know your nature, and your background, quite frankly, worries me. After seeing what I have in regard to your temperament, I worry about our future."

May opened her mouth to explain there would be no future for them, but he shot her such a sharp look she closed her mouth again.

"Let me tell you what has brought me here to make what most would consider an outrageous decision." He paused until May gave a little nod. "You don't know your uncle well. I suppose it is no surprise, though. You have spent very little time with him. Despite what you think, he is a good man."

May scoffed at the thought. Her uncle was a bounder of the worst kind. He was a bully and a tyrant who took enjoyment from tormenting her to the point of tears.

"Five years ago I would have lost my lands. The reason is no longer important. What is important, though, is how your uncle supported me until the debts were cleared. I owe him everything I have.

"When he came to me in need of help, I gloried at the opportunity. Your aunt is ill. Dying, possibly."

"I know only too well my aunt's condition." May turned her gaze down to the neatly scythed grass growing under her feet.

"Though the earl has a difficult time expressing it, he too is deeply concerned. He also knows that your aunt will not come to live with him. They are cut from the same stone, those two. He had hoped that if your aunt saw you married and settled nearby, she would naturally follow."

A lump settled in May's throat. "Winnie's welfare is very important to me. I would never do anything to hurt her."

"Then agree to marry me." He sounded so reasonable. "If your aunt doesn't wish to live with her brother, she can live with us."

The temptation to accept was great. With one simple word, May could vanquish her troubles.

But marriage? The lump in her throat threatened to straggle her. Her dreams, her silly womanly dreams of love, marriage, and happily-ever-after had somehow become hopelessly entwined with that handsome rake, that devil who had already set his cap for another. The pain ripped at her heart.

"Please, Mr. Tumblestone, do not rush me." May needed time alone to think. "Give me a few more days before asking me to make such a decision."

How had it happened? She never wanted it. It felt like

the worst thing in the world, in fact. But the truth was wedged between her and Mr. Tumblestone like a very sharp sword, keeping the only rational option at bay. No matter how hard she tried, she could not deny what had become only too real.

She was hopelessly in love with Radford.

Chapter Eleven

A raucous clamor erupted from the front of the cottage and drowned out Mr. Tumblestone's response to May's plea for time. A sudden shout of laughter turned her attentions from his withering gaze.

"Portia said I might find you sitting under your favorite tree," Iona called out as she bounded down the narrow path through the side yard, her skirts raised. A goodly portion of material was bunched in her fists. She looked delightfully young and playful, running at breakneck speed.

Iona hadn't behaved so unladylike since before her come-out three years earlier. May couldn't help but wonder, while feeling a bittersweet pang for the past, what intrigue had prompted this burst of hoydenish behavior.

"You must come around right away. You simply must—" Iona crashed to a hasty halt. Her face paled and she dropped her skirts. "Oh, dear. I didn't realize you weren't alone." Iona's sweet lilting voice had flattened into the soft, proper tone both women had been trained to make great pains to use. "Forgive me for intruding."

Although Iona made a great show of being embarrassed, she made no move to leave. Mr. Tumblestone bristled at the intrusion and looked ready to bite Iona's head off. He restrained his irritation, May supposed, only because he was making a grand effort to paint such a pleasant picture of himself and marriage.

His hands tightened into large fists. With a stiff back, Tumblestone gave a short bow. "Lady Iona," he said. "A pleasure to see you again. Please, do join us."

"Oh no, I couldn't possibly stay," Iona said and fluttered her hands about her breast. "What I mean to say is that you must come and see. You may come too, of course, Mr. Tumblestone."

May rose from the bench, her curiosity peaked. "See what?"

"Lord Nathan has a new phaeton and Lord Evers has followed in a handsome landau. You simply must come and see."

May found it hard not to get caught up in Iona's infectious enthusiasm and join in the fun. Though she had never been a great fan of coaches, she always did enjoy a friendly ogle.

Even Iona appeared surprised when May abruptly sobered.

May clasped her hands while her gaze bounced between Iona and Mr. Tumblestone. For Aunt Winnie's sake, she needed to curb her impulses.

"Mr. Tumblestone," May said and cast a longing eye toward the front of the cottage. "Perhaps we should continue this discussion inside? I am sorry, Iona, but I cannot join you today. Perhaps another time?"

"But it is the fair's last day today and the weather is ever so lovely." Iona refused to budge and it would be rude to leave her standing in the back garden alone. "Perhaps you would wish to come as well, Mr. Tumblestone? You would be most welcome, I assure you. There should be plenty of room in Lord Evers' landau. Oh, please say you will come."

"What is this about a fair?" Uncle Sires ambled toward them. "Child, you must know there is a group at the door inquiring after you." His gaze latched on Lady Iona's. "Oh, I see you have already announced yourself, my lady," he said rather rudely.

The earl and the Duke of Newbury had never rubbed well together. May's finding such a close friend in his daughter and acceptance with the Newbury family had only rubbed salt into the tensions separating the two men.

"Lord Nathan and Lord Evers are escorting Lillian and myself to the country fair in Widcombe. I had hoped May and Mr. Tumblestone were available as well."

"A fair in Widcombe?" Sires rubbed his chin.

"I had already declined the offer, Uncle." May had no desire to be scolded unfairly since she had done the mature thing and refused the tempting invitation.

"You refused? Stupid child," he muttered. "Of course Tumblestone will escort my niece to the fair. The delightful couple could use some time away from the doddering old folks in this cottage."

Iona looked about ready to choke. May had a difficult time keeping from sputtering a laugh herself. Tumblestone was Uncle Sires' age. The old farmer was doubtlessly hoping to escape back into the cottage and return to the *doddering old folks* instead of trying to get away from them.

"I would be delighted," Tumblestone said, not sounding at all pleased. He entwined his fingers with May's and forced a vicious smile.

Regardless of anyone's wishes, Sires had made up his mind. He handed May twenty pounds and declared she should spend the miniature fortune on useless baubles. May stared at the boon, feeling utterly flummoxed.

"Promise to keep a close eye on these two lovebirds, Lady Iona. I cannot allow anything untoward to happen that might besmirch the child's reputation or rush the wedding date."

May glanced up, expecting to find the ground above her and the clouds at her feet. Uncle Sires was acting so out of character, it made her head ache.

Even Iona was at a loss for words.

But her uncle wasn't the sole cause of May's topsy-turvy feelings. She had no idea what to think about riding in a landau with Mr. Tumblestone by her side while having to watch Radford pet and coo over the delicately beautiful Lillian.

The afternoon promised to be torturous. And yet, her heart

could not help but slam against her chest in silent anticipation. Spending another afternoon in Radford's company was her dearest wish . . . and her greatest fear.

Why in blazes had he let Wynter talk him into this mess? Though the weather was pleasant and the air fresh, Radford longed to be anywhere but in Widcombe, spending time with not only the woman he was to wed but also with the woman he could not seem to get out of his mind. Unfortunately, those two women were not one and the same.

So far, he had a miserable time riding in his landau with Lady Lillian pressed to his side and twittering on about the fashions she'd spied in the Edgar's Building shop windows that morning. He had a miserable time watching Miss Sheffers sit without letting her back touch the squabs and averting her gaze from both himself and the scowling Mr. Tumblestone. She was dressed in a lovely gown with a white-and-red spotted pattern that was cut specifically to display her generous contours.

If she wore such a garment every day, the poor gel would be overset with marriage offers. There was a lovely gem hidden underneath those ill-fitted, faded gowns after all.

The realization made Radford all the more miserable. Why in blazes had he agreed to step one foot out of his house?

The country fair in nearby Widcombe was crowded into the Widcombe Crescent common, a large grassy expanse, and spilled over into the neighboring fields. Many familiar faces filled the crowd. It appeared as if over half of Bath had decided to join in the frivolities.

Wynter and Lady Iona led the way past singing acrobats, street performances of popular morality plays, and street stands selling savory smelling meats and sugarcoated pastries.

"There is an ancient lady at the edge of the field, I am told," Wynter explained. Mischief sparkled in his bright blue eyes. "She will tell your future for a mere two pence. Isn't that a lark? We must all let her peek at our palms."

"The devil, you say?" Tumblestone did not sound at all pleased. "'Tis a sin to deal with fortune tellers or witchcraft. I shall not partake in this folly . . . nor shall Miss Sheffers."

"Indeed?" Radford drawled, trying his best to make the word sound bored instead of strained. The brutal pace Wynter had set pained his foot since pride had kept him from bringing his cane. He stopped on the path to catch his breath.

"Do you agree, Miss Sheffers? Are you not curious what future this old woman sees for you?" He slanted a pointed glance in Tumblestone's direction.

May turned her head away, apparently too smart to fall into the trap Radford had ungallantly set for her. A free spirit like May would undoubtedly enjoy the amusements of an old gypsy witch. "Would be a waste of money, my lord," she mumbled.

"What nonsense, May," Lady Iona said. "Your uncle gave you ample funds to waste today."

"Not on sinful behavior," Mr. Tumblestone snipped.

"I don't see what the fuss is about," Lady Lillian said. She dug her claws into Radford's sleeve. "May doesn't need a gypsy witch to read her palm. I daresay such a skill is inborn with the likes of her. The old witch might even be her grandmother. You can divine your own future, can you not, May? It is in your blood . . . your father's gypsy blood."

Her father a gypsy? "Preposterous," Radford blurted. "Her mother is the daughter of an earl."

"Believe what you like," Lillian said with considerable spite. The emotion was most unbecoming on the lady's youthful features.

Iona stuffed a fist into her mouth. Wynter blushed and muttered incoherently. No one really knew what to say. Radford half expected Miss Sheffers to burst into tears and run away.

Yet the young miss was much too strong to do something as weakly feminine as that. Instead, Miss Sheffers stood her ground and stared up her nose at the taller, lovelier Lady Lillian. Without speaking one word, she effectively erased any lingering doubts from Radford's mind.

This was Miss Sheffers, the one woman who ever dared call him a fool and who read not only the most horrid novels but soaked up all the classics. Above all, this was the woman who had forced him to see the harm he was doing to his body by rejecting that infernal cane. How could such a gently bred, courageous woman be tainted with feral gypsy blood?

"What a spiteful thing to say," Radford scolded in a soft tone in a desperate attempt to break the tense silence. "You should not utter such lies, my lady."

"You think I lie?" Lady Lillian squared her shoulders and looked immensely pleased with herself. "Ask May yourself. If she denies what I say, then you will witness firsthand a truly accomplished liar."

Tumblestone was taking a keen interest in what Miss Sheffers might have to say for herself. "Well, miss? Deny the lady so we may continue on. People are beginning to stare," he said.

May's violet-colored eyes darkened several shades. She opened her dainty mouth a number of times to speak but never made a sound.

"This is foolish. Apologize, Lillian, for saying something so vicious." Iona quickly came to Miss Sheffers' defense.

"I will not." Lillian tilted her head up. Tears were threatening her eyes.

Radford could only shake his head. No matter how hard he tried, his comprehension of the female species never improved.

"Perhaps we should continue then," Wynter suggested. He sounded as uncomfortable as Radford felt. Moving on and putting the accusation behind him suited Radford just fine.

Unfortunately, Tumblestone had other thoughts on the matter. "Miss Sheffers, say something. Deny or affirm what the lady claims."

May's nervous glance danced from face to face. Finally

she sighed, her shoulders slumped in defeat. "I can do neither," she said. "You will have to speak with my uncle if you wish to know the truth."

Ah. Another mystery surrounds the dear elfin princess.

Radford found himself perversely intrigued. He hoped his man-of-affairs returned soon with all her dirty secrets uncovered.

With nothing left to discuss, Radford took Lady Lillian's arm and plodded a slow but steady path down the line of booths.

There was a gypsy witch waiting to be consulted.

The old woman was hunched and wrinkled. Her shaky fingers were gnarled like the limbs of an ancient oak. Her patched clothing flowed about her, displaying an array of bright colors. She wore a woolen kerchief on her head and had a large golden hoop piercing her earlobe.

Lady Lillian laughed nervously as she slipped the witch a few coins and offered her hand. The cloudy-eyed woman stared not at Lillian's palm but into her face. She stroked Lillian's long fingers and hummed softly for several moments.

The witch bent forward and whispered in a thickly accented voice, "You are so lovely, dear. You turn so many men's hearts, do you not? But what is beauty? What will it bring you? Oh dear, not much. Many frustrating years will pass before you find happiness."

Lillian snatched back her hand and clutched it to her chest. "Is that all you have to say, you old fraud?"

The old woman shrugged. "Do not despair overmuch. You are yet young."

Iona took Lillian's hands and cooed gentle words to the sensitive girl while Wynter slipped the witch two more coins. When she reached out to take his palm, Wynter captured Radford's hand, peeled off his glove, and held it for the old woman to peer into.

"What in the devil?" Radford protested.

"Just listen to what she has to say."

Funny thing, the witch had nothing to say. Her eyes grew wide as she stared deep into the center of Radford's palm.

"Perhaps I'm supposed to be dead already," he quipped.

"Oh no," she said, shaking her head violently. "You have a very strong lifeline. Only"—she traced a path down the center of his palm with her crooked finger—"you are not living it."

"Not living it? Then what am I doing here, if not living?"

"Hiding, I suppose. Hiding from everything that should be important to you. Use that limp as a shield, do you not?"

She pulled on his arm with a surprising burst of strength, forcing him to crouch down so she could whisper into his ear. "Beware, my lord. There is no hiding from your heart. The universe will not allow it."

Just like Lady Lillian, Radford drew his hand back as if the witch had stung him. Something wicked curled in his stomach as her words wound their way through his body. He shook himself and gave a short laugh. The witch was good. Her theatrics rivaled the best actors he'd ever seen grace the stage.

"How droll," he said. He laughed again to cover up a sense of foreboding sneaking up inside him, warning him that the witch had hit the mark. "You have earned your money." Radford tossed her a few extra coins before jamming his hands into his pocket and returning to Lillian's side.

He lavished his pretty lady with attention and listened with only half an ear while the gypsy witch promised Wynter he would soon make his father proud and find love in a surprising quarter. Lady Iona's reading was just as benign and vague as Wynter's.

When the witch turned her watery gaze on May, Mr. Tumblestone renewed his protests against the sinful activity. "You will not gain a cent from me, you old crone. So stuff your filthy hand back into your skirts."

A wry, otherworldly smile creased the old woman's features. May had the grace to give the poor soul a gracious nod before letting Tumblestone lead her away.

"Perhaps we could move farther away from the farm animals," Lillian suggested. "The smell is disgusting."

Before the group could agree on a new activity, the old witch hobbled up and wrapped her withered hand around May's arm. The woman's wild gaze was a frightening sight.

"It is dangerous to pretend to be something you are not," she hissed the words before anyone could come to May's rescue. "You would be wise to cease playing such games, dearie—especially with yourself."

Chapter Twelve

The witch vanished into the crowd. Her departure left May gaping like a fool. The old woman had voiced the words she had refused to let her own heart speak for far too long.

She *was* pretending to be something she wasn't.

"Did that gypsy harm you?" Radford had cupped her cheeks and crouched slightly so he was eye level with her. His fingers gently traced the line of her jaw.

"What?" May felt suddenly overwhelmed by his close, masculine presence. "I am fine."

"She doesn't look fine," Wynter said.

"She is fine," Tumblestone argued. With a heavy hand, he yanked May away from Radford and hooked his arm with hers. "This is nonsense, I say. Utter nonsense spouted by a crazed crone. I do not like the atmosphere here. It is not a proper place for a young lady. I demand we return to Bath at once."

That was the last thing May wanted. To return to Bath would mean her adventure with Radford would end. Her return would put her in a position where she felt compelled to accept Mr. Tumblestone's suit.

It is dangerous to pretend to be something you are not.

They should return as soon as possible. To pretend she was a lady—to pretend she was someone Radford could love was dangerous. She could lose her heart if she wasn't careful.

"I would like to stay." The stubborn words rolled off her tongue despite all of May's good judgment. "We have only just arrived, and there is still so much to see."

She should enjoy the afternoon. What else did she have to lose when Radford already owned her heart . . . whether he wanted it or not.

Refined and young, Lady Lillian hailed from a good family. She was everything Radford wished for in a wife. It wasn't as if he really needed to like the girl. He lingered behind while watching Lillian and Iona flit through the crowds from stall to stall, admiring the simple wares and buying whatever made them smile. Iona had locked arms with May and dragged the elfin princess along with her. May rarely smiled as they shopped. Though she admired many swaths of colorful, exotic fabrics and volumes of battered old books, she never once opened her reticule to make a purchase.

After a while, the group wandered back out into the field where the gypsies had made their camp. Some passing acquaintances had mentioned a collection of antiques for sale from the mysterious lands of the East.

The trail to the battered wooden caravan led them down a dusty path where tall grasses reached out and brushed against their legs. Lillian, the fair-haired beauty who perfectly suited him, whimpered with every step. She despaired over the dirt clinging to her gown until Radford begrudgingly agreed to lift her into his arms.

May uttered no such complaints. For a woman who admitted to being frightened of animals and uncertain of what to do in the wilderness, she plodded through the tall grasses as if her small body was made to spend long hours strolling in the out-of-doors.

Strands of her amber hair slipped from their pins and hung loose down her back. Her straw bonnet sat askew on the top of her head, bobbing with each step. She was truly a creature of the earth. Perhaps she did have a touch of gypsy blood in those veins. Perhaps that was why she'd been able to bewitch him with those haunting eyes.

His desire for her was strong enough to make him rethink his values. A man in his position could use a solid woman like Miss Sheffers as a mistress. Having her by his side would make him a better man.

What could be the harm with that? He would take care of her and protect her from leering old men like Mr. Tumblestone.

"Oooo." Lady Lillian squirmed out of his arms. "They are lovely." Her eyes glistened at the sight of three unusual figurines on a small table in front of a colorful tent. They were crafted from the finest bone china.

For once Radford had to agree. The figurines, a trio of wood sprites, were frozen forever in the middle of some pagan dance. Heads thrown back, limbs light and jaunty, and gowns flowing, they appeared to be moving to some ancient tune in the liquid-smooth china.

Radford studied them while sneaking glances toward his own personal mystical creature. All three smiling faces were the very image of Miss Sheffers.

"They are quite well made," he commented. He picked one up, turned it over in his hand, and stroked the figurine while thoughts of Miss Sheffers tripped through his mind.

She leaned forward and peered at the figurines. A broad smile brightened her features at the sight of the fairy creatures.

A naked longing lurked deep in her eyes and could not be overlooked. Had she seen something in the way those figurines danced freely? Did she too long for such freedom? Perhaps she too saw the image of herself in their lovely faces.

"They remind me of an amazing woman I happened upon not long ago on Beechen Cliff," he said just loud enough for her ears. "She possessed a spirit as free as these imps, do you not agree?"

"I am sure I don't know what you are talking about, my

lord," May said, her entire being bristling. She didn't step away, though. She continued to silently admire the small statuettes.

"Perhaps one day you will let your hair down and dance with such abandon for me?" He knew the suggestion would scandalize her, but he could not stop his tongue. Goading her prudish façade proved far more enjoyable than any thoughts of restraint.

She slanted a questioning glance in his direction. "You mock me," she whispered. With a single step back from the gypsy's treasures, May tried to fade into the surroundings.

Well, hell, that was the last thing he wanted her to do.

"You don't have to run away," he turned around and said to her.

Mr. Tumblestone inched closer to May in an overt show of ownership. His glare fixed on Radford. An unspoken challenge lay on the ground between them. Radford had a mind to stand up to the old fool and win May for himself.

It took Lady Lillian to remind him of his duty to both her and his mother. She tugged on his arm and pouted prettily.

"What is it, my lady?" he asked. Heaven help him, Lillian's neediness tried his patience.

"I have spent all my money," she said softly. She wrinkled her button nose and batted her long lashes. "Oh la, and I simply adore those figurines."

Radford patted the hand she had latched onto his sleeve. "It is never wise to make your selection before considering all your options." His gaze unwillingly traveled to May.

Her ribbons were drooping. Her curls were fast becoming a riot of tangles. And she was glowering at him with the most honest expression of dislike he could ever hope to see. All and all, he found her quite irresistibly adorable.

"It is unwise to ruin your one chance for happiness by acting rashly, don't you agree?" he said.

Lady Lillian's frown deepened. "But, Lord Evers, you could buy me the figurines if you truly wished to."

He had a feeling his wishes didn't merit in this case. His

feelings would never merit when it came to Lady Lillian. She was a selfish child.

Not a woman prepared to . . . to . . . What did he expect from marriage other than children?

In trying to hide from a future with a leg that would never heal, he had failed to picture his life in the years and decades ahead of him. What would he want from a wife?

"I will buy you one of the three, my lady, to teach you a lesson. You cannot always have what you want. Sometimes you have to make a choice. I wonder. Which one will you choose?"

"You are a tease, my lord," she purred. The perfect coquette, the lady literally dripped with sensuality.

Oddly, her charms bored Radford. He watched with disinterest as she lifted each figurine and explained what about it she simply adored. Lady Iona joined in the fun.

Wynter wandered off in search of more interesting entertainments while Lillian remained undecided.

May battled a tiny baby goat that wanted nothing more than to eat the silk flowers stitched into the hem of her gown. Her nudging the little brown and white scamp with her gloved hand only made it more determined to play with her. She let slip a husky laugh when the little guy rammed her leg.

Tumblestone ruined the fun. He swung his stout leg at the playful beast and would have struck it if May hadn't put herself in his way. The toe of his boot struck her shin.

She rubbed her leg and laughed off the pain. But there was a definite limp in her step when she clapped her hands and chased the little goat back into the field.

Radford ground his jaw, aching to kick that bounder Tumblestone a few times in her defense. He couldn't, though. His interference wouldn't be welcomed or appropriate. Miss Sheffers had already made her feelings abundantly clear. She wanted nothing to do with him.

But what did she want?

Certainly she couldn't seriously be considering marriage to a man like Tumblestone. He was too old, too staid for her.

Such a marriage would break her spirit. Her rare smiles had grown strained and her unpredictable personality had turned subdued after only a few hours in his company.

"This one." Lady Lillian held up a figurine. The porcelain wood sprite was curtsying with her head thrown back in a laugh.

"Very well," he drawled. He considered offering to purchase one for Lady Iona as well, but she had wandered away from the figurines and was busy speaking with one of the gypsy traders about a necklace with a large purple gem. Wynter had joined her and looked prepared to guide the lady in her purchase.

Radford had no wish to leave without the other two wood sprites. As unbelievable as it seemed to him, the lithe figures charmed him.

"And you, Miss Sheffers, what do you wish for? Do you by chance long for one of these treasures?"

She appeared startled by the question. She quickly blinked away a sheen of tears and turned away.

He'd expected her to tell him his charity was unwelcome, though he had secretly hoped she would beg prettily for the pair of fairy figurines. Never, not in a world of possibilities, had he dreamed she might grow misty-eyed.

"It is getting late," she said, refusing to answer his question. "Aunt Winnie will be worrying after me."

"Very well." He paid for Lady Lillian's present and offered the simpering miss his arm. As they worked their way through the crowd, Radford could not keep his mind off the two stranded figurines.

May deserved to own them.

They were nothing more than a pair of simple baubles—naught but toys for adults. He must have lost his mind.

"Please excuse me a moment." He unhooked his arm from Lillian's. "Wynter, please look after my sweet confection," he said and graced his companion with an indulgent smile. "I believe I see an old acquaintance. I won't be but a minute."

"But I would like to meet—" Lady Lillian started.

Radford pressed a finger to her lips. "Not this time."

"Don't be too long, Evers," Wynter said rather impatiently. "We'll wait for you at the landau."

With a jaunty step, which was quite a feat considering the pains in his swollen foot, he returned to the gypsy caravan and purchased the two remaining figurines. *A gift,* he thought. Surely there was nothing improper with him wanting to give May a symbol of his gratitude. She had talked him into using his cane.

That blasted cane. He dearly wished he'd overcome his pride and brought it with him to the fair. His concern over what Lady Lillian might think if she saw him constantly dependant on it had stopped him.

"Buying your intended the other two ornaments, I see." Tumblestone fell into step with Radford.

"Something like that," Radford muttered. Gentleman or not, he had no desire to converse with the old farmer. "Where is Miss Sheffers?"

"She was happy giggling with those two silly hens. And I wanted to have a word with you in private."

"Indeed?" Private wasn't an accurate description of the crowded Widcombe Commons they were crossing. "Wynter said he would look after all three of them? I'll owe him for that. He is a bachelor who enjoys his women, but not all at once. And definitely not the marrying variety."

Tumblestone chuckled. "S'pose I envy him. We're on the same quest, you and I. Here we are, two confirmed bachelors, and now marriage looms heavy on the horizon, does it not?"

"Family responsibilities require it." Radford stiffened. He had no desire to have this discussion with Tumblestone. Morbid curiosity forced him to ask the question though. "Why would you wish to change your ways?"

"You could say the right offer came along." A curious expression darkened Tumblestone's stark features. He had the smug look of a man emerging from a gambling hell with his pockets filled with blunt and a deck of marked cards tucked up in his hat.

"I see," Radford drawled.

"I am afraid you might not," Tumblestone said. "I have watched the way she looks at you."

"The way she scowls, you mean?" Radford used his devil-may-care tone. He'd spent many years perfecting his roguish manner and could call it up at will. "Miss Sheffers would wish to curse me, I'm afraid."

"You don't believe that, do you?" For a thunderous moment Tumblestone reminded Radford of his father. He half expected the man to cross his arms and sigh. "She has developed feelings for you, the foolish girl. I don't appreciate your encouraging her unschooled impulses. I don't know what you have in mind, but she will not be your mistress." Tumblestone raised a large fist. The old man possessed a workman's strength and could no doubt hold his own in a fight.

Radford had no desire to test his mettle. "You mistake my intensions, sir. I do not even find the imp attractive."

"Forgive me, my lord." Tumblestone backed down immediately. Apparently the frosty glare and the little lie did the trick. "I meant no disrespect. Just—and I'm sure you can understand—I am unable to give Miss Sheffers the discipline she sorely needs until after the marriage. I must woo her . . . win her trust. But she is such a flighty, empty-headed chit. She sorely tries my patience, I'm afraid. Fortunately, there is nothing about her that a heavy hand cannot correct."

Merciful heavens. And Radford had been worried about Tumblestone breaking May's spirit? She'd be lucky not to be physically broken after just a few months living with this monster.

Chapter Thirteen

"Please tell me you have some news for me about Miss Sheffers' situation," Radford said in place of a greeting as his man-of-affairs hurried into the study with a bundle of papers tucked under his arm. After having suffered a sleepless night, he'd sent a messenger to fetch Bannor at first light.

He had to stop May's marriage plans. He simply had to. If not for that blasted eviction letter, she wouldn't have given a man like Tumblestone the time of day. She was an independent woman, lively and vivacious.

The simplest solution to her problem was the very one that had kept Radford from finding sleep. Not because it was impossible, nor because it tossed logic out the window. Just considering it made his blood race.

He could marry Miss Sheffers.

"I wasn't able to uncover much about the young miss, my lord. But I did learn some interesting things about her family." Bannor adjusted the glasses on his nose and settled into a chair. He took his time organizing the papers in front of him on the desk.

Radford had too much energy to sit still. Leaning on his cane, he paced the length of the room. His patience quickly ran thin. He didn't have time for Bannor's efficiency. "Well? Don't hold me in suspense. What have you found, man?"

Bannor fiddled nervously with his glasses again. "Just—

just a couple of wills." He scrambled his papers in search of a particular sheet. "I don't have a copy of the documents, mind you. Just pieces of gossip from a boy I hired to glean information from the servants working at Redfield Abbey."

"Redfield Abbey?" Bannor's thoroughness impressed Radford. He wouldn't have thought to send someone to snoop around the Earl of Sires' servants.

"Yes, my lord. I hope you don't mind," Bannor said nervously.

"No, of course not. What did you find?"

Bannor cleared his throat. "Appears the Redfield's ladies and the current earl rarely see eye-to-eye. When the earl severed ties with his youngest sister for marrying without his permission, his grandmother wrote him out of her will. She left her small fortune instead to this sister."

"And this sister is—?" Radford asked.

"Lady Viola, Miss Sheffers' mother. I still haven't been able to uncover why these funds have been recently seized by the courts, but I have a niggling feeling the earl is responsible."

"Keep working on that, then." Radford resumed his pacing. "And what else have you discovered?"

"Another interesting story. The earl's mother is still alive. And though very old and feeble by all accounts, she still possesses her wits. Not long ago, she and the earl had a falling out, and she changed her will, leaving Lady Winifred all her worldly possessions."

"All her worldly possessions? And what would that entail?"

"Much more than a few diamond necklaces, it would seem. According to my source, the dowager countess holds ownership to a small estate in London and to a vast amount of farmland adjacent to the Redfield Abbey estate."

"I see."

"I don't think you do, my lord. The property the dowager countess is so willing to give over to her eldest daughter accounts for more than half of the earl's income. His lifestyle could change considerably upon his mother's death."

Uncle Sires' manner toward May had softened considerably the next day. Though he still never smiled in her presence, his scowl was less defined.

"I am pleased you enjoyed your outing with Mr. Tumblestone yesterday," he said to her during a brief encounter at the Pump Room that morning.

He was *pleased*?

Nothing involving May had ever pleased her uncle Sires. This was truly a momentous occasion. Though May had long ceased wishing for his approval, this small crumb thrilled her.

She smiled like a dimwit as she took her turn around the Pump Room with Winnie. Everything would be perfect that morning if not for her aunt's health. Poor, dear aunt Winnie was feeling weak again today. She leaned heavily on May's arm and kept her lips pressed tightly together.

Iona and Lillian joined them as they approached the glaring statue of Beau Nash located at one end of the Pump Room.

"You look absolutely bedraggled, Iona," May gasped. Her friend's hair was slipping from its pins and her dress was splattered with mud.

"A wild horse nearly ran her down," Lillian explained in that whisper soft voice of hers. "Just outside the entrance, no less. Mamma suffered a fit of vapors and had to be carried home in a sedan chair, the poor dear."

"Oh my," May gasped. Horses could kill a person.

"The wild beast reminded me of that monster Lord Evers had purchased. He's going to sell that horse, you know. Mamma said he would. Said his mother heard him curse the vilest words and decry how it had nearly killed me." She batted her eyes and looked immensely pleased. "He sent me a roomful of flowers as an apology."

A knife turned in May's gut. "How wonderful," she said. Her pleasure at her uncle's approval faded away.

"It was just a simple vase full of posies," Iona muttered.

"It was a rather large vase though. No matter, Mamma says he plans to offer for me. He is smitten. I don't think I will give him an answer right away. I am only nineteen, after all. Perhaps I shall let him pine for a while and make him prove himself worthy of my interests."

May didn't think she could listen to another word.

"I'm so very happy for you," she lied.

"There is more," Bannor said.

"More?" The thought of the earl's sudden interest in marrying off his sister's caretaker was chilling enough.

"I took the liberty of asking around about Mr. Tumblestone. He is the fellow who has—"

"Yes, yes." Radford waved his hand. "I know bloody well who he is."

"Did you also know that some thirty odd years ago Lady Winifred had run away with Mr. Tumblestone? They would have been secretly wed over the anvil in Scotland if the earl hadn't intervened."

"And now the earl is parading Tumblestone under his sister's nose and forcing her dearest niece to marry the one man she once loved? That must be torture for Lady Winifred. How will that help him after his mother dies?" Radford resumed his pacing.

"I don't know, but there is rumor running through the servant's hall that Mr. Tumblestone will receive a pretty penny for agreeing to take Miss Sheffers to wife."

Lord Nathan Wynter bowed grandly and made a big show of greeting the women in the middle of the Pump Room. "The viscount sends his apologies. He had some pressing business come up this morning."

Lillian glowed and latched onto his arm. "How thoughtful, Lord Nathan. He didn't want me to worry after him so he sent you, the considerate man. I will have to scold him for neglecting me, of course. Though I think I know what business he might be attending to." Her gaze flitted to her empty finger.

May could only watch with growing despair. To remain in Bath and be forced to feign happiness for Lillian and Radford's nuptials would be more than she could bear. Heaven help her, she needed to escape.

And Aunt Winnie needed caretakers more able than she. Her aunt's steps slowed until they were nearly at a stop.

Lillian, Iona, and Lord Nathan plodded forward and were drawn into a conversation with one of Lord Nathan's acquaintances. Iona gave May a little wave before strolling on ahead.

"Let me take you home," May said, worrying over her aunt's flagging step. "I have had quite enough for today myself."

"I am sure you have. Has that silly chit truly enchanted our Lord Evers?" Winnie whispered the question. For the briefest moment color flooded her aunt's cheeks, turning them a healthy pink. She looked more animated than she had in days. "He's more the fool than I initially suspected. What shall we do?"

May's heart dropped down and landed in the pit of her stomach. How could she tell her aunt that there was no hope for a relationship between her and the viscount? She led Winnie from the room and into the bright sunlight. The day promised to be as warm and inviting as the last—a sharp contrast to the storm brewing in May's heart. They walked silently down the colonnade toward Cheap Street.

"He has said we could remain in the cottage for as long as we want," May said finally. "He said he was not interested in our money."

"Oh dear." Winnie picked up her pace and pinched her niece's arm. "You haven't done anything foolish, have you, May?"

May's cheeks stung from a sudden rush of embarrassment. "No, Aunt, no. I would never."

Winnie sighed. "Has he asked you to?"

"He says he doesn't want me like that. . . ."

"But?"

"He kissed me at the Newburys' concert." May felt utterly wicked. A decent lady should never confess such a thing, not even to her loving aunt.

Still, Winnie wasn't satisfied. "And?"

"And nothing. It was naught but a simple kiss." A simply wondrous thing that had set her body on fire.

"There is no such thing as a simple kiss between a young woman such as yourself and a man like the viscount. What shall we do?"

The bright gleam in Aunt Winnie's gaze was identical to the look Iona would get when she was hatching a scheme. There was trouble afoot. May needed to proceed with her plans with great caution.

Uncle Sires was right. Aunt Winnie needed someone better able to care for her. Unfortunately she wouldn't willingly leave May's side unless she knew May wouldn't be left alone and penniless. Marriage was the only logical solution.

By all accounts, Lord Evers would be proposing to his Lady Lillian this evening. There was no reason for May to continue to torture herself. He was never a man she could ever hope to have. Her uncle had taught her that lesson only too well. Because of her birth—because of who she was, respectable society could never accept her. She was not a worthy candidate for such a fairy-tale marriage.

And there was Mr. Tumblestone.

He was willing.

She would send a note around to her uncle. "Please don't worry overmuch about me, Aunt. I am a sensible woman. Matters of the heart are problems for simpletons and fools. I am quite immune."

"Very well." Winnie did not sound convinced.

May would have to act before her well-meaning aunt

could set a plan into motion. She would never own Radford's heart. She didn't need to, either. After tonight, her future would be set. There was truly no other viable option.

"I will be happy," she said, not at all confident she spoke the truth. "I promise, Aunt, I will be happy." Marriage to Mr. Tumblestone promised to be a great challenge to those bold assurances of happiness.

"What about Miss Sheffers? Were you unable to find anything more about her background?"

"Besides the fact that her parents recently died abroad, no." Bannor paused and looked as if he were carefully weighing his words. "The servants are tight-lipped about her. The earl can't abide to be near her, that much was made clear. My boy thinks there is something buried in her past. Something no one is brave enough to even whisper."

Something like her father's gypsy heritage? Could it be true? If it were, his wild idea of marrying May just grew several degrees more impossible.

"Dig into her father's background. Find out who he was, and who his parents were."

"Yes, my lord." Bannor gathered up his papers and started for the door. "Oh, my lord. Please do accept my fondest congratulations."

"For what?"

"Your mother says you are to marry one of the Duke of Newbury's daughters. You couldn't pick a wife from a more respectable family."

Chapter Fourteen

Radford studied the two porcelain woodland sprites he'd set on the mantel, unable to decide which one to keep and which one to give to May.

One sprite had shamelessly pulled up her skirt and bared her leg as she danced, frozen in time by the hardened clay. A truly free soul. Her hair flowed about her shoulders and flowers wreathed her head. This was how he wished to see May. This was how a fairy princess should appear. He lifted the tiny statue and turned it over in his hand. Even the dimples on the sprite's round cheeks looked like May's.

The second figurine appeared much more subdued by contrast. Her slender hands covered her mouth and she was turning away to cover a blush. The artist had been adept at capturing detail though. The dainty woman's eyes were peering back, as if perversely drawn to whatever had made her shy away.

The artist could have used May as a model for this figurine. She hid from her joyous nature, only allowing precious glimpses to occasionally escape.

So which one did May deserve? The image of her shrinking away from society . . . away from love and life? Or the image of the free spirit she should no longer deny?

He could give her both.

Presenting her with even one, no matter how trivial, would be viewed inappropriate. He was a bachelor contemplating marriage to another. She was a maid rushing into a disaster he felt honor-bound to stop. The gift wouldn't be well received. He wasn't going to fool himself on that point.

What was wrong with giving her both figurines?

Selfishness, Radford supposed.

A strong desire to keep both for himself burned in him. He wanted the reckless elfin creature and the shy, frightened innocent fey princess. Both charmed him. And, he suspected, one couldn't exist without the other.

Since he'd already decided to give her one, he forced himself to come to a decision. Just like the gypsy witch had suggested, May deserved her freedom. He picked up the wild, dancing woodland sprite and held it so it shined in the ray of sunlight streaming through a large window. She needed to be given the opportunity to dance and shine in full view.

Radford would give it to her and keep the memory of the other hidden away. To cherish . . .

And love.

He carefully wrapped the shy woodland figurine in a linen handkerchief and tucked it into his breast pocket so she could rest just above his heart.

He scooped up the other and jammed his beaver hat onto the crown of his head, with the intention of paying May a visit straight away. Whether she wanted to or not, he would make her accept his gift.

"There you are, Radford." His mother sailed into the room. She wore another light gown that floated about her ankles as she crossed into the drawing room.

Lillian's mother, the Duchess of Newbury, lagged a mere step behind. Good manners had Radford removing his hat and greeting the women politely. He dropped May's figurine into his pocket.

"That lazy butler of yours should have brought the tea up by now. You really must have a word with him." His mother shot a troubled glance in the duchess' direction. "Bachelors are such helpless creatures. They really do need a strong-willed lady to take the servants well in hand."

Never, not even in his wild youth, had Radford been careless with his servants. He was fair but stern, expecting they return as much effort and respect as he gave them. The accusation against Jeffers grated his nerves mainly because she'd criticized a butler worthy of praises.

"Mother, I will not—"

"You don't have to do anything, my dear. We have the matter well in hand."

"You do?" Radford picked up his hat again. He would worry about the women's scheming later. Someone had to warn May of Mr. Tumblestone's not-so-honorable reason for wanting to marry her.

It was his experience that young women in such dire conditions often acted in haste. Time was definitely of import.

"Very well. You can get along well without me then."

"Radford!" his mother screeched. She latched onto his arm with an amazing strength. "You must be a part of this. We are planning your marriage."

Of course they were. He gritted his teeth and tossed his hat onto a nearby chair. Why else would his mother and the duchess gather together and search him out? The new-bride shine in their eyes should have set off all sorts of warning chimes in his head. He'd seen the glow in the eyes of dozens of young besotted ladies and their beaming mothers before his injuries turned him into a creature to be pitied.

"Heaven forbid I miss such a momentous discussion. Remind me, Mother. Who, pray tell, have you decided to marry me to?"

"Radford," his mother scolded while the duchess sucked in a deep breath and looked quite unabashedly shocked. "He's joking, Duchess. Not in good taste, mind you."

Radford stood his ground. "Since I have yet to formally declare myself to any woman, you must understand my confusion."

"I certainly do not understand you." His mother shook a slender finger at him. "Your jest has gone too far. Apologize to the duchess at once."

The duchess did appear on the verge of a fit of apoplexy. Her cheeks were turning beet red as she continued to gasp for air.

"Are you choking?" he asked, truly concerned. "Perhaps some water would help?"

"She is in need of an apology, Radford."

"I apologize then. I am sorry to cause you such distress, your grace—though I certainly haven't a clue why you should be so concerned over your youngest daughter's prospects. She is young and beautiful, and she possesses the refined qualities any gentleman would desire in a wife."

"She is so young and impressionable," the duchess managed to sputter between gasps.

"Are you certain you wouldn't want me to fetch a glass of water?" Radford pressed, his concern growing. "You really must sit down." He led her to the closest chair and helped lower her into the seat.

"She—she is in love with you, my lord," the duchess whispered as she continued to struggle for a smooth breath. "I would hate for her innocent heart to be broken . . . shattered. She has such tender emotions."

Lady Lillian with tender emotions? They must be well hidden. Radford rubbed his chin. A sizzling dread landed in his chest. Could he have misread the silly girl? Could he have completely overlooked her hidden depths?

Possibly . . . probably . . .

He was a bounder. His interests had been too focused on the very unsuitable May Sheffers. What a wreck he'd caused. Both ladies were in danger of having their hearts bruised, thanks to him.

Radford leaned heavily on his cane as he plodded his way to the closest window. The sun shone brightly on the fields. He glimpsed his star horse, the lively Princess, frolicking with one of his younger geldings.

His future stretched out before him in that field. But with his old life gone, nothing but disappointment waited for him out there. He was trapped in a world where he could no longer enjoy the freedom only riding a horse could bring him.

What kind of husband would he make any woman? No one, not even the trying Lady Lillian, who was his perfect match, deserved to suffer so.

"Are you certain of her feelings toward me?" he asked the duchess. The thought that the young lady might be in love with him was met with a great deal of alarm. "She couldn't possibly be in love. We have only just met."

The duchess mournfully wagged her head from side to side. "She sees only bliss and happiness. She is young yet, Evers. Your attentiveness to her has completely won her regard. I pray your rejection will not inflict irreparable harm."

"Rejection?" Lady Evers called. "What is this nonsense about rejection?"

"I just wish to slow down. I had hoped to woo the lady without—"

"Hush, boy," his mother said sternly. "You have created enough havoc for today."

Radford heaved a deep sigh and crossed his arms over his chest. There was no hope for it. He'd gotten himself in deep this time. Let the women make the marriage plans. Such matters failed to hold his interest anyhow.

He set the dancing figurine he intended to give to May back on the mantel and listened with only half an ear to the two mammas prattle on. His hopes for winning Miss Sheffers' favor had suddenly degraded into something unfathomable. The wild idea of asking her to marry him could never come to pass. There were too many people involved with his marriage plans . . . too many fragile hearts to be considered.

But what was May to him? If she was not wife material, but too honorable to be considered a mistress, he would just have to settle for friendship. As a friend, he would warn her. He would do everything in his limited power to stop her marriage to that old money-hungry goat, Tumblestone.

Friendship would have to be enough for him.

* * *

"Surely you're not suggesting men and women cannot be friends? I'll have you know that Miss Sheffers is a most uncommon woman with a mind surpassing a goodly number of men's."

Wynter had only laughed, claiming that Radford, a man, could never hope to be friends with May, a most sumptuous woman.

After enduring two hours with his mother and the duchess, Radford had been more than ready to escape his home and venture out in search of May. He may have agreed to visit the Duke of Newbury and officially declare his intentions that evening, but he had not agreed to forget his desire to help a friend in need.

Leave it to Wynter to burst into his home and keep him from his task while demanding an explanation at the same time. Wynter's scowl had grown more fierce as Radford explained his situation. He made light of the confusing feelings he felt toward May and protected her reputation by not mentioning the money Mr. Tumblestone had been promised for taking her to wife.

"Miss Sheffers is an honest woman. I would be proud to be able to call her a friend," Radford declared. He tried again to make it to the door, jamming his beaver hat low on his head. He'd wasted too much time in the house already.

Wynter moved swiftly to block his escape. "Are you being purposefully obtuse? Of course I believe there are instances where a man and a woman can develop a friendship akin to a man's bond with his peers. All I am saying is that men don't look at friends the way you look at her. You are besotted. You *love* Miss Sheffers and yet are on the verge of proposing marriage to a lady you can barely tolerate. As your closest friend, I have to ask: Have you lost your bloody mind?"

Chapter Fifteen

May clasped her hands together to keep them from visibly trembling. What she planned to do went against every one of Mary Wollstonecraft's feminist teachings. An independent woman would never give up her freedom this way. She would have fought a better battle.

If only Aunt Winnie's health wasn't a concern . . .

Too late to back down now. She had set her course, had already sent for Mr. Tumblestone. Portia had already hurried away to answer the door and let the caller in.

May held herself as still as a statue, desperately wanting to appear calm and in control. The burgundy silk gown, neatly pressed, hung nicely on her round frame. It was important to look her best, to present a pretty image to Mr. Tumblestone. He should be happy with her decision and pleased with her manner.

Happiness was too lofty a goal for herself, May conceded. But since marriage seemed unavoidable, she planned to do everything in her power to make the situation as painless as possible.

"We will get along well enough," she muttered. Her heart raced and her mouth grew dry as she listened as a pair of heavy boots banged against the hardwood flooring.

"The Viscount Evers, miss," Portia announced.

The viscount? Here?

The housekeeper appeared as surprised as May felt. Radford had no business coming to her home. Not now. Not when she expected Mr. Tumblestone's arrival at any moment.

"I apologize for arriving unannounced." He didn't appear the least bit contrite. The viscount filled the room with his manly presence until May felt as if she had to struggle for a breath. His eyes met her skittish gaze. He smiled. It was a predatory expression that sent her heart pattering anew.

"I am expecting Mr. Tumblestone, my lord." She had meant to sound frosty. Her breathlessness let a note of despair slip under her words.

"Indeed." He raised an eyebrow. "In that case, it appears I have arrived just in time. That dress complements your figure. You look truly lovely, Miss Sheffers. I suppose the extra effort you have taken with your looks is for your elderly goat?"

"How dare you." His words had struck like a dagger to her heart. "You have no right to judge me, my clothing, or my choice of husband. I did not ask for nor do I wish to know your thoughts on the matter. My life is my life. You hold no power over me." She drew up her arm and pointed toward the door. A long, slender finger, one like Lady Lillian's, would have painted a much more convincing picture. "Get out."

Radford kept his feet planted in a wide stance on the worn Oriental rug. "You will hear me out first."

"I will hear—? Oh, no. If you won't leave, I will." May started for the door.

Radford caught her in his arms and hauled her up against his chest. "You will listen."

"If you don't unhand me this instant, I will scream."

His grasp only tightened in response to the threat. He pulled her up until she was straining on the tips of her toes. And his mouth closed over hers.

At his prodding, her lips parted and granted his questing tongue free access to tease the soft interior of her lips. May turned limp under his sweet assault. The press of his chest against hers, the sharp hold of his hands heating her arms even through the fabric of her gown, and the gentle touch of his lips on hers all overwhelmed.

Her dreams and secret prayers were being answered. He wanted her. He'd come—just in time—to declare his undying passions.

Oh la, for just this moment, she allowed herself to believe in the magic of fairy tales and in that elusive happily-ever-after.

"Oh, May," he whispered on a heady breath when he peeled away from her. His rough fingers caressed her cheek. These weren't the hands of an idle gentleman. The coarse calluses only made her love him more. "My dear, stubborn May."

He tilted her chin up and turned her head until she was gazing straight into his warm gaze. "What you do to me . . . you can't imagine. . . ."

His heart thundered under May's hand. She drew her palm away from his chest and stepped back. "Why have you come here?" she asked, hoping beyond hope he would declare his love.

Radford blinked several times and cleared his throat. He jammed him hand in his pocket and drew out a shiny porcelain figurine. May recognized it right away as the one she'd admired at the fair.

"For you." He placed it in her hand and curled her fingers around the cool, smooth statuette. "A token of our friendship."

Friendship?

May didn't know what to think. She stared blankly at the laughing woodland fairy child he'd given her.

He came to offer *friendship*? That kiss had heated parts of her and left her longing for more. Certainly there was more than just friendship in the way he'd touched her.

Of course he couldn't offer her anything else.

May raised her chin and swallowed her feelings. The circumstances of her birth made her ineligible to marry someone as respected and sought after as Radford.

A single tear splashed on the fairy's joyous expression. "Thank you, my lord. I will cherish it forever."

Worry creased Radford's brows. He captured May's wrist and closed his hand over her fist and the figurine. "Well, hell. You seem less than pleased . . . and it is not at all proper for you to be alone with me here in this room."

Keeping a sharp hold on her, he led the way from the parlor and out the front door, his cane clacking on the hardwood flooring. The bright sun streaming down into the small yard burned May's tearstained eyes. She rubbed them with the back of her gloved hand.

"Please unhand me," she said as he led her through the yard and toward the street. "Where are you taking me? Unhand me. I expect Mr. Tumblestone to arrive in any minute."

What a disaster she would have on her hands if Tumblestone were to see her alone with Radford. In addition to a broken heart, she would lose the only offer of marriage given to her. What a disaster!

She twisted free of his grasp and set her fists on her hips. "I am not your puppet. Tell me what this is about or leave. Either way, I don't care."

Radford raised a single brow. "You don't care?" He dragged a finger over her cheek, wiping away a stray tear.

May bit the inside of her mouth and prayed for strength. She would not let him see any more of the excited and painful emotions swirling in her stomach. He didn't have a right to know how her heart pained for him.

Her silence appeared to frustrate him. Radford bit off a muttered oath and drew a deep breath. "I came to warn you and seem to be doing a poor job of it," he said, dropping his cane. He clasped his hands behind his back and strode a crooked gait a few steps toward the neighboring field. Tall grasses waved at them. "I don't know how to tell you this."

"Tell me what?" Since he wasn't going to declare his undying love or beg for her hand in marriage—that much was certain—May was wary of what Radford wished to tell her. "I will not agree to be your mistress, my lord. I have too much self-respect to become a kept woman."

"Good Lord, no." He kept his back to her. "I have too much respect for you to suggest such a thing. Oh, damn . . . this is a deuced difficult thing to say."

He turned around then. The hard planes of his aristocratic features made May's breath catch in her throat.

"You can't marry that old goat." The words tumbled out of his mouth. "Your uncle is paying him a small fortune to offer marriage to you. Do you understand me? He is being paid to take you away from your aunt."

"What an ugly thing to say," May hissed. Only a monster would think to stomp on her shattered heart.

No malice, only candid concern haunted his eyes. "I'm so sorry, Miss Sheffers. But it is the truth. Your uncle has a very good reason to want Lady Winifred back under his control. You stand in his way. Hence, the marriage proposal."

"You lie." May backed up a step. She didn't want to hear this. To believe him would be too painful. "You claimed to be my friend. Why hurt me so?"

Radford approached, holding his arms out to her. "I am your friend. My only wish is to protect you from your uncle. Mr. Tumblestone just wants the small fortune he's been promised . . . not you."

"No," May whispered as if denial could drive his words away. The thunder of hooves drowned out the nervous pattering of her heart. May's gaze flicked over her shoulder. Uncle Sires' crested carriage was rolling up to the cottage. The note she'd sent had promised Tumblestone a pleasant reply to his marriage proposal.

But what if Radford were telling the truth?

"No." She returned her tear-blurred gaze to Radford's pleading expression and shook her head from side to side, uncertain what to do—uncertain what to think, even.

She needed time.

Gathering her skirt up into one hand, May ran as fast as her short legs could carry her into the tall grasses.

Nothing was ever solved by running away. May should have stayed and demanded the truth from her uncle. She should have stood her ground with Radford and demanded he explain why he had kissed her with such naked passion.

Running away was the coward's choice, and she never considered herself a coward.

Not caring about grass stains or dirt or messing the careful arrangement of her hair, she dropped on her back in the middle of the field and sprawled out on the cool ground. She stared up at the puffy clouds floating above in the deep blue sky. After a time she closed her eyes and just breathed the warm country air.

A lifetime of days in London had robbed her of such simple pleasures. She found herself enjoying the feel of the earth underneath her back and the rich, musty smell of a fertile soil. She'd grown tired of the endless balls, routs, and teas where she was largely overlooked. The bustle and excitement of a crowded city only offered disappointed dreams.

She was ready for a change.

Marriage to the tall, plump Mr. Tumblestone offered her that change. He lived a quiet, bucolic life. Even if Radford were telling the truth and he only wanted her for the money her uncle had to offer, the offer of marriage still hadn't changed . . . nor had her feelings toward Tumblestone been altered. He was a kindly old man who offered her nothing but a stable future.

There could be no harm in accepting his suit, could there?

If only she knew what Radford had meant by saying that Uncle Sires was trying to get Aunt Winnie under his control. He wanted to provide better medical care—that much was clear. Could there be another reason for her uncle's sudden interest in their lives?

What about her parents?

They were not dead. May could feel the truth of it deep in her soul. They might be lost . . . but they were far from dead.

Why was her uncle so adamant about declaring dead the two people he'd once wished completely out of his sight? Why dredge up a connection he so dearly wanted to ignore?

So many questions . . .

Damn Radford all the way to the tips of his adorably arched eyebrows. He'd brought those questions to light. And worse, for a fleeting moment he'd made her feel loved. And that was what she desired most . . . to simply be loved.

Her birth and her unconventional manner frightened respectable gentlemen away. She had accepted her empty heart, had told herself that her aunt's affection was enough—but it wasn't.

May felt paralyzed by grief. She needed help—needed someone with whom to discuss those unanswerable questions.

A hot wind blew in her face, tickling her nose. The crunch of nearby grasses warned her she was no longer alone. The skin on her back prickled as she realized someone was silently watching her.

How dare an interloper sneak up without a word of warning! A flood of harsh words filled her troubled mind. They would have spewed past her lips if she hadn't realized what a shocking picture she must have made lying flat on her back with her legs and arms sprawled out at the most absurd angles.

Gracious, whoever was watching her must think her mad.

With no hope to preserve her dignity, May pried her eyes open. A great brown nose attached to a strange, long face slowly came into focus. It snorted, spraying her with its hot breath.

May bolted up. A scream strangled in her throat.

Chapter Sixteen

"Gone? What do you mean, gone?"

Lyles, Radford's stable manager, wrung his cap in his grubby hands and danced from foot to foot, apparently at a loss for intelligible words. The man's strange behavior did nothing to sooth Radford's already foul temper.

The simple task of warning May had turned into a complete disaster. The memory of her running away with fresh tears filling her eyes tore at his heart. He'd charged after her, of course. But his leg had collapsed under the strain. After taking a hard tumble to the ground, he'd conceded defeat.

Instead of befriending her, he had kissed her. He was naught but a blasted fool . . . a blasted, besotted fool.

Wynter had been right, again.

His knuckles ached for the chance to beat his friend's smug face into the ground. And since Wynter was nowhere to be found, Lyles unfortunately became only too convenient a target. He took a broad step toward the quivering man.

"Speak up. What do you mean she's gone?"

"She—she must have jumped the fence, m'lord. I've searched the countryside for her. She's nowhere to be found."

Just like Wynter.

"Blast it, what am I paying you for? I thought you understood her importance. You were supposed to watch her. You were supposed to guard her." He slammed his fist into his open palm. Years of hard work and dreaming were slipping away. His life, his wants and desires were harder to hold on to than the fairy-footed maiden, May Sheffers. "Someone must have taken her, damn it."

Lyles paled considerably. "I took great care, m'lord. No one went near her. I swear it. No one."

May scrambled up into an awkward sitting position. Her breath hitched in her throat. Those shiny hooves, just inches from her chest, looked so large. One wrong move could startle the curious beast and her powerful legs. Even if the animal meant her no harm, May could be crushed under its weight just the same.

"That's a gentle Princess." May forced the whisper past the lump of fear lodged in her throat. "You don't want to hurt me. You must have come looking for your Lord Evers." She could only imagine Radford's worry. This young filly had given him nothing but trouble and yet May had clearly recognized the dreamy gleam in his eyes when he gazed on his beautiful beast.

Princess tossed her head and snorted. *Heavens above, she's going to kill me!* May's heart skittered to a stop as her gaze latched onto those hooves again.

Fate sure had a knack for painful irony. She'd stumbled into love only to have another offer her marriage—only to have the man she loved crush her heart. And now his horse was poised to finish her off.

In her grief May might have lain down and given Princess free rein to stomp her to bits. Yet concern for Aunt Winnie wouldn't allow her to simply give up. She had to fight and be strong despite the hollow pains piercing her heart. Despite all that was rational, Aunt Winnie resisted Uncle Sires' offer to let him take care of her. May needed to find out why.

Was Radford telling the truth or just trying to hurt her?

"Please, Princess," May said, feeling a shade braver. She gently nudged the velvety nose that continued to hover all too close to her head. "Please, don't be startled and stamp me into the ground when I try and stand."

It took all her daring to get out from under the horse—most dredged from long-ago feelings tucked away after scores of sleepless nights, worrying why her parents didn't love her enough to return to their only child. May drew a deep breath and slowly rose to her feet.

She brushed off her gown. It was ruined. The burgundy silk was smudged with grass stains and dirt. Portia would scold and work for hours trying to salvage the material. But like May's, the gown's future looked grim.

Princess nudged May's shoulder, reminding her that she still wasn't out of danger. Unlike the other day, there were no leading reins hanging from Princess' halter. More to the point, the beast wasn't wearing a halter.

She was as wild and free as the summer wind.

May backed away from the horse, hoping to increase the distance between them and eventually escape. For each step May took, Princess took an equally measured stride. After several minutes of stepping in one direction and then another only to find herself leading Princess in a stiff dance, May gave up all hope for it.

The horse was lost and looking for a friendly face. Who was May to deny the poor thing?

"You might as well follow along," she said. Through the fields, across a delicately arched bridge, and up the gentle Sion Hill lay Longbranch House, Radford's home. Leading his prize filly home was the only honorable thing to do.

Besides, somewhere in the back of her mind May dreaded returning to her little cottage and her uncle's scowls.

What in blazes could she say to explain her behavior? She'd run off without a word to anyone. Once again, her hot gypsy blood had led her to mischief.

"I just hope you will not attempt to display that dry wit of yours tonight," Lady Evers said as she settled into a settee in the drawing room. A moment before, Jeffers had delivered a pot of piping hot tea to the room, sniffed haughtily, and quietly slipped out with a glower tugging down the corners of his lips.

Radford declined the tea and barely acknowledged his mother. His thoughts were still on his missing filly. Teams of men were out searching, literally beating down the tall grasses, for her. If not for his injuries, he too would be out riding through the fields. Like a hobbled pony, he was stuck listening to his mother prattle happily about his future.

"Well?" his mother said sharply. "Do I have it or not?"

"I beg your pardon, Mother." Radford sighed when he realized he didn't have a clue what she was asking him. "Do you have what?"

"Really, Radford. I do worry that your war injuries have addled your mind. You have been acting so strangely since returning home from that dreadful place. Will you please attend to me?"

Radford gave a curt nod and pushed his thoughts of Princess out of his head.

"Very good. Now, as I was saying . . . do I have your word that you will behave like a complete gentleman tonight? No more jests about not wishing to marry Lady Lillian?"

Ah, so she'd been schooling him on how to ask for a lady's hand in marriage. Radford ground his jaw and stood. He walked, letting the cane take the weight off his damaged foot, and crossed the room to stand in front of the large floor-to-ceiling window.

A figure in the distance caught his attention. Amber curls bounced with a delightful dishevel. Tempting hips swayed as May sauntered up the road. A gentle smile brightened her pursed lips.

What in blazes? Radford blinked twice to convince himself his eyes weren't deceiving him. Princess, his errant filly, followed behind May like a truant pupil, wagging her head from side to side with each easy stride.

Lyles, the stable manager, rushed out and greeted May, his arms gesturing wide arcs. Like a dark cloud passing in front of the sun, May's smile faded. She glanced nervously toward the house. Radford stepped away from the window.

"Do you intend to ignore me completely? Is this how you aim to honor your mother and all I have endured?"

"I should go down to her," he muttered. His mother's shrill voice barely registered in his head. His thoughts were so completely wrapped around the sight of May that everything else in his life disappeared—especially his injuries. "How in blazes did she manage to bewitch my horse?"

"Radford! Attend me this instant!"

He turned in response to the shout. His mother had risen from the settee. She floated across the room like an angered specter. "What is distracting you? What do you see?"

Her eyes narrowed as she peered out the window. "Who is that dreadful-looking young woman? Something about her seems familiar."

Dreadful? The sight of May's pretty form added new colors and a new depth to the world. How could anyone describe such a miracle as dreadful?

"You met her the other day," Radford said rather stiffly. "She is Miss May Sheffers."

"Sheffers? I don't know that name."

"She is a friend of Lady Lillian's."

His mother's brows furrowed further. "And what is she doing here . . . without a proper escort . . . and looking as wild as a hoyden? Certainly she will not seek to speak with you."

He could only hope.

Lyles had draped a loose rein over Princess' neck. He pointed toward the house, no doubt inviting her inside. May raised her hands in front of her and stepped back.

She didn't want to see him.

How could he blame her? He'd confused her with his brash kiss and then clumsily blurted out why she shouldn't marry that money-hungry Tumblestone. Of course she refused to believe him. Only a fool would believe a tale presented so callously.

She thinks you want her for your bed.

"There is nothing improper about Miss Sheffers," Radford explained to his mother. The elfin princess was far too proper to even consider becoming his mistress. If only there were some other way . . .

The marriage list he and Wynter had created burned in his pocket. There was no need to retrieve it and review the qualifications he required from a wife. The words were seared in his head. He could recite them in his sleep.

According to every point on that list, May was ineligible. She could never make a proper wife.

Lady Lillian could.

"She won't come up." Remaining a passive observer and watching her turn away from the house was the hardest thing Radford had ever done. "I don't believe she wants even a crumb of my friendship."

"As well she shouldn't." Lady Evers breathed a sigh of relief. "It's shocking enough to see her appear at your door like that."

"I believe she found my horse." Something precious inside him spiraled down into a bleak hole. "I owe her a debt of gratitude. She's afraid of horses, you see."

"Your horse, Radford? The spirited, wild filly that attacked your affianced? I thought we agreed you would get rid of that troublesome beast."

"I didn't agree to any such thing." He jammed his hands into his pockets. His gaze followed May as she retreated. He found it impossible to turn away from the window and the sight of her delightful swaying gait.

His mother's gaze bounced between the window and Radford. "Oh dear," she said quietly, "I really must do something about this."

"About what, Mother?" he asked. His thoughts returned to that cursed list. Something felt fundamentally wrong about it. But perhaps it wasn't the list at all. Perhaps there was something fundamentally wrong *with him.*

Even if he were to throw propriety and logic to the wind

and dash after May to declare undying love, nothing would change. She spurned his friendship, his offers to help, his overtures for passion. Her rejection kept him planted firmly in the drawing room.

A man so broken, so confused about his worth in life, could never hope to lure a fey spirit like May's into his soul. She deserved a man with the ability to unlock the gilded cage that held her. She deserved to soar with the clouds.

As he watched through the window, May glanced back at Longbranch House. Was it his imagination, or did he see the same longing that burned in his chest reflected in her bright eyes? Could there possibly be a chance for a future with her?

No. No. No. The answer had to be no.

There was no love between them, only longing and a curious emotion Radford didn't quite know how to describe. His passions toward May felt as comfortable as a friendship, only more heated.

What a blasted mess. He dragged a hand through his hair, tugging at the strands.

Lady Evers captured his wrist and kept his manicured fingers from further mussing his hair. "Don't fret about the future, Radford. I will keep the path clear for you. You will see. Your decision to marry Lady Lillian is the right thing. This match is something that would make your father proud."

Her eyes glistened prettily. "And you will make me proud tonight—and bestow happiness on a very lucky young lady."

Happiness? Why hadn't he thought to put anything about *his* happiness on that marriage list? The list, so like his life, had become muddled by the limitations of logic and duty.

Chapter Seventeen

Life would be so very different if she possessed Lady Lillian's delicate looks or Lady Iona's gentle manner. May stiffened her chin and sniffed back some unruly tears. If men refused to see past her birth, her nature, and her looks . . . well, she wanted no part of such a world.

She would survive.

Her parents abandoned her. And she somehow managed to survive. Society matrons treated her like a servant. And she barely blinked. Her aunt's health weakened. And she was forced to become something stronger than she ever imagined she could be. She more than survived.

Why should a little trifling like a broken heart trouble her?

Back straight, head held high, and prepared to face her uncle, May marched back to her cozy little cottage. She would confront him with Radford's accusations and insist that Aunt Winnie demand her brother's assistance and support.

Although this moment felt tragically like an ending, May reminded herself that it wasn't. This was a wonderful, glorious beginning. A new adventure lay before her on the horizon.

Things would be different, and she would be stronger without a certain dashing viscount meddling in her life. Things would be better. . . .

May drew to a sudden stop. Uncle Sires' carriage was no

longer waiting in front of her thatched roofed cottage. The shades inside were drawn, the windows dark.

A crimson-tinted cloud reached out overhead, signaling the approaching end of an utterly perplexing day, and May could not stop a feeling of dread from snaking through her veins. The cottage looked different, somehow. Something was wrong.

Horridly wrong.

"May!" a breathless voice called out to her. Lady Iona waved her arms as Lord Nathan deftly steered his new curricle down the road. May tilted her head back and looked up at the pair as the curricle pulled to a halt on the road in front of her. Pins were slipping from Iona's hair, and her dress was smudged with dirt. Tears stained her rosy cheeks.

"Whatever is the matter?" May asked. Her friend would never appear in public in such a state unless something was terribly amiss. "Please tell me it isn't—"

"Your aunt, May. She's collapsed. We've been searching everywhere for you. Where in Heaven's name have you been?"

"No," May gasped. She charged into the stone-still cottage, tears streaming down her face. She should have never run away. She should have never . . .

"Aunt! Please, please, no . . ."

Portia appeared in the foyer. Her lips tightly drawn, her hands in constant motion, she lowered her head. "I am so sorry, Miss Sheffers. You poor, little mite."

May heard Lady Iona and Lord Nathan follow her into the house. She felt supportive arms hugging her shoulders. But her mind could not take it all in.

"Aunt Winnie?" How would she survive without her aunt? Her legs melted beneath her, and she sank to the Oriental carpet covering the foyer floor and silently wept. "I must see her. I must ask her to forgive me for not being here."

Lord Nathan cleared his throat. He padded nervously around the small entranceway. "It seems your housekeeper bravely tried to keep Lord Sires from carrying her to his town house, but he would not be dissuaded."

"Oh, that is correct, Miss Sheffers. Your poor, poor dear aunt was so weak. He insisted he care for her." Portia heaved a weepy sigh. "He cursed something fierce until I thought my ears might bleed."

May lifted her head slowly, fearing sudden motions might wipe away that small bud of hope. "Aunt Winnie is alive?" With a sheer force of will, she made her legs support her. "I must go to her. She needs me."

"Of course." Lord Nathan took May's arm and led her back outside.

"But—but Lord Sires . . ." Iona sputtered.

"Blast the man. He will just have to tell her himself," Lord Nathan grumbled.

May was much too upset to wonder about that exchange. She let Lord Nathan help her up into his curricle. Iona snuggled in beside her, and within a minute, they were racing through the paved streets toward her uncle's town house in Queen's Square.

Aunt Winnie was strong. She would recover. She would simply have to. . . . May wasn't prepared to accept any other ending.

"I was told not to let anyone enter." Uncle Sires' butler sneered down his nose at May as he spoke. She recognized him from Redfield Abbey. He'd been the Abbey's head footman the last time she'd visited. In no way did his off-putting manner dissuade her.

"I beg your pardon," she said, keeping her voice dangerously level. She made sure her devilishly violet eyes glared daggers into his. "I care not one whit about what you were told. My aunt is inside and I intend to see her." She paused for a dramatic beat. "Step aside."

"I would do as she commands," Lord Nathan said. He folded his arms across his chest. Lady Iona, bless her, did the same. A united front poised for battle.

"Very well." The butler stepped to the side of the doorway. He made no attempt to lead them to a parlor or to Aunt Winnie's room. Instead he left them stranded in the impressive marble foyer. "I will tell his lordship that you have arrived."

May had no intention of standing around while the butler and her uncle discussed ways to deny her. Aunt Winnie needed her. She would open every closed door in the house, if need be, to find her.

As the butler scuttled off toward the back of the house, May took to the stairs. Lord Nathan and Iona followed along silently.

A low murmur of voice rumbled behind a closed door at the end of a long hall. May rushed toward the sound. She tossed open the door, not worried about anything beyond seeing to her aunt's welfare.

Two men were bent over her aunt, who was lying all too still on an elegantly appointed bed. The room looked like it had been decorated to house a fairy-tale queen. At least her aunt was finally getting the comfort she had always deserved, May thought as she rushed to her side.

"How is she?" May asked. She knelt beside the bed and gently lifted her aunt's hand to hold it against her chest.

"Only time will tell," the white-haired man closest to her said with a slight shake of his head. "She is weak."

"She has been overtaxed with worry," Uncle Sires' voice boomed into the room. "I will not have you and your unseemly manner endanger her further, child."

May carefully laid her aunt's hand on the soft bed. She lovingly stroked Winnie's smooth cheek and said a small prayer for her recovery before rising to face her uncle.

"I have more right than you to stay with her," she said in an oddly calm voice. "You may be able to take away my money. You may be able to take away my future. But I will stand up to the forces of hell before letting you take Winnie from my life."

"Please," the doctor said, ushering everyone to the door. "She needs quiet. She needs to rest."

The instant May stepped her toe outside the bedroom door Uncle Sires captured her wrist. He mercilessly dragged her through the hall and down the stairs. May tripped over her feet as she tried to keep up with the brutal pace. Lord Nathan stepped in and attempted to save her but was swiftly pulled away by two burly footmen draped in bright red livery.

"What do you mean to do?" May asked. She twisted her wrist, trying desperately to break free. There was a murderous gleam in her uncle's eye that made her heart slam against her ribs. "What do you mean to do?"

"Something I should have done years ago," he said and gave her arm a vicious tug. She stumbled down the last three steps. Her knees slammed against the hard marble floor in the foyer. He didn't give her time to pull herself back to her feet. His pace unbroken, he dragged her across the floor and into a dark oak-paneled study.

The door slammed closed behind her. The lock clicked.

"You are an abomination . . . just like your father. I can't stand to look at you, a grotesque mixture of his blood with mine." He loomed over her. A menacing grimace transformed his features into a mask of pure hatred.

He leaned down until his lips were a mere hairbreadth from her ear. His fiery breath struck her cheek as his voice crackled. "I cannot allow this willful existence of yours to continue, child," he threatened, jamming a leather horsewhip just under her nose. "I intend to beat it from you once and for all."

Where were the blasted rains? The skies were darkening as evening approached, the pale moon rising, and not one blasted cloud to be seen. Radford didn't wish to gaze on the moon as his open landau carried his mother and him to the Newbury town house in the center of Bath.

The moonlight reminded him of May and the night he first kissed her. She'd been bathed in the spectral glow of Heaven flowing in the tall window in the Newburys' darkened library. A fey goddess illuminated by natural elegance.

An unattainable spirit, who would soon be engaged to a man very anxious to beat all that was special and loveable from her small body.

His hand curled into a very tight fist as the carriage bounced over a rut in the stone-paved road. Just picturing May married to another man . . . entering the marriage bed with another . . . it was too much to bear.

He much preferred the rains and the aching muscles and misery the damp weather brought with it than to gaze on the shimmering, oval moon and think of May.

A family ring, an ancient piece of art with a miniature crest etched into a cabochon-cut ruby, sat nestled in the breast pocket of his coat. Within a few hours he'd slide that ring onto Lady Lillian's slender finger and pledge himself—body and soul—to a woman he may never be able to love.

His mother snuggled up beside him and cooed happily.

"Tonight will be magical," she whispered. The landau's driver slowed to turn onto Bennett Street. "Just a few more blocks, Radford. Your future waits for you in the Royal Crescent. I couldn't be more proud."

She squeezed his hand. Her grasp felt light, fragile through his leather gloves.

This night was for his mother. He would give himself to Lillian, vowing to her fidelity and security in exchange for a brood of children.

This was his gift to his mother. She'd suffered so much because of his injuries. Marriage to a beauty like Lady Lillian was no great a sacrifice in order to fulfill his duty to his family.

If only the rains had fallen. With that blasted moonlight shining down on his face and the stars twinkling mysteriously all through the nearly black sky, he couldn't seem to keep his thoughts from straying to May, a most unsuitable woman.

Ah, May . . . a future with you is naught but a pretty fairy tale. Children may believe in such a romantically outrageous ending. Adults are trained to be far more practical.

His future waited a few blocks away.

"I am pleased you find pleasure in my decision," he said warmly to his mother. "Your happiness is very important to me."

"As yours is to me, dear." She gave his arm a gentle pat. "As yours is to me."

Lady Evers craned forward then, tilting her head one way and then the other. "Whatever could that be about?" she whispered while craning forward further still. She'd scooted so far off the bench she was in danger of falling off.

Radford searched the road. His landau was rounding The Circus. A few pedestrians, three young women giggling as they followed an older couple, were strolling on the sidewalk. A carriage rolled by in the other direction. Two carriages sat motionless in front of a couple of town houses, with grooms attending to the waiting horses. Other than that, he could see nothing. Certainly none of the activity visible on the street was out of the ordinary.

"What is it? What do you see?" he asked when his mother gasped and fell back on the squabs in a near swoon.

"Shameful . . . disgraceful," she muttered. "A harlot being tossed from a home, here, in this respectable area? I cannot believe my eyes."

"Really? Where?" Radford asked more to placate his upset mother than out of any kind of perverse interest in viewing another man's dirty affairs.

"There." An accusing finger shot out to identify a town house a few doors into the circular row of houses known as The Circus.

What the devil?

Radford perched forward on the bench to get a better view. Time moved at a painfully slow pace as he watched a nightmare unfold.

May, dressed in the same burgundy gown she'd been wearing when he'd met with her earlier in the day, stood at the open door. A long, elegant sleeve had been ripped away. Part of the ruined bodice hung open. She tugged wildly at the wide, masculine arm holding her. A look of naked terror on her elfish face, dimly illuminated in the yellowy lamplight, froze the blood in his veins.

He rose shakily to his feet, prepared to leap from his landau while it still moved.

"Hold there," he called to his driver and swung open the door.

"Radford!" his mother screamed and wrapped her arms around his strong leg. He fell back onto the bench as his damnable weakened leg collapsed under the strain from his sudden shift of weight.

He watched in horror as May tore free from her attacker, tripped down the steps, and ran blindly into the brick road. His horses, startled by her sudden appearance in front of them as they were slowing their pace, whinnied and reared. The landau creaked and jolted forward.

May screamed.

A deadly silence followed.

No! Radford pried his mother's hands from his body and jumped down to the ground. *No!* He dragged his weaker leg behind him, not caring what he looked like or how he moved. All he cared about was getting to May . . . to seeing her safe.

"There was naught a thing I could do to save 'er, m'lord. I swear it. I didn't even see 'er," his driver cried, wringing his hands as he gazed down at May's crumpled body.

A trickle of blood oozed from high on her forehead.

"No," Radford whispered. He dropped to the road and gathered May into his arms. Cradling her, he hugged her against his chest and felt for any sign of life, no matter how small. She was still in his arms, too still. "Live, damn it. If I have to cling to this cursed mortal coil, you do too."

He glanced up pleadingly at the sky. His gaze chanced on the open door and the man who'd tormented her, the man who'd driven her to run in front of his horses.

The Earl of Redfield.

A horsewhip hung in his hand. A murderous gleam darkened his face. Why hadn't Radford seen it? The bounder had been set on ruining May's life from the start. His power and his comfortable lifestyle were being threatened. Radford should have worried about May's safety after telling her the truth about her uncle. She must have confronted him and roused the greedy man's wrath.

"I should have protected you." He brushed her hair away from her bloody brow and pressed a handkerchief to her forehead. He'd never forgive himself if she died. Losing May would leave a gaping hole in his heart, which, like his leg, would never heal.

With a shout, Wynter pushed the earl aside and charged down the steps and across the road. Lady Iona followed closely behind, pausing only long enough to stomp the earl's toe on her way past.

After that, time began to gush at a hell-or-high-water speed. It took all of Radford's concentration just to keep up.

"Is she dead?" Lady Iona wailed and tossed herself into Wynter's arms.

"No." Radford pressed his palm to her chest and felt a strong, steady heartbeat move underneath her tattered gown. "But she does need immediate care."

He glanced up again. The door to the Earl of Redfield's town house had closed. The light in the front parlor had been extinguished. He'd get no help from that villain.

"Wynter, fetch the best doctor you can find. I'm going to take May back to Longbranch House. She'll be safe there."

"My father—" Lady Iona started to say only to be hushed by Wynter.

"Let Radford handle this." Wynter unfurled his arms from Lady Iona's shoulders and bent down to pluck May from Radford's arms. Radford refused, holding tightly to May's body. He unreasonably wanted to keep his woodland sprite pressed against his chest until he knew she was truly safe.

As if he could protect her. Hah! Her weight trapped him to the ground as surely as his dying horse had on the Peninsula. Radford reluctantly released his hold. As it was, he'd have a struggle to stand with his arms empty, which he started to do as inelegantly as anyone could imagine. He floundered like a fish out of water until Lady Iona offered him a hand. Swallowing pride and a goodly portion of his manhood, he reached out and allowed the slight woman to assist him back into the landau.

"Oh my, oh my," his mother was muttering. She weaved on the bench. Her skin was as pale as the moon, and she appeared to be on the verge of a collapse. Wynter and Lady Iona looked fairly ill themselves.

"I will come with you, Lord Evers," Lady Iona said. She dabbed at her tear-stained cheeks. "I can help with May and your mother."

Radford was grateful for the assistance. "Of course, please do." He moved aside to make room while pulling May into his lap.

"Go, Wynter! Get a doctor!" he barked the order, and as soon as Lady Iona was settled, he gave a nod to his anxious driver to put the horses back into action.

A block into the drive May's eyes fluttered open and she sighed roughly when they bounced over a loose stone. Radford's chest contracted tightly as she stared up at him with wide eyes. Such confusion tainted her lovely violet gaze. If only he could bathe her with kisses and wipe her fears away.

"Aunt Winnie . . ." May whispered, turning in his arms. Fighting him. A perfect round breast looked as though it might fall free of her ripped bodice. "Please, Winnie . . ."

"Hush, my love. Let me take care of you." With no thought about the sharp gazes of his mother or Lady Iona watching his every move, he reverently cupped her breast and the soft velvet of her gown. Her chest rose and fell with deep regularity with each smooth breath. Radford took comfort in feeling her warm satiny-soft skin. She felt very, very alive.

He didn't realize how inappropriate it must look for him to continue touching her, lightly caressing her, until his mother, her lips set in a thin line, reached over and moved his hand. She placed his fingers so he'd clasp May's shoulder instead.

Radford shifted slightly, embarrassed. What the two ladies with their set stares must think of him.

May blinked heavily. Her gaze settled on his face, and a slight smile creased her lips. The adorable look left Radford itching to cover her petal-soft mouth with his.

Here he was, a gentleman mere hours from proposing marriage to another, goggling over a half-conscious woman whose weak smile sent his heart tripping like some helpless lovelorn swain.

This was madness. Pure madness.

Chapter Eighteen

May woke up in a strange bed feeling quite out of sorts. Her head throbbed, her arms felt painfully stiff, and her knees burned as if they'd been scraped raw. The strange bed had a full and luxurious down mattress that vexed her. She clutched the heavy comforter to her neck and worried her mind trying to remember what had happened.

"Aunt Winnie!" She jolted up in bed, only to be confounded by a spinning room. "Aunt . . ."

Her head settled back to the silky pillow. A fire smoldered in the fireplace across the room. Clearly the coals had been recently tended. A painting of a happy sheepdog hung on the wall between two floor-to-ceiling windows. Snatches of sunlight stole into the room from around a pair of heavy burgundy drapes . . . drapes nearly the same shade as the velvet gown she'd worn.

Still feeling dreadfully confused, May slowly lifted the bedding and peered underneath. Her gown was gone. A soft lawn chemise with a satin tie at the neck now covered her.

A stranger's house wearing a stranger's nightclothes. The last thing she remembered—or had that been a dream—was being cradled in Radford's arms. Had he truly called her *his love*? No, those fantastic memories could only be from some wondrous dream.

May closed her eyes and tried to conjure real memories . . . and push away those gentle thoughts created purely by some anomaly brought on by a blow to the head.

"Aunt Winnie had collapsed," she said aloud as the events of the previous day slowly returned. A sob burst out as she remembered seeing her aunt lying on her uncle's bed. She'd looked so pale. So very weak. "Oh, Winnie."

Be brave. For Winnie she'd have to be brave and figure this all out.

"I'd quarreled with Uncle Sires. He was being most unreasonable." Oh yes, she remembered now. Her heart raced as she recalled how he'd threatened her. He'd been so angry. Out of his head, really. He'd been poised to beat her with that leather horsewhip when she'd bit him and fled like a banshee from his town house.

From there her memory turned fuzzy. Dreamlike. Had she been trapped in a nightmare or a fantasy? A horse had frightened her. Hooves kicking up to kill her!

With a shout, May shot up in the bed and scooted toward the rosewood carved headboard in an attempt to escape the terrifying images.

"Hush, hush, dearie." A slightly crooked maid hurriedly placed a platter on a small dresser and rushed to May's side. "Just lie still now. That's what the master said you needed to do to get well again. Just lie still and all will be well."

The room was spinning again, but less so than before, thank goodness. May let the older maid arrange the bedding around her until she was tucked in as tightly as dough in a pan.

"Thank you, um . . . um?"

"The name's Lottie, miss." The smiling lady lightly caressed May's forehead. "I've been the lady's maid for thirty years now. And she told me to take real good care of you. His lordship, you see, is worried something fierce. He didn't sleep at all last night. Since it wouldn't be proper for him to step foot inside this room, he paced the hall just outside until dawn, the poor cove. And the lady doesn't like to see him upset. She tells me she wants you well as soon as possible."

May wiggled from under the covers so she could sit up against the mound of pillows at the top of the bed. "The lady you speak of? Who is she?"

"The Viscountess Evers, Miss Sheffers," the words rolled very properly off a refined tongue before Lottie could answer. May's gaze darted toward the bedroom's open door. Lady Evers, dressed in a stark black gown, glowered as she surveyed the room. "You may leave us now, Lottie. I will call for you when Miss Sheffers is ready to eat the porridge you've brought up."

Lottie murmured promises to return soon and curtsied deeply for the viscountess before scurrying from the room. A clock somewhere nearby chimed the hour.

Ignoring her aches, May raised herself higher in the bed and smoothed her hand over the comforter. "May I inquire the hour, my lady?" May asked somewhat sedately.

"It is eleven in the morning."

"Eleven? Oh, dear. I have never slept so late."

The viscountess smiled tightly. "You were ill." She stepped inside the room and closed the door behind her with a snap. "I trust you are feeling better."

"I am still a little dizzy—" May started to explain.

"That will soon pass. The doctor did not appear at all concerned last night. I trust his judgment and so should you." A bitter edge to her soft voice caught May off-guard.

"Yes, of course. I didn't mean to complain."

"Of course."

"My aunt, Lady Winifred?" May ignored the matron's cool demeanor. She had much more pressing concerns to think about than the reason for the viscountess' unhappy mood. "Is there any news on her condition? My uncle took her to his town house after she collapsed."

"Lady Iona Newbury arrived early this morning with all sorts of information." Lady Evers lowered herself to sit on the edge of the bed and continued to glower. She produced a note from a fold in her skirt.

"Yes? I beg you, tell me of my aunt. She is all I have."

"She is, isn't she, you poor dear?" There was no compassion in the sentiment. "Your aunt is stronger this morning. Her doctors are confident that with diligent care she should recover much of her strength."

May breathed a sigh of relief and felt her taut muscles relax into the fluffy bedding. "Thank God," she whispered.

"You will want to visit her right away, I suppose?"

"Oh, yes. She depends on me, and I love her very much."

Lady Evers clucked her tongue and wagged her head slowly. "The earl is most upset, however. That shocking scene you orchestrated in front of his home mortified him. I must admit I was horrified having to witness such base behavior from a young lady. Such screaming and blatant displaying of your body . . . I shudder to think upon it."

"He was trying to harm me. I only wished escape," May tried to explain. She remembered the horse again . . . and its great hooves poised to crush her. Her mouth went dry.

"Radford saved me?" Could he really have called her "his love"? Did he truly hold her tightly in his arms? "Please, I don't remember what happened once I fled my uncle's."

"It is just as well that you don't." The viscountess leaned forward. She placed the letter she'd been holding on her lap and took May's hand to cradle between her frosty palms. Her slender fingers rubbed the tops of May's knuckles. "You are fond of my son."

Lady Evers had stated May's feelings toward Radford as if they were common knowledge. Certainly May's behavior toward him in public hadn't betrayed her deepest feelings. Certainly she'd acted more carefully than that.

May tried to draw her hand away. "I don't understand what you mean."

The lady tightened her grasp. "Now, now. Let's not play the coquette. You do not have the personality or the delicate physique to succeed with such games. I've watched you. I know."

She knew? May fought a desire to crawl under the covers and hide. "Very well," she forced herself to say calmly while tightening her chin. "I do feel a certain warmth for the viscount."

"As does he for you, foolish boy. I don't know what you've done to him, but he seems quite captivated."

Radford captivated? Could it be possible? May's cheeks stung as a blush bloomed over her face and down her neck to touch her chest.

Lady Evers lifted the letter she'd set aside and tapped it against May's hand. "I've corresponded with the Duchess of Newbury on this matter just this morning, and she assured me that you are a reasonable girl."

Praise from the duchess was a rarity. Iona's mother had never approved of May's attachment with the Newbury family. She'd made it plainly known that if she'd had her way, May's entire existence would be ignored.

Luckily, the duke heartily disagreed.

Hearing that the duchess had actually called her "reasonable" gave May cause for alarm. "What else did she say?" May asked, eyeing the letter with grave concern. With the brush of a quill, the duchess could make her life even more difficult. May might be completely rejected by the *ton* if they knew the full truth of her father's past.

Such a man has no place in polite society, Uncle Sires had always insisted.

"Her grace is not pleased, you must know. My boy was to propose to her daughter last night. That scene you created ruined those plans. Despite my pleas, Radford remained here to worry over your trifling injuries instead of keeping his dinner appointment with the Newbury family."

"Oh?" Then he wasn't engaged to Lady Lillian yet? Knowing that he was still an eligible bachelor shouldn't have lightened May's mood, but it did.

"Miss Sheffers, you cannot truly believe that my son, a viscount, could possibly marry you. You must see that such a match is impossible."

Of course she saw that. She knew her place only too well.

Yet she jutted out her chin and tried to look as defiant as possible as if she could scare the truth away.

"What do you think would happen if my Radford were to marry you, a woman with a history of finding disasters?" Lady Evers asked. Her voice grew a little shrill. "Do you think society would stand for such an ill-advised match? Do you think he would be able to keep the political influence the Evers family has cultivated for generations after proving he cannot even be trusted to pick a proper wife? If you care even a little for Radford, you must let him go."

May's shoulders slumped. No matter how defiantly she held her chin, the truth would never go away.

Lady Evers slipped the letter from its envelope. "Her grace was kind enough to share a little of your background with me. Your father's mother was an unmarried gypsy. She and her people raised your father until his twelfth year. You were born to a bastard gypsy father who'd stolen your mother despite the Earl of Redfield's efforts to protect her. Your father befouled a gently born lady and produced *you*."

That last word hung in the air, dripping with layers of contempt. May had trouble separating the disdain Lady Evers felt for May from the lifetime of disapproval she'd had heaped on her by her uncle.

"I wonder. Will you call her grace a liar? Will you deny that this is your heritage?"

May slowly turned her head from side to side. "The duchess is well known for speaking the truth," she whispered. "I do not dispute her words."

Lady Evers smiled broadly. "It pleases me to see that you are indeed a reasonable girl. Tell me, then. Are we in agreement? Do you see now how marriage between you and my son would be a disaster?"

May nodded as tears flooded her eyes. "I do, as does he. He has never offered such a boon."

"Please reconsider, miss. I beg you to reconsider," Lottie said, wringing her overworked hands while May continued to stubbornly fuss with an unruly strand of hair. A slab of plaster covered a small wound high on May's forehead. Though pulling a brush through her hair tugged at the injury, making her feel like sharp needles were pricking her scalp, May felt it was a small price to pay. She wanted to make herself appear hale and hearty for her aunt. Nothing should upset Winnie or her recovery.

"His lordship said you were to remain abed," Lottie complained. "I would've never brought up the walking dress Lady Iona Newbury had delivered if I'd known you'd insist on wearing it. His lordship will be most upset when he learns of this."

May brushed her hands over the skirt of the faded violet gown she'd hastily donned. "I have no wish to upset the viscount. He has been most kind."

May just needed to escape. Quite simply, her aunt needed her. Radford didn't. Staying under his roof for a moment longer would only damage her heart further. Just admitting her feelings to his mother had been torture. Hearing Lady Evers put voice to how wrong May was for him nearly killed her.

All her life, she'd been wrong. Unsuitable.

She could not stay.

Despite the slight dizziness, May was determined to straighten out the messes she'd made and move on with her life. Her mind had cleared after Lady Evers' visit.

All she required was courage.

"No one ever complained I was lacking for want of courage."

"What's that, miss?"

"Nothing, Lottie." She wrapped her arms around the small maid and gave the beleaguered woman a tight hug. "You've served me well. You've made me feel comfortable, and I thank you."

May marched from the room and down the stairs with her head held high. A bout of dizziness interrupted her pace only once . . . and that was after she chanced to catch sight of Radford through a window.

He was strolling alongside the house with Wynter at his side. They looked to be heading toward his stables. A gold-handled cane thumped on the ground with each step. Bless him, he had finally committed to treating himself right and giving his leg time to heal. May could barely discern a limp as he deftly relied on that sturdy cane. Like Wynter, he was impeccably dressed, though somewhat less formally. A pair of brow-raising buff-colored doeskins hugged his legs. A subdued green-and-white-striped waistcoat covered a crisp white shirt. He carried a plain olive frock coat draped over his arm and his shimmering beaver hat between two fingers. His cravat was tied in a relaxed four-in-hand style.

All and all, May thought he looked devastatingly handsome. She could see why the ladies of the *ton* used to speak of him in scandalized whispers.

She stood transfixed while watching the distance grow between them. A great pressure built in her chest. She was right to flee. Staying hurt too much.

With a stiff upper lip, May continued down the hall and met Iona, who'd been waiting for her in the front parlor. Her dearest friend took one look at her disheveled appearance and burst into tears.

"I was so worried," Iona wailed. "Whatever would I do if I lost you?"

"Oh, don't be a silly fuss-pot," May scolded, feeling suddenly embarrassed by the trouble she'd created. "Don't speak as if I'd been on death's door. I suffered nothing more than a slight knock to the head." She gave the top of her head a rap with her knuckle, which she instantly regretted. Sharp sparks of pain rippled through her skull.

"See?" May said through gritted teeth. "Nothing to worry about. Please take me home now. My housekeeper must be beside herself with worry."

Iona hooked her arm with May's. "I will do no such thing.

Portia's already been moved to my family's town house. Papa insists you stay with us while your aunt recovers."

Stay at the Newbury household and watch the wedding preparations up close? May doubted her heart would be able to bear it.

Iona stomped her tiny foot. "You know this is the only way. It's improper for a young lady to live alone . . . unchaperoned."

Of course May knew that. How foolish for her to believe she could suspend the rules of society.

The sooner she accepted her fate, the better.

"Very well," May conceded. With a sorrowful Jeffers watching on, she and Iona walked arm in arm through the front entranceway and down the front steps of Radford's Longbranch House. A ducal carriage waited on the road just a few steps away. Two footmen dressed in crimson livery leapt down from their perch to sweep open the carriage door and lower the steps.

Iona gave May's arm a tight squeeze.

"You will survive this," she whispered.

May swallowed hard, realizing then, after stealing one last glance up at Longbranch House, that tears threatened yet again.

"What's this?" Radford called from the side of the house. Appropriately dressed now with his olive frock coat buttoned up and his beaver hat firmly set on the top of his head, he approached quickly with a hopping gait, letting the cane do most of the work for his stiff leg. He took May by the arm and pulled her several feet away from Iona and the carriage. "What in bloody hell are you doing out of bed?"

His voice shook.

May blinked heavily, praying he wouldn't scrutinize her too carefully and notice how close she'd been to letting those blasted tears in her eyes spill.

"I am well enough, thank you," she said.

"You are—?" He tossed off his hat and dragged his fingers through his dark hair. "You—you are ungrateful—

that's what you are. How dare you sneak away from me like a thief?"

He flicked a nervous glance toward Iona and a longer, more predatory look in the direction of the fast-advancing Lord Nathan Wynter.

Still glaring at Lord Nathan, he moderated his voice. "It would please me if you'd grant me a moment of your time, Miss Sheffers." He turned his sharp jade-colored eyes on her then. "Just a few minutes to listen to what I have to say."

May's heart thundered in her ears as she considered the request. Of course she'd agree to listen to him. She'd happily listen to whatever he wanted to talk about for the rest of her days.

"For just a minute," she managed to say coolly with a glance at the sky as if she could read the time from the position of the sun.

Radford acted as if she'd just agreed to give him the world. With the most glorious smile, he scooped his discarded hat from the warm grasses and led May back into the house, rudely leaving Iona stranded outside with Lord Nathan.

Neither Iona nor Lord Nathan, who were grinning like fools, appeared upset in the least.

"Please, sit," he said softly, motioning to a petite chair just steps inside the front parlor.

With a sharp nod, May did as he bid. She took several deep breaths, desperately trying to slow her racing heart before deliberately folding her hand primly on her lap. She turned her head up and stared at him with a carefully executed blank expression. "What is it you wish to say?"

Radford looked so serious. What grave matter did he wish to discuss? Was he, like his mother, planning to scold her for her shocking behavior the evening before?

Probably.

Her fearful escape from Uncle Sires apparently caused quite a stir. Even Iona had muttered that recalling the scene had occupied the gossips in the Pump Room that morning.

She held her breath, praying that Radford, a man who'd once begged for her to consider him a friend, wouldn't join with society and condemn her out-of-hand.

"That violet color brightens your eyes," he said with utter sincerity.

"What?" Certainly Radford hadn't brought her back inside the house to comment on the color of her—her—

What in the devil was he commenting on?

"Your walking dress." He made a vague, almost embarrassed, gesture in her direction. "The material is faded. But the color, it suits you."

"Thank you," May said, stiffening. There was more. His blurted compliment came from nerves. She knew him well enough to recognize that he needed to build up to whatever he planned to say.

"How are you feeling?" he asked after a brief silence. "You are free from suffering severe pains?"

"Yes, yes." May held her hands in front of her like a shield. "Please, do not fret over me. You have much more important matters—"

"More important?" His brows creased. "Nothing could possibly be more important than your well-being, May. Nothing at all."

Oh, if only that could be true . . .

Radford started pacing then. His cane thudded on the Axminster carpet with a regular tattoo. "You don't understand."

May was afraid she understood too well. "Oh, Radford," she said with a sigh, "you must think of your family first. I'm like a new toy. This fascination you have in me is fleeting. The shine will wear off far too quickly."

"You don't understand." He kept a steady pace as he continued methodically across the room. "I knew of your uncle's plans. I knew he might cause you trouble. And yet . . . yet, I failed to protect you. In fact, my own damned horse nearly killed you."

"I wasn't nearly killed," she whispered. Watching him

take all the blame for her troubles pricked her deeply. No man had ever acted so gallantly or made himself her champion.

Mary Wollstonecraft would not approve. A woman should always serve as her own champion. As much as she wished for him to take charge and fix her horrid messes, she could not allow him to do so.

If you love him just a little, you must let him go, Lady Evers' words echoed in her head.

"I never asked for your assistance," she said.

"That is true." He stopped and turned toward her. "You didn't ask, you demanded. That first day you stormed into my study like a delightful harridan, you demanded I help you."

Oh dear . . . she had done exactly that.

"I—I never intended . . ."

"May, my lovely overlooked May," he said. He began to slowly return to her. "I've considered this for quite a while and can only find one solution. You and I must marry."

The words hung in the air like a dream teetering between sleep and forgetfulness. If she were to wake up and acknowledge his proposal, the magic would all but disappear. Reality would sadly return.

"No." May rose from the chair slowly, afraid her legs would be too watery to support her. "Please, I cannot." She backed toward the door.

Radford advanced with a determined glint sparkling in his eyes. "We must."

With a steady gait he moved closer, moving as assuredly as a hungry falcon stalking his prey. "It's the only way I can honorably protect you from your uncle and his scheming."

The breath caught in May's throat as his burning gaze kept her pinned to where she stood.

"Besides, May, we will suit, you and I. You will—"

"No." May said forcefully. No matter how much she wished for it, no dream could replace reality. She shook her head from side to side to deny his words. "No. You would only grow to hate me. You deserve better than what I have to offer. Much better."

His jaw dropped slightly as he tilted his head. "You do not hold yourself in high esteem?" Radford asked. He sounded genuinely surprised.

His question cut deep in her soul. "I have eyes . . . and ears. I know very well what I am. I have no pretensions about it."

"Pretensions?" He tilted his head. If only he didn't make her long to be the beautiful, graceful woman he wanted for a wife. Perhaps then, the truth wouldn't be so hard to voice.

"I am a small, stocky woman more suited to the role of washerwoman than gently bred lady, my lord." Tears burned in her eyes. She would not let them fall. Not for this, not ever for this. "In fact, I am not a gently born woman. My father, you see, is naught but a bastard—his father was a careless gentleman, his mother a wild gypsy." She turned her head away and regained control over a quivering breath. "I refuse to be ashamed," she whispered.

"Nor would I ask you to be." He was suddenly standing in front of her, cupping her face with his gloved hands. "I don't care about your past. It is your future that concerns me. And you are presently out of options. You are powerless against your uncle's machinations. I am not."

Her eyes fluttered closed as she rubbed her cheek against his warm touch.

"Let me do this for you, May. Consent to become my wife."

If only . . . if only . . .

His touch ignited a host of feelings. Her head spun in the spiraling confusion. The man she loved with her whole heart was proposing to her. *Her!*

How easy it would be to say yes. She opened her mouth to agree to the madness when she realized what was holding her back.

Though Lady Evers' words had made an impact, it wasn't May's disgraceful birth that was acting as a roadblock. May hadn't lied when she'd said she wouldn't be ashamed. Though her parents weren't much more than a faint memory, she loved them dearly . . . and cherished how they loved each other.

Her parents had defied convention to marry, not out of honor or a desire to champion the other. They had made that difficult decision because of passion.

Though this moment would always live as a miracle in May's memories, she would also remember the reason she pushed away his hands and kept him at arm's length before his lips could touch hers. Nowhere in his sincere proposal had Radford mentioned love. He'd vowed to protect her, to do the honorable thing and rescue the maiden in distress. Perhaps he'd even convinced himself that he loved her.

No doubt the constant frustrations over his injuries left him feeling helpless, compelling him to act like St. George and do battle with her dragons. He'd said it himself—in this he felt powerful.

"Please, Radford," she increased her distance from him. "Please, don't press me for an answer."

To deny him would be too painful.

To accept him would be a mistake May couldn't afford to make.

Chapter Nineteen

Radford watched with utter confusion as May fled his home. Her body trembled as she let a footman convey her up into the Newburys' ducal carriage.

Lady Iona cast a nervous glance in his direction before following May into the carriage. Within a matter of a few shocked heartbeats the horses were spurred into motion and the wheels were rolling, carrying May out of his life.

"What did I do wrong?"

"What did you say to her?" Wynter aggressively pushed Radford back up the front steps and into the house. "Miss Sheffers looked crushed, absolutely crushed. Not to mention Lady Iona. She's out of her head with worry for her friend. What in blazes did you do to make things worse?"

Radford led the way to his study where he tore off his frock coat, peeled away the gloves, and tossed his hat onto a chair. The late summer heat was getting to him, making him crazy.

He poured two glasses of claret and took a deep sip from his glass before offering its twin to Wynter. After muttering something about getting himself in too deep with Lady Iona, Wynter drained the glass with one try.

"Now tell me, Evers, what did you say to upset Miss Sheffers . . . and Lady Iona?"

Radford pulled at his hair as he remembered how May

had paled when he'd detailed the reasons they should wed. "I was rational, calm. I cannot understand her reaction."

"What exactly did you say to her in this rational, calm manner?"

"Why, I told May that we should marry. To hell with the requirements of the perfect wife, Miss Sheffers needs me. I can help her stand up to her uncle."

"Bloody hell," Wynter muttered. He helped himself to another glass of claret. "You actually told her you wanted to marry her to protect her?"

"In a manner, yes." Just like May, his friend was getting emotional over what should be clear-cut, rational reasoning. Wynter stomped around the study like a wild beast while grumbling curses under his breath.

"Miss Sheffers is a proud woman," Wynter said after he'd apparently worn himself down. "You saw that the first time she barged into this very room and demanded you listen to her. She does not wish to be coddled or told what is best for her."

"And when did you become the expert on proposing marriage?" Radford shouted. "I thought you'd vowed to become celibate before agreeing to make such a unbearable commitment."

"I remember I'd spoken those words less than a minute after you had made a very similar oath. We were both deep in our cups . . . and young, and foolish."

Radford dropped into his leather desk chair and pursed his lips. "Perhaps we weren't so foolish. I don't think I was fated for marriage." At least not the kind of open, honest partnership he now desired. Meeting May had changed him. Before her, marriage with a woman like Lady Lillian would have fulfilled his family obligations. Now . . . the thought of such a future left him feeling empty.

"Giving up on marriage doesn't solve our problem," Wynter pointed out.

"No. It doesn't," Radford agreed.

"So what do you plan to do? You've created a heap of trouble by upsetting Miss Sheffers."

Radford considered his options carefully before answering. He had no wish to inadvertently make matters worse for May. "We should include my man-of-affairs in this discussion. He's been gathering information for me about the earl and his family. Information that isn't commonly known. I believe we'll be able to use the closet filled with skeletons Bannor has been digging through to keep the Earl of Redfield from causing Miss Sheffers any more stress."

Not one to back down or let others defend her, May felt uneasy the next day as she strolled with Lady Iona and Iona's father, the very powerful and more than a little intimidating Duke of Newbury. This outing had been the duke's idea. He planned to confront the Earl of Redfield on May's behalf.

May's pace slowed. She lagged several steps behind while fidgeting with the ribbons on her bonnet. Oh, how she longed to visit with her aunt and see for herself that Winnie was getting well again. But what would her uncle say seeing her arrive unannounced?

Tongues were wagging through the streets of Bath. According to the Duchess of Newbury, word of May's disastrous encounter with her uncle and of Radford's somewhat puzzling rescue was well known by all the Bath residents. Such a public airing of a family matter would have mortified her uncle. He put family pride and appearance above all things.

May would be lucky to be permitted to step foot within Uncle Sires' town house.

"You have nothing to worry about," the duke said. He'd stopped on the pavement and waited for May to catch up to him. "You will not be denied. The earl has a duty to you, his niece. I'll see to it that he treats you with the utmost respect."

Much to May's chagrin, Iona had recounted to her father every horrid detail of how Uncle Sires had completely lost his head and attacked. Why should Iona keep her lips sealed, though? To hear the duchess speak, all of Bath knew how her uncle had tried to take a horsewhip to her. It was as if an audience had watched the frightening drama.

Well, an audience had . . . only, May expected her uncle's servants to behave more discreetly than that.

Her temples began to pound as the group stood on the stoop and waited for the butler to answer the bell. If it weren't for her Aunt Winnie, she would have never agreed to see her uncle ever again. Since he was Winnie's caretaker now, she had no choice but to humble herself and beg for her uncle's audience. She'd beg all day if that was what it took to see her aunt.

Iona squeezed her hand as the ornately carved wooden door swung open.

"Fetch the earl," the duke said, handing his card to the frowning butler.

"I am sorry, your grace," the butler said gravely. "The earl is presently away from home."

"He may feign his absence to anyone else in this town, I don't care. He will see me." The duke crossed his arms and glared at the butler's stern expression.

For a moment May thought the duke had finally met a man brave enough to resist his severe façade. Gradually the man's shoulders slumped, and the corners of his lips dropped.

"Very well," the butler said as he backed out of the doorway. "I will inform the earl of your arrival."

Before leaving them, he led the trio into the very study where May had brazenly bitten her uncle in order to escape his madness. The drapes were drawn and the candles unlit. The room was dark and silent.

The duke laid a hand on the butler's arm and delayed him before he could scurry away. "You will tell him to not keep me waiting."

The butler gave a quick nod and disappeared.

Not five minutes later the Earl of Redfield appeared at the doorway, dressed in the very finest buff pantaloons, colorful waistcoat, and black frock. His gaze flicked from May to Iona to the duke.

"Newbury," he said.

"Redfield," the duke replied.

May stepped forward to intervene. This was her battle to keep Aunt Winnie in her life and she intended to fight it.

"Ah, what a surprise," a booming voice echoed through the hall. Mr. Tumblestone sauntered into the room, wearing a broad smile and a rather baggy country outfit. He maneuvered around the earl and, with his thick hand outstretched, approached the duke.

"Your grace," he said jovially, "it is a pleasure to see you again." He turned and gave a nod toward Iona. "And you, my lady." His watery gaze then landed on May. "And especially you, Miss Sheffers." He swept May's hand into his and placed a kiss on her gloved knuckle.

"How do you do?" May said as she tugged to regain possession of her hand. She turned away from Mr. Tumblestone and returned her attentions to her primary target. "Uncle, I wish to make amends."

"Hush, May," the duke said lifting his hand. "Let me handle this."

"But, your grace—" May started to say.

"Let the men talk." Mr. Tumblestone's thick fingers wound around her arm. He pulled her until she was nestled close to his side. "While your spirit enthralls me, I doubt a man of either the duke's or the earl's stature are amused by such antics."

May tilted her head up at the portly man and frowned. "Did you just say you were enthralled?"

She noticed then that both Uncle Sires and the duke had fully turned around and were gaping at them. The duke's manner took on a fatherly tone as he stepped forward to intervene. Iona gave May a wink and settled into a comfortable armchair, looking as if she were getting ready to enjoy a play.

"Perhaps you should take care and remove your hands from Miss Sheffers," someone growled.

May's head snapped toward the study's doorway. Her heart stopped. What was he doing here? Lord knew she certainly didn't need any more complications standing in the way of her seeing to Aunt Winnie's welfare. For his sake and Winnie's, May had left him and her heart at Longbranch House. He shouldn't be here, interfering with her life. He didn't have a place in her life . . . nor she in his.

Yet there Radford stood at the threshold, as handsome as ever, dressed all in black with a cane in one hand and the earl's lanky butler dangling by the collar in the other. Wynter served as an imposing second at his side. Both men's gazes were fixed on Mr. Tumblestone, especially on how his hands were tightly curled around May's arms.

May's heart lurched. She'd lived in London long enough to know that wild rakes had the troubling tendency of challenging each other to duels over such trivial matters. By no means did she want a duel fought over her.

"What in blazes is going on?" Uncle Sires roared. "I will not abide my home being treated like a public house!" His face darkened to a deep puce color that couldn't be healthy.

May attempted to pull herself from Tumblestone's grasp, but he only closed his farm-hardened hands more fiercely around her arms.

"I said unhand her." Radford's voice carried the force of his military background with it. "You have no right to touch her."

"Please, this is too much," May said, still squirming to free herself.

"There is no need for these theatrics," Mr. Tumblestone said with a nod to Radford and a second, deeper nod in the duke's direction. "If you would but let me explain, all would be well."

"I doubt that," Radford murmured. He released the hapless butler, crossed his arms, and glared as if the devil had taken him.

"Please explain yourself then, Tumblestone," the duke said soberly.

Uncle Sires grunted and gave a nod. His skin tone began to return to its normal pale pallor.

A large grin spread across Tumblestone's wide lips. He traced the rim of his slick bottom lip a couple of times before proceeding. "Miss Sheffers and I have an agreement."

May watched as Radford's hands closed into a pair of very solid fists.

"No," Tumblestone was quick to add. "There hasn't been a formal announcement. Quite honestly, there hasn't been time. The earl and I were calling on Miss Sheffers to make the final arrangements when Lady Winifred suffered a collapse because of her weak heart."

"That's a lie," Radford said, biting off the words. His fists clung tightly to the stout golden-headed cane at his side. "She would never willingly accept a marriage proposal from you."

"Ah, but she has."

May's head began spinning. She had accepted his suit. That graceful letter she'd penned just hours before her aunt fell ill had said as much. Her eyes grew wide as Tumblestone released her arm so he could pull that very letter from his waistcoat pocket.

"Isn't that so, Miss Sheffers?" he asked.

With her gaze fixed on that cursed letter, she nodded slowly while her mind worked furiously on trying to figure out what best to say.

"Is this what you truly wish, May?" the duke asked in that paternal tone of his.

"Before you answer," Mr. Tumblestone rushed to say just as May opened her mouth to gently tell him that she'd changed her mind, "let me remind you of the situation." He turned to the Duke of Newbury then. "She's been unduly influenced, and I'd say, confused by a man who desires only to make her his mistress."

"Indeed?" The duke's eyebrows rose. "Is this charge true, Evers?"

"Indeed it is not." Radford tossed down his cane and

peeled off his gloves as he advanced. "You will pay for that insult."

Tumblestone tugged at his gloves, pulling them off one finger at a time.

Oh dear, trouble was brewing. Trouble she didn't have time for. All she wanted was to see her aunt. If the men's actions were to continue in this vein, a challenge for a duel would no doubt be issued. May planted her feet when it became clear that she stood between the two men and their dangerous folly. She held up her arms.

"Stop this right now." Her voice rang with such chilly hauteur that both men froze where they stood. "I will not permit any man to fight in my presence or on my behalf. Up until now, I haven't needed a man in my life, and nothing has changed to compel me to cling to the nearest strong arm. I am my own person and I intend to make my own decisions."

Tumblestone appeared vastly amused by her speech. He slapped his gloves against his arm and chuckled. "Very well, Miss Sheffers."

Radford, on the other hand, wasn't going to be so easily dissuaded. His jaw tightened as he glared daggers at her. She felt like she'd slapped him in the face. The anger burning behind his tense expression was familiar. Just like the day in the Pump Room when he'd nearly fallen and she'd taken the blame for the mishap, she'd punctured his pride.

And that was the last thing she wanted to do. No matter what—despite their lack of a future—May loved Radford as dearly as she loved her parents and as fiercely as she loved her aunt. Though she may never see him again, after today, he would always be a part of her heart and her thoughts.

"Please, my lord, you need to worry about your own affairs. As you can see"—she gestured toward the duke—"I am being well looked after."

"But I—"

She pressed a gloved finger to his lips. Shameful behavior, she knew, but still she needed to touch him, to feel his warmth just one more time. What she was about to say was guaranteed to tear at her already tattered heart. "Go back to Lady Lillian. You have chosen well with her. She is worthy of your title and will make you a good wife. Worry about her, my lord. Not me. Your name has been sullied enough by connecting it with my problems and me. Think of your family name and do what is right."

Radford captured the finger May had pressed to his lips and held the slender digit fast in his palm. "What is right?"

The question struck her dumb.

"Family duty," Uncle Sires answered for her. "I must congratulate you, child, for having put voice to a point I hold dear. One's duty to the family must always come first, do you not agree?"

May felt trapped between Radford's intense gaze and her uncle's encouragement to blindly obey and satisfy her obligation to honor the Redfield family name.

"Think of your aunt," Mr. Tumblestone said. "Lady Winifred will wish to have you nearby during her long recovery."

Again, her head spun. Drat that bump on her head paining her temple. If she could only have some time to think clearly . . . if only there wasn't a crowded room waiting to hear her decision . . . if only her life were different.

But that wasn't exactly true. Before she felt her heart beating and learned of its existence, she'd been content. She'd enjoyed living with her aunt and taking care of her needs. Her life wasn't perfect, but whose was? She'd been happy.

And could be happy again.

The choice was hers to make.

"I am sorry, Radford." She drew her hand away.

Independence had made her happy. That was one choice she could make. Her aunt was another. Family duty weighed heavily on her shoulders. After years of hard work supporting her aunt, she knew her shoulders could bare the weight. "My aunt comes first. I will do what it takes to be in her life, to be there for her."

"What is this poppycock?" Aunt Winnie leaned heavily

on her rarely used cane as she slowly entered the room. She was wearing a heavy wool wrapper over her white nightgown. A frilly cap framed her face, covering all but a few stray wisps of gray hair.

Everyone in the room turned to watch her make a grand entrance.

"Winnie?" May gasped. Her hands flew to her chest. Her aunt looked so pale, so weak. May charged across the room and caught her aunt's free arm to help support her. "Winnie, you should be abed."

"Poppycock!" Winnie banged her cane against the floor. She did, however, permit May's continued support. "There is too much chicanery occurring in this house for me to lounge around now."

"Please, take my chair," Lady Iona offered. Wynter assisted May as she led Winnie to the soft-cushioned seat. Her aunt's feet moved painfully slowly. The poor woman should not have been allowed to stray from her bed. By the time she was settled in the chair, she was panting from the effort.

May hugged Winnie and could not stop the tears from spilling down her cheeks. "I was so worried. You cannot believe how worried. I feared I was going to lose you."

Winnie, true to her proud self, didn't allow May's gushing to last. She patted May's arm before slamming her cane against the floor to silence the room.

"Although it is heartwarming to see you, May, you are not the reason I came down here." Winnie's voice sounded as regal and strong as ever. She reached out her heavy arm and pointed toward Mr. Tumblestone. "You," she said, rolling the word. "We must speak."

The grin faded from Mr. Tumblestone's face. He bowed his head. "Yes, I suppose we must."

"Aunt?" May couldn't understand why Winnie would feel the need to drag herself from a sick bed just to speak with her niece's suitor. She'd almost always allowed May to handle her own affairs. It was rare indeed for her to step in and take charge like this. She firmly believed that May needed to learn to handle problems as they came and not to expect someone else to fix them for her. May agreed wholeheartedly to that philosophy.

What did her aunt intend to do?

"I once loved you with all my heart, all my being," Aunt Winnie said to Mr. Tumblestone.

May's jaw dropped.

"This is not the time, Winnie," Uncle Sires said through clenched teeth. His color darkened again as his gaze tripped across all the members of the *ton* standing in his study and witnessing yet another drama, thanks to May.

"When you were ripped away from me so many years ago, I'd thought my life would end. You were the world to me. Oh, you knew exactly how to speak to a lady and make her feel as if there was no one else in the world but her."

Mr. Tumblestone had courted Aunt Winnie? It was possible. He lived only a few miles from Redfield Abbey, and they were of similar ages.

"Years later I learned the truth. I now know you accepted the money my brother gave you to stop the relationship. The truth tore at me even worse than the mystery of your sudden disappearance. When you arrived in Bath with Sires, I thought you had come to beg my forgiveness." Winnie lifted her chin proudly.

"You don't understand the circumstances," Mr. Tumblestone said tightly. "You have never gone without money."

Winnie raised a brow. "Nevertheless," she said. May shivered at the frost in her aunt's tone. "You came to marry my niece, not to settle with me. Naturally I assumed May would refuse. Yet a part of me agreed that she needed a husband. My deepest desire is to see her raise a family of her own, to have someone to love and care for when I am gone."

"Oh, Winnie," May whispered, unable to bear the thought of a world without her aunt.

Winnie stiffened. "Up until now I have held my tongue, giving fate a chance to take its course. I will do so no longer. Other paths to fulfillment are now possible for my niece. And you, Mr. Tumblestone, are cold and heartless, longing only for wealth. I would have been miserable in marriage to you.

"I thank my brother for doing me a favor all those many years ago. I, in turn, will do the same for my niece. She will not marry you. I will not allow it . . . nor will Sires."

The room fell still with stunned silence. Only Radford had the audacity to grin like a victor returning from a hard-fought war.

"Lord Redfield?" Mr. Tumblestone said finally. "Do you agree with your sister on this?"

Uncle Sires looked as if he'd just swallowed a lemon whole. He twisted nervously. His crisply starched cravat appeared as if it were beginning to strangle him.

"I do," he whispered.

"But we had an agreement." Mr. Tumblestone paled. "You had said that if I—"

"Never mind what I said," Uncle Sires said loudly. "I would thank you to leave now. In fact, I'd thank everyone to leave my home. I have much to do."

No one moved. Not even Tumblestone.

"What will you do now, dear?" Winnie asked. She gave a sly glance in Radford's direction.

"She will marry, of course," Uncle Sires answered for her.

"Of course," Winnie said, much to May's chagrin.

"I will find her another, more suitable gentleman," Uncle Sires said.

May raised hands in alarm at the prospect of being bartered away to yet another penniless gentleman. "No, uncle, I will not agree to such madness. I have no need of a man in my life. In fact, my mind is made up. I will never marry."

"If you not marry, child," Uncle Sires said as he poked May in the chest with his stubby finger, "what shall you do? Starve?"

Chapter Twenty

Radford looked on as May denied her need for passion in her life. She had been pushed to the background for so long that she'd all but forgotten how to be herself. Radford saw her as she'd been forced to become. Her spirit dampened. Her urges restrained. Just like the shy ceramic sprite hiding in his pocket, May had completely withdrawn from the exciting world calling to her.

He could not let such a crime continue. As long as he still breathed, he'd free her. Not an easy task, he knew. His help wasn't exactly welcome. Wynter had been right in his assessment of that one. Radford had bruised May's pride when he'd boldly announced that she should marry him and let him solve all her problems.

No matter how deep she hid herself, her independent spirit would always shine through. That was one reason he loved her so fiercely.

Love.

The mere thought of being under the control of such a tender emotion scared Radford all the way down to his aching toes. Admitting to such soft feelings was a peril he wasn't ready to face. She'd rebuffed his attentions more than once. May would have to prove her feelings for him before he'd risk the humiliation of declaring himself in love.

Radford stood stiffly in the middle of the Earl of Redfield's study and watched helplessly as May faced down her uncle. He took some comfort knowing that with so many protectors she wasn't in danger of suffering injury from Redfield's hand.

Though Radford hadn't been permitted to see to May himself two nights before, the doctor had recounted the bruises lining her arms and legs. Wynter had described in detail how the earl had dragged May to this very study while everyone in the household worried after her.

Her life had been in danger. Radford planned to use every power available to him to see that she never faced the same threat again.

The night before, Radford and Wynter had closeted themselves in Radford's study while they met with Bannor. The three agreed that their strongest weapon against a man like the earl would be the threat of exposing the changes in his dying mother's will.

Like many in the *ton*, the earl lived an expensive lifestyle. Bannor had produced a long list of creditors to whom the earl owed money. With the income from his family's estates, he'd have no trouble paying his bills. But if he were to lose a large portion of that income to his sister, as stipulated in this new will, the earl would find himself in a real pickle.

If that tidbit of information were to become common knowledge, the earl's creditors and shopkeepers would all be lining up to demand cash payments. Sires would lose his creditability. For a man of his self-importance, such a scenario would be like suffering a mortal blow—exactly the kind of weapon Radford had hoped to find.

He and Wynter had forced their way into the earl's town house today to warn him that they were prepared to share the details of his mother's new will with his creditors if he continued to cause trouble in May's life.

They hadn't expected to find a crowd.

The Duke of Newbury standing beside May like a lion protecting his cub had certainly been a surprise.

A welcome one at that.

The night before Bannor had reported another interesting

piece of information . . . this one about May's father. As Radford had feared, her father had indeed been born to a wandering gypsy. The father of the ill-conceived birth, who in turn was May's grandfather, was the eighth Duke of Newbury, the current duke's father.

May was the Duke of Newbury's niece? That information, combined with a favorable nod from the duke, would give May full entrance into fashionable society. A favorable nod—one that the stingy Earl of Redfield had never deigned to give his niece—would make a marriage between her and a viscount a socially acceptable possibility.

I will never marry, she'd just declared. Radford would have to dredge up all his forgotten charms to win her trust and her hand. The very thought of fighting such a battle made his every breath surge with new life . . . this was truly a woman worth living for.

"No matter what happens, I will never starve," May said to her uncle. There was a delightful fire smoldering behind her violet eyes. Small as she was, she stood straight and tall before her uncle. A valiant David standing up to frightening Goliath.

Radford could not feel more proud. She was special, one of a kind. Capturing such an elusive fey spirit wouldn't be easy. He would start the pursuit by proving his loyalty.

"Redfield, I have come to seek a private word with you," he said with great authority. He tugged on his waistcoat. "It concerns a matter of utmost importance, and no, it cannot be delayed further."

May's frown deepened. "I don't see how you could have—"

Radford pressed his finger to her lips. He'd rather enjoyed it when she'd done so to him, so he only happily returned the gesture. She colored prettily as she looked around and took notice of the room filled with raised eyebrows.

She'd done it to herself, setting the intimate tone between them in such a public way. Proper ladies did not press their fingers to a gentleman's lips. Nor did they call a gentleman by his given name. Such scandalous public behaviors only alluded to more intimate happenings behind closed doors.

After today, a swift marriage would no doubt be expected.

"I insist," Radford said softly.

Her blush deepening, she gave a sharp nod.

"I wish to take part in this," the duke said. Though his tone was amiable, the accompanying expression conveyed his unbending demand to be included. His interest in May's future pleased Radford enormously.

With a grimace twisted enough to make a baby scream, the earl led Radford and the Duke of Newbury into a small adjoining library.

Radford kept his demands short and to the point while the duke looked on, nodding occasionally. The earl remained silent, a grim expression fixed on his face.

"I don't understand why you'd trouble yourself so over the child," Redfield said after a lengthy silence. "She's a gypsy bastard's daughter . . . not good for anything."

Radford's knuckles itched for violence. "Do I have your cooperation?"

Redfield chewed his bottom lip for several more silent moments. A highly polished brass clock on an oak mantel ticked loudly. "Yes, damn it. Take her away from me. I wash my hands of the chit."

"And Lady Winifred," the duke said, "you will treat her with the greatest kindness or you will find the *ton* learning of her impending fortune."

Redfield bristled. His chin shot in the air. "Everything I have done, I have done for the betterment of my family. I have always taken care of all its members."

"Then you will have nothing to worry about," the duke said as he inclined his head slightly.

Of course Radford had no intention of waiting to see if the earl was a man of his word. His mind was already churning as they returned to the study. If May ultimately refused his suit, he would simply have to pay for a Bow Street runner to keep an eye on her.

After the second chance she'd given him at living, Radford was determined that May would never find herself in a position of being alone again. She'd never be forced to act out of desperation and beg for charity as she had on their first meeting.

"Is this mystery matter cleared up to your liking, my lord?" May asked crisply upon his return.

Radford pursed his lips, barely able to contain a smile at her futile attempt to separate herself from her previous slip, demonstrating her affection for him to the room. "I believe so, Miss Sheffers."

He retrieved his cane from the floor. Bending down to fetch the damned stick proved difficult with his stiff leg. Out of the corner of his eye, he caught Lady Winifred placing a staying hand on May's arm when she moved to assist him.

Smart woman, Lady Winifred. A wedding date would have to be set before the end of the week if May had acted so uncharacteristically and provided him—the very man she had once vowed to never assist again—with a kindly hand. Radford trusted Wynter, the duke, and Lady Iona to keep their tongues from wagging. Mr. Tumblestone, however, might not be so discreet. He'd just lost a promised fortune by losing May's hand. The picture he could paint would be less than flattering for both May and Radford.

There was no need to further feed the speculation already blazing through the tearooms. The gentle wooing he planned for May would have to be conducted in public and conform to the strictest dictates of propriety.

"Miss Sheffers," he said as soon as he straightened, "if you are agreeable, I would wish to call on you at the Newbury residence this afternoon."

Her jaw stiffened, a feat Radford had thought impossible. Her features already appeared sorely strained. She opened her mouth to object. He could see disapproval bright in her eyes.

"Of course, Evers, Miss Sheffers would be delighted to entertain you," the duke answered before May had a chance to utter what surely promised to be a crushingly wicked refusal.

"Delighted?" she blurted, her ire truly pricked now. Her eyelids snapped several times as she huffed. Lady Winifred pinched the back of her niece's hand.

Radford winced in sympathy for the sharp pain she must have suffered . . . to her hand and her pride. May obediently bowed her head. "I would be delighted," she murmured.

She was quite the accomplished liar, Radford thought with a quick grin. He gushed his fondest wishes on Lady Winifred, Lady Iona, and the duke before sweeping from the room. Wynter followed like a happy pup.

"I beg a moment," the duke called just as Radford worked his way down the earl's front stoop.

Radford turned and waited for the duke to join him. Wynter, with incredible tact, wandered over to his landau and pretended to inspect a wheel.

"Yes, your grace?" Radford tensed at what promised to be an awkward discussion. Lady Lillian's heart would be broken. There was simply no way to avoid it.

The duke might even wish to punish Radford for causing his lovely daughter such pain. And who could blame him?

"I do apologize for any embarrassment that I might cause," Radford said quickly, hoping to stave off the worst of the duke's infamous anger.

"About my daughter," the duke spoke as if he hadn't heard a word of the apology. "When she is to marry, it will be to a man whose heart isn't otherwise occupied. I no longer approve of your interest in her. You will no longer be permitted to escort her to any future affairs."

Radford couldn't believe his luck. "Thank you, your grace."

The duke, by putting an end to the courtship himself, had just spared Lady Lillian from the shame of being considered jilted. Though no formal announcement had been made, everyone had expected the engagement. If Radford had called on May before the matter with Lady Lillian was settled, it would have left a nasty blot on Lillian's reputation, one that would be considered by many as shocking as being left standing alone at the altar. Vicious tittering would persist far beyond this summer season as the *ton* continued to speculate on what Radford had found lacking in Lillian..

He clasped the duke's hand and shook briskly. "Thank you. From the bottom of my heart, I have never been so pleased to have a father find fault in me and in my desire to wed his daughter."

"You needn't continue to watch for the bounder like some excitable spaniel," the Duchess of Newbury said to May with considerable disgust. "He won't be coming."

May was seated near one of the two large windows in the Newburys' drawing room. The cool, sage-colored walls created a false air of calm in the room. The duchess was correct on one account: May's heart was beating like a nervous spaniel's.

For the last hour she'd been gazing at her newest book, a discourse on American flora and fauna, but not reading a word. Every sound drew her eyes to the front garden, where a storm was brewing overhead. Dark clouds rolled across the sky like great dragons.

Radford had said he'd come and call on her. Though it was the last thing she thought she'd wanted, May found herself turning breathless as the day drew late. It was Iona who had convinced her to don the bright violet gown, a dress May had never before worn.

"A messenger arrived several minutes ago. The viscount sends his regrets. I am sorry." The duchess' tone told another story. The Duke of Newbury had returned home and announced that he'd told Radford to look elsewhere for a wife. Never had May witnessed such dismay. The duchess had collapsed when she'd been unable to change the duke's mind.

"The viscount is not good enough for Lillian," the duke had said with finality. "She will just have to find another man to whom to cling."

At first Lillian took the news calmly, shrugging elegantly and declaring there were many more fit men on the marriage block. But after her mother had fallen into a fit of hysterics, Lillian followed.

The poor duke had to soothe two wailing ladies while standing firm on his decision. May felt lucky to have such a strong-willed man on her side. She'd too been close to tears by the end of the ordeal.

Consequently, neither the duchess nor Lillian took a favorable view of the idea of Radford paying a call on May that afternoon.

"You must agree that his wishing to come here was in very bad taste," the duchess said as May continued to stare out the window. She still couldn't believe that Radford would ask to call on her and then suddenly change his mind. Had something happened? Whatever could be wrong? "Of course, after suffering Lillian's rebuff, he'd want to find a new woman to parade on his arm. You were likely the most convenient. His pride must have suffered quite a blow. He was so devoted to Lillian, you must realize, ready to marry her."

"Yes," May agreed in the hopes of getting the duchess to just leave her to brood in peace. She certainly didn't need anyone to remind her how she wasn't quite up to crack when it came to the marriage mart.

When the duchess continued to hover, May closed her book and stood. "Pardon me, your grace," May said sedately. "I believe I'll go change. If you wouldn't mind, I believe I should spend a few hours at the cottage helping Portia pack up the household."

"Of course, dear. You must be feeling anxious to begin your new profession."

Dressed in a plain calico cotton dress with a kerchief in her hair, May assisted her housekeeper in packing up the shabby belongings she'd grown to love. The battered silver candleholder she'd bartered from a shipping merchant had become an old friend. May ran her finger over the pitted and dented metal and remembered the nights she and her aunt had spent in their cozy parlor, laughing while playing card games with a ruthless abandon.

Those days were over. The reminders were being packed away in soft cloths to be cherished sometime in the distant future.

May's hand then stilled on the tiny porcelain figurine she had carelessly left sitting on an occasional table two days before. At the time, she'd rejected the dancing fairy figure Radford had purchased at the fair for her. The events of the past several days had been so chaotic, she hadn't been able to take a moment to wonder about the gift. Why give her such a lovely present?

It wasn't at all proper for a gentleman to be giving presents to an unmarried woman . . . not unless his interests in her were well known and accepted. It was even more improper for May to have accepted the gift.

Yet he hadn't let her reject it.

Just looking at the laughing sprite, a figure lost in a world of bliss, burned a hole in May's heart. She set it aside but couldn't bring herself to wrap the creature in a strip of linen and hide her away in a box.

She was doing the right thing, she assured herself. Her aunt had reluctantly agreed with the decision to leave. And though she'd miss her aunt dearly, this was the only way. Staying so close to Radford would hurt far too much.

Leaving Bath was truly her only rational option. Too many memories lived on the streets of this charming town. Staying in the city and having to relive them everyday would eventually stain those beautiful scenes.

Radford would eventually move on . . . and so should she.

"Oh dear me," Portia called out from the back of the house. "Oh dear, oh dear."

May dropped the packing linens she was holding and dashed to the kitchen. Portia stood with her hands clutched to her chest while a creamy-colored horse craned its neck through an open window. Its long lips covered a bright orange carrot and sucked it into its mouth.

"Princess," May whispered.

The filly, hearing its name, jerked its head up and stared at May. Its long lashes fluttered as it blinked its great big eyes.

"Whatever are we going to do?" Portia asked. "I can't seem to scare the beast away, and she's making a shambles of my kitchen."

Earthenware canisters on the worktop lay toppled on their sides, contents spilling out. Fresh vegetables were scattered all over a flour-coated floor.

"I'll keep her occupied," May whispered, cautious not to startle the large horse. "Go fetch the Viscount Evers. He must be terribly worried about losing this troublemaker here."

"Yes, miss. You be careful, miss. I've never seen a horse act so queerly." Portia picked up her skirts and ran toward the front door as fast as her legs could carry her.

May kept Princess calm by singing a bedtime song she vaguely remembered hearing her mother sing. A fresh set of painful memories rode into the room on the backs of the long-forgotten notes she produced.

Princess seemed to calm in response to the soft sounds. The filly lowered her head and nibbled happily on a head of cabbage as May repeated the chorus.

May remained frozen in the center of the kitchen while battling a mad desire to rush upstairs, fix her hair, and change into a newer gown. Radford would soon be on his way. She didn't want his last memory of her to be one where she was dressed like an overworked servant.

But if she were to move, Princess might bolt. The young filly might look strong, but as Radford had said, she was still very young and spirited. She shouldn't be allowed to run wild through Bath. There were too many dangers she might encounter. She needed to be cared for, protected.

May's voice grew sore as she sang the same gentle lullaby. Luckily, her tune kept the horse's interest. Princess continued to nibble.

The front door squeaked as it opened. The filly's ear twitched. Her attentions, however, remained fixed on the feast before her.

A minute later, Radford limped into the kitchen, his cane clattering loudly on the stone floor. "Thank God," he said between several deep breaths. "I thought I'd lost her for good this time."

His cravat hung loosely around his neck. He wore a black oilskin cape smudged with dirt. He looked adorably mussed. May couldn't help but be drawn in by his larger-than-life presence in her kitchen.

"I'm afraid she's going to startle and run," May whispered. "I've been singing to her."

A strange grin turned up the corner of his lips. "I heard. It was charming." He spared May a quick glance. "She likes you, you know. I've never seen a horse so besotted before."

The thought of a horse in love with her had a strange effect on May's mood. It pleased her to think that such a lean, graceful creature could find favor with her.

"Come with me," Radford said as he gathered the few remaining carrots from the kitchen cutting board and stuffed them into his pocket.

"Where are we going?" May asked. She didn't want to leave the filly. The silly horse needed her.

"Outside." Radford took May's hand in his. "You are going to catch Princess for me."

"I am—what?" He had to be mad. She couldn't catch a horse. What was to stop Princess from getting startled and kicking up her heavy hooves? May would get trampled . . . again.

"No, no, don't fret, May. I'll be right beside you." He led her around the house to where Princess stood in the backyard. She'd completely trampled Portia's herb garden. The ground vibrated underneath May's feet when Princess jerked her head from the window and sidestepped away from them.

Distant thunder rumbled. Princess tossed her head up and down and sidestepped again, the storm obviously making her edgy.

What to do? What to do?

Radford needed her. Princess needed her. And all May could think about was how a horse had kicked her two days ago. She couldn't brave the danger. It was madness.

Radford pressed a carrot into her palm. She drew a deep breath. Madness or not, Princess and Radford needed her. She stepped forward and hummed the song she'd already used once to calm Princess. Her voice cracked as her nerves began to wan.

"I'm right here," Radford said quietly as if coaxing a skittish kitten. "Trust your instincts."

He set his cane on the grass and drew out a long leather lead line. "Keep doing what you are doing. You've won her interest. Now lure her closer with the carrot."

May clicked her tongue in her cheek as some carriage drivers would do before setting the horses into motion. The sound captured Princess' attention. The horse lowered her head and flared her nostrils.

"Hold out the carrot." Radford's cupped the back of May's hand as he slowly guided her to reach toward the giant filly. He stepped directly behind May, his body conformed to the curves of her back. He folded an arm around her chest and held her safe within his cocoon. The leather lead line hung loosely in his grasp, brushing against the front of her threadbare calico gown.

"Sweet Princess," May sang. "Sweet, lost Princess, come home."

Step by step the horse approached. May swallowed hard and closed her eyes, fully expecting a loud clap of thunder to send the horse on a murderous rampage.

Thunder did roll high in the sky. May's eyes flew open. Princess didn't seem to notice the rumbling sound while her flaring nostrils guided her to May's hand.

"Draw the carrot closer to your chest now," Radford whispered.

Her hand trembled as she coaxed Princess' large head to hover inches from her own.

"That's a good girl." May couldn't tell if Radford was speaking to her or the horse. Not that it mattered. The tender space behind her ear tingled in response to the caress of his gentle voice. Her legs grew watery.

Radford raised the lead line and very carefully laid it over Princess' neck. It felt like forever as he very methodically looped the line around the filly's broad neck.

"Beautiful," he breathed. His arms tightened around May. "Beautiful."

May released the breath she'd been holding and let her head fall back his chest, thrilling in the feel of his body touching hers.

His lips brushed her neck, nudging her to tilt her head to one side as his warm lips worked their way up toward her tender earlobe. He drew off the kerchief covering her hair and ran his fingers through her thick curls.

"Hmmm . . ." Radford purred. "You've been such a passionate student. I cannot wait to teach you how to ride."

May teetered on the verge of losing herself. It would be only too easy to open her heart to him again. She started to turn her head and accept his kisses when a large drop of rain landed on the center of her forehead.

A second drop fell on her shoulder.

And then the sky opened up.

Radford tightened his hold on the leading rein as a constant patter of cool raid pelted them, effectively washing the magic away and returning life to as it was. Radford stepped around May to settle Princess.

"Let me secure her to the post out front and then I'll join you inside."

Chapter Twenty-one

Why hadn't Radford called on her earlier in the day? Just a moment ago he'd acted as besotted as his filly. A complete change from a few hours ago when he'd sent that impersonal message to explain his absence. Was it his worry over his missing horse that had kept him away? Or second thoughts?

May worried over those questions as she moved stacks of boxes from the parlor's chairs. The whole cottage was in a sad state of disarray. The thought of entertaining anyone mortified her. She ran her fingers through her tangled curls and smoothed her gown several times while waiting for Radford to join her.

"What is this?" he asked when he finally entered the room. He shook the water from his cape but didn't bother to remove it. Instead he lifted the heavy box from May's arms and set it aside. "You are leaving, aren't you?"

He sounded utterly crushed by the idea.

"Aunt Winnie and I discussed the matter at length after you left this morning. She plans to stay with my uncle. He can provide for her much better than I."

Radford gave a sharp nod. "And yourself?"

She found she couldn't look at him. "Why didn't you call on me this afternoon?" She'd had a pretty speech all planned for him. She'd worn her best gown . . . and he hadn't appeared. No note, only a brief message conveyed by a footman to the Newburys' butler.

"Princess had jumped the fence. There were spots of blood on the boards and I was concerned she'd done herself injury. I asked my mother to—" He suddenly began to pace. "I suppose you never received a proper explanation. I am sorry to have disappointed you."

May shrugged. "I needed to help Portia pack our belongings anyhow. I—I am leaving Bath."

"You can't," he whispered, his expression falling. "I won't let you."

She caressed his cheek. "Oh, Radford, I cannot stay. The Duke of Newbury's eldest daughter has three children and no governess. She has graciously invited me to go live with her and her husband in London, and I have accepted."

"But what about us? I can't believe you would walk away from our friendship. I . . . I . . ." He turned away suddenly. "I need you, May."

Oh, how she longed to believe he truly needed her. Hearing those words only punctuated the reasons she could not stay. She believed he found her attractive. But attraction was not enough. Mere attraction was not what had held her parents together for more than twenty years.

What would happen to their relationship when his leg healed and he no longer felt as if he needed to be her champion in order to regain a morsel of self-worth? He would declare his hasty marriage a disaster, that is what.

Oh la, if only she could peer into his heart and see what it was he loved. Did he truly want her or was he simply drawn to the feeling of strength he got from rescuing her?

"I don't know you well enough to know if this is right between us. Unlike my gypsy ancestors, I cannot read the future. What happens when the shine of our attraction begins to dim and you realize that I'm not someone special?" May drew her hands down her short, slightly squat body. "I am not willing to risk ruining your life for a few moments of bliss."

"A few moments, May? I don't want just a few moments.

This is a lifetime I'm talking about. You might not be able to see the future, but I can. For the first time since the accident I can actually visualize a tomorrow without dark clouds."

"That hope you feel is because you are taking care of yourself now. You are healing, becoming stronger. Soon you'll be able to prove the doctors wrong and ride again."

"No," Radford insisted. "It's you who have transformed me."

If you care even a little for him, you must let him go. His mother was right. He was confused, scared that he may never be the strong man he once was. He needed time to heal and see for himself that there were scores of women who could make him happy.

"Please do not press me," May said. Her voice wavered as she held back a flood of tears. "My mind is set. I will not marry you."

The affection flew from his expression. His gaze was as cold as the jade stones his eyes resembled. He slapped his white-gloved hand against his thigh, a sure sign of his agitation.

"You can drop the act." He laughed then. It was a mirthless, pained laugh.

May's heart stopped. "I don't understand—"

"You must be the most skillful coquette I have ever met, ma'am. Imagine, I had believed you the most innocent of creatures."

Innocent? May had never thought herself innocent. She'd suffered enough rejection and heartache to understand the harsh realities of the world. She splayed her hands in front of her. "I am who I am, Radford. I have never played any games."

"Hah!" He tossed a hand in the air and paced, his cloak billowing out behind him. "You look at me with those large sorrowful eyes and see my disabilities. Admit it, you find me lacking."

"Lacking?" Like an empty-headed parrot, she could only repeat the outrageous charge.

"One favorable nod from the Duke of Newbury and you'll become the rave of the season. Every beau of the town will be panting after you. That is what you want, isn't it? That's why you choose London over me."

May shook her head, unable to believe her ears. The anger dripping from his tongue singed them. "I don't understand, my lord."

"My lord, is it now? You retreat to that prudish formality I once thought attractive? Well, it no longer wields the same power it once did, ma'am. I now know who you are. I'd been kidding myself. You are no different than Lady Lillian. All you care about is increasing your social position."

"Social position?" The thought was laughable. May would have laughed too if the hurt hadn't cut so deeply. How could he believe such a thing?

"And I was tearing myself apart trying to figure out how to convince you to be my wife!" He rounded on her then with violence brightening his eyes.

May refused to cower while her heart was breaking. What hurt worse than his words was the solid conviction with which he'd uttered them.

May sighed deeply.

"Before your uncle, the duke, took you under his wing, you must have thought I was the best you could do. I needed a wife and you were so kind to me, pretending to be so blind to my infirmities, weren't you?" He grabbed her arm and shook her. "I thought you had tender feelings for me. More's the pity, I actually believed you."

May stumbled when he pushed her away. Her foot caught the corner of the tiny occasional table, toppling it. The woodland sprite figurine Radford had given her plunged to the floor and shattered.

A tear tumbled unbidden down her cheek at the sight of the poor broken fairy creature. She had done nothing to deserve such a bad end.

Nothing at all . . .

"My lord," May said. She drew a deep breath, blinked

back what felt like a flood of tears, and straightened her shoulders, making herself as tall as her squat figure would possibly allow. "I would thank you to leave now."

He gaped at her for a moment and appeared unwilling to budge. It took all of May's willpower and considerable pride not to throw herself into his arms and beg his understanding.

If only their friendship didn't have to end this way, shattered on the floor in so many pieces like the ruined figurine. Repair would be impossible.

They were from two different worlds.

"Good-bye, Miss Sheffers." His voice was as stiff as his lame leg. He dipped a half bow before leaving her little cottage forever.

The morning sun shone so brightly it nearly burned Radford's stinging eyes. The early heat quickly dried up all evidence of the storm that had raged through the night.

How dare the sun shine? The earth should be shrouded in darkness. That's how he felt. Why shouldn't the world share his grief? A brightly liveried footman had arrived shortly after breakfast and handed him a folded piece of foolscap bearing the Duke of Newbury's seal, along with the missing teacup from his set wrapped in a dainty handkerchief.

The sight of the lonely teacup crushed his aching soul.

He'd sat up all night wasting page after page of foolscap in a desperate attempt to recapture the flowery words he'd once spoken to charm the young ladies, words that could win back May's bruised heart. Those words were no longer his to spout at will. That carefree young man had died on the Peninsula. His words were now fatally tinged with bitterness . . . and pride.

His pride had ruined him yesterday. He'd wanted to sweep May into his arms and kiss her until she was gasping for air. Her open dismissal of his need for her had killed the impulse. For a horrifying moment he felt like he was again sprawled and split open, helpless on the battlefield.

Out of fear, he'd fought back. Anger had done well to hide

his fears . . . and had managed to push away his first glimpse at regaining a pleasant life.

After setting the delicate teacup on the desk in front of him, Radford broke the ducal seal and unfolded the foolscap. The note, signed by the duke, was brief and terse.

"Miss Sheffers has asked me to return this teacup to your person. She sends with it her regrets for having kept it so long. Upon her leaving Bath this morning, Miss Sheffers also personally requested that you make no attempt to contact her. I am to assure you that she bears you no ill feelings."

Radford read the letter through several times, each time feeling emptier than the last.

She was gone . . . and wanted nothing from him.

He'd been a damned fool not to pursue her in the first place. He tore the dratted marriage list from his pocket and smoothed it out on the desk beside the Duke of Newbury's letter.

None of the requirements of the list seemed to make a bit of sense anymore. The check sheet had led him down the wrong path . . . if not for fate, he'd presently be engaged to a lady most unsuitable for him.

He lifted the list and tore it neatly down the center. He'd forgotten to factor in so many intangibles such as passion, caring, and love. Those were the qualities he should have been looking for when beginning this fool's search for a wife. And those qualities weren't to be found in any one young lady. As May had shown him, he needed to find those qualities first within himself.

Her compassion and understanding had opened his heart . . . now she was gone and he felt raw inside. He rose from the desk and limped across the room. With an angry flick of the wrist he tossed the cursed list into the fireplace and watched as the corners of the paper that had once outlined his future curled and burned.

A gentle pressure touched his shoulder. Radford reached up and cupped his hand over his mother's frail fingers.

"I knocked," she said. "I grew worried when there was no answer."

Radford didn't say a word for a long time. He just continued to watch as the foolscap slowly burned in the banked coals.

"I have made a mess of my life, Mother," he confessed after the last evidence of the marriage list was destroyed.

"No, dear, you are doing just fine. You are just unhappy right now." She choked back a soft sob. "I was wrong to press the suit between you and Lady Lillian. I see that now. She wasn't right for you."

Lady Lillian, a fine woman by all accounts, would one day make a lucky man very happy. Just not him. He needed a very special woman to lift him out of his dark moods. He needed a woman to teach him that life was worth living again.

How had he let his pride chase such a woman away?

"I apologize for my behavior, son. I should have never let the prestige of connecting our family with one as respected as the Duke of Newbury's get in the way of your happiness. Your happiness is all that is important to me. Please tell me you believe that."

Radford drew a long, deep breath. His life wasn't over. That gypsy at the fair had told him that he'd been hiding instead of living. Today, he believed it. "I do, Mother. I want the best for you as well."

"That Margaret Sheffers," his mother said, "she is the lady whom you love?"

Radford limped over to the window and watched as his horses pranced and played in the fields. It was time he began to live again. Even if it meant he'd have to subsist as a lonely man, he would embrace each new day with all the challenges the rising sun brought with it.

"The gel is by no means a diamond of the first water. But," his mother sighed deeply, "I suppose if the duke embraces her as family . . . then, with a little polish, she might just be able to be brought up to crack."

May was perfect. He wouldn't wish her to change at all. She had taught him an important lesson with her fey spirit. She'd taught him to live. It was a piece of her he'd cherish in his heart for the rest of his days.

Chapter Twenty-two

The carriage swayed gently as a warm breeze blew through the open windows. The early-autumn sun was shining brightly on the City of Bath. It had been a month since she'd seen the gothic spires of Bath Abbey or enjoyed the calm flowing of the River Avon. May could hardly believe how fast the time had passed.

She wouldn't be coming now if not for the urgent letters she'd received from both Iona and Aunt Winnie urging her return. Iona's sister and husband had been most supportive, insisting she leave right away and giving her use of their carriage.

She clutched both letters and worried. Neither letter provided a drop of important information beyond stressing a need for her presence. What if Winnie had fallen ill again? What if the playful Iona had somehow gotten herself embroiled in a scandal? May prayed that the emergency was not too great that she couldn't handle it.

She also prayed that Radford would not be in residence this late in the season . . . while wishing with all her heart she could see him again.

For several days she lived her life in London on pins as she half expected him to come after her. When running an errand or strolling the streets, she had always watched for him. Hoping, dreaming, fancying she'd catch a glimpse of him in a crowd, but always finding she was mistaken. Those dreams had faded into pleasant memories. She enjoyed teaching the young children in her charge and believed herself moving on with her life.

Now, upon returning to Bath, May realized she'd not moved on at all. It felt like only yesterday she'd told Radford to leave her alone. Nothing in her life had moved forward. Her running to London had solved nothing.

It had been easier to hide than risk chasing a happiness she might not be able to keep. But no more could she let such foolishness continue. May realized she'd have face her unresolved feelings for Radford and put them to rest so she could truly begin a new life.

"I just pray Aunt Winnie and Iona are both well. I will need all the help they can offer with this one."

"I beg your pardon?" a man asked from outside the carriage.

May blinked. She hadn't noticed that a finely dressed gentleman on horseback had been passing her carriage at the same moment she carelessly spoke her thoughts aloud.

Such a lovely horse he was riding, too. A light cream-colored mare with a dark mane and tail . . . and brown speckles on her rear flank. She looked exactly like—

May blinked again.

"Lord Evers?" she asked, praying her wishful eyes weren't once again deceiving her.

The man slowed his horse to match the pace of the carriage. He turned to look at her. His eyes sparkled as recognition lit them from within.

"May?" He drew a quick breath and seemed to quickly regain his composure. "Miss Sheffers, what a delightful surprise. What brings you to Bath? I hope you are well."

May simply stared at Radford, unable to trust her eyes or her ears. Certainly Radford wasn't really here, riding beside her carriage. She had to be dreaming again. But this couldn't be a dream . . . she was far too worried over the reasons she'd been summoned to Bath so urgently and over her Aunt Winnie's health for this to be a pleasant dream.

She rapped on the roof of the carriage and called for the driver to stop. As soon as the wheels ceased turning, Radford awkwardly lowered himself from Princess' saddle and swung open the carriage door. He reached inside and lifted her to the ground.

His arms lingered around her waist even though her feet had touched solid ground. Her hands lingered on his shoulders as well, she noticed with a start.

"I cannot tarry long," she said as she hurriedly pulled away from him. There was no reason to get herself worked up over a dream she'd already refused to chase. "Lady Iona Newbury and Aunt Winnie have both written me, begging I come to Bath as quickly as possible." Her hands shook as she showed him the letters she'd crinkled beyond repair. "I fear Winnie's health has taken a turn for the worse."

Talking about her concerns helped vanquish the frivolous butterflies flittering in her stomach and the shortness of breath she suddenly experienced from standing so close to him again.

He smoothed his thumb over her furrowed brow. "I spoke with both your aunt and Lady Iona at the Pump Room just this morning, Miss Sheffers. Let me assure you, they both appeared to be in high spirits."

May felt her frown deepen. "They were?" Why then would they write with such urgency? At least there was no dire disaster awaiting her. She took comfort in having learned that much.

"They were walking arm in arm chatting merrily and charming everyone in the crowded room." Radford smiled. His cheeks had the most adorable dimples. He took her chin and tilted her head up so she was staring directly into his eyes. "You are as lovely as ever." His voice grew soft. Obliviously he didn't notice her wrinkled and dusty carriage dress, her drooping bonnet, or the unmistakable exhaustion etched beneath her eyes. "I've sorely missed that impish expression of yours."

He did? "You did?" Her heart raced as hope flooded her

chest. Before he could answer, she rushed to change the subject.

"You are riding again. I'm so very glad you've proven your doctors wrong. Not that I'm surprised, mind you. I knew you would."

Radford's smile remained as brilliant as the sun as he continued to focus on her and nothing else. "I'm able to ride for short distances," he said somewhat absently. "Ever since I stopped pushing myself so hard—thanks to your scolding—my leg started to grow stronger. No great changes, mind you. It's a slow process."

His thumb continued to caress her cheek. He inched closer. May felt her face heat as she realized how shocking their behavior must look to the carriage driver and to anyone who might pass by. She ducked her head away from his magical touch.

"You look healthy and content. I'm happy," she said in place of a dismissal and turned to climb back into the carriage. She let him lift her since no steps had been lowered.

"Right now I'm better than content," he confessed. "I'm tremendously happy." That determined focus of his nearly tripped her as she nervously settled on the carriage's narrow bench. "If you are agreeable, I would like to call on you tomorrow afternoon. There is much I would like to explain . . . and to apologize for."

May gave a brisk nod just as the carriage lurched forward and began to roll down the road.

Yes, yes, yes, she could barely refrain from shouting. She would dearly love for Radford to call on her. His leg was stronger and yet his expression still softened when he'd first set eyes her. Perhaps his affections for her did go beyond his need for her troubled situation to give his injured pride a sense of worth. Her spirit soared. It had been far too long since she'd allowed herself to feel so recklessly special.

Certainly such a rare happiness was worth the risk she'd just placed on her barely healed heart.

* * *

No one would tell her anything. Iona would stare at May with a funny grin but kept her lips tightly sealed when pressed for answers. That evening, Aunt Winnie had come to the Newburys' town house for dinner and, like Iona, would only smile when asked about the vague but urgent letters.

"Tomorrow," was the most anyone would say.

Tomorrow.

May sat in the Newburys' welcoming, sage-colored parlor the next afternoon and fidgeted. Radford was due to appear any moment. This waiting felt only too familiar. A sick feeling turned in her stomach.

What if he didn't come?

She'd donned the same deep violet gown fashioned from the sheerest muslins that she'd worn a month ago as she'd waited nervously in this very same parlor for his visit. Iona had helped her to tame her ruddy brown curls and pile them on the top of her head.

As she spied her reflection in the window, she thought she looked surprisingly elegant. Last summer had changed her. She'd grown even more confident, more comfortable with herself. Unlike before, the gown's stunning color didn't discomfit her. Gone was the shy creature who had felt a need to hide behind the curtains.

She was who she was. Nothing was going to change that. Radford had taught her she had no need to feel ashamed. She straightened a book sitting on a small, elaborately carved rosewood table and glanced out the window again. Hopefully he would keep his word and arrive on time. She so wanted to thank him for this new confidence she enjoyed.

"May?" Iona stood at the threshold of the parlor, nervously twisting her hands.

"He's not coming, is he?" May said, feeling suddenly tired.

"What?" Iona's hands moved all the more nervously. "Oh, I don't know. There are some people in Papa's study waiting to see you."

"Who?" May crossed the room to follow Iona to the

study. Iona grabbed her and pulled her into a tight hug. Tears dampened May's shoulder. "What is wrong, Iona? You are scaring me."

"Nothing." Iona dabbed her eyes with a handkerchief and tried to smile. "I'm just happy, is all."

May imagined she understood the apprehension men felt when being led to the gallows. Her heart thundered erratically. She knew Iona. Those nervous tears were not born from simple happiness. Something earth-shatteringly big was awaiting May in the study . . . and Iona was terrified for her.

May straightened her spine, drew a deep breath, and opened the door leading to the duke's oak-paneled study.

Three faintly familiar, darkly tanned figures beamed smiles in greeting. They were clearly a family. The gentleman stood with his arm lovingly around the lady's waist. A much younger man with unruly black hair tugged at his boots as if they were paining him.

"May, darling? Winnie didn't lied. You have grown into a beautiful woman," the gentleman said.

"May, my sweet May," the lady wailed. "We've come home to stay."

The voice rang like a whisper in a dream. May covered her mouth while staring, unable to believe.

"I think she's in shock," the duke said.

Someone began patting her hand vigorously. May looked and saw it was Iona.

"Who are you?" May whispered the question from behind her hand. She didn't know why she asked such a foolish question when she already knew the answer.

Despite the gray streaks in their hair and the deep bronze hue of their skin, they were the very image of the tiny portraits she'd always worn in her locket.

"Who are you?" she shouted when her gaze latched on to the young man. He couldn't be much older than fifteen or sixteen. His face was a tan, masculine version of her own.

He swaggered up to her and gave an awkward bow. "I am your brother, Perseus."

"Brother?" May was amazed at how calm her voice sounded. "It is a pleasure to make you acquaintance, Mr. Sheffers."

"Oh dear," said her mother, who suddenly felt more like a stranger to May than this boy calling himself her brother. "You're angry."

Angry was a blasted understatement. Her parents had a son. They'd traveled the world while heaping their love on this boy. She hadn't been good enough to keep by their side. They'd left her behind, let her fear they were dead.

Let them go back to their exotic, far-off lands and love *their son*. She'd been happier without them in her life, anyhow.

"May?" Iona whispered. "Lord Evers has arrived."

As if sensing May's need for support, Radford placed his hand protectively on the small of her back. "You look stunning," he murmured in her ear.

May tore her gaze from her parents and slowly turned toward Radford. He was dressed in his finest black suit. His beaver hat gleamed as it sat at an angle on the top of his head. His cane was tucked underneath his arm so he could hold the largest bouquet of wildflowers May had ever seen.

"Would you care to introduce me?" he asked with a nod toward her parents.

"Viscount Evers, I am pleased to introduce Mr. and Mrs. Gaylord Sheffers . . . my parents."

Oh God, her parents were finally home, and she felt absolutely unloved and miserable. This was not at all how she imagined their homecoming.

Hands and arms were smothering her as her mother and then her father embraced her, crying as earnestly as she wished she could. Her eyes remained curiously dry throughout the emotional ordeal.

"I suppose we should explain," her father said after the

duke had ushered them all into the upstairs drawing room where tea had been served.

Radford had directed May to sit on a small sofa. He set the flowers on a sideboard and sat beside her with his hand protectively holding hers. She let him feed her strength while she steeled herself for whatever her parents had to say.

"We wrote," her father said. "We wrote letter after letter explaining our delayed absence. I'd send the letters to a small fishing village in Brazil along with the specimens I'd collected. Only recently did I learn that neither the letters nor the specimens ever found their way to the trading ships in the Caribbean. A man we trusted took payment for this service and threw away our packages. When I confronted him, he tried to kill us and steal what little money we had left. We escaped only to lose our way in the jungle. Years passed before we happened upon a captain of a ship willing to carry us home."

May heard the very logical explanation and accepted it as true. Still, she felt miserable. If not for Radford's steadying presence, she was convinced she'd have stormed from the room like a spoiled child.

"When I heard how Sires had treated you . . ." her mother said. "I cannot tell you how his behavior angers me. I am so sorry we weren't here to protect you. To give you a better life."

"I am content," May said softly.

Her father's gaze narrowed. He looked at Radford as if seeing him for the first time. "Viscount Evers," he said, a lilt of raw emotion alive in his tone, "what interest do you have in my daughter? I am not sure it is at all appropriate for you to sit there and cradle her hand like that."

Radford's protective hold remained firm. "I disagree."

May's father, a tall man who appeared as fit as a man many years his junior, peeled off his gloves. "I don't give a fig if you disagree or not. She is my daughter and I will protect her."

The dam broke. May charged across the room and tossed

herself into her father's arms just as she had when she was four years old and begging him not to leave.

"All these years I feared you didn't love me," she cried. "I feared I wasn't good enough and that's why you didn't take me with you."

"Oh dear God, May." Her father held her tightly in his arms. "We have always loved you. Leaving you was the hardest thing we ever did. I fought against it, but Sires and Winnie convinced us that it would be wrong to endanger you by bringing you along. You deserved a better life than the one a wandering scientist such as I could give. You deserved to be raised as a lady." He set her down and looked her square in the eye. "Never has my love for you wavered. You are my dearest, sweetest little Mayflower."

Those were the words May had somehow forgotten but desperately needed to hear. The day her parents set sail, her father had made her promise to always remember that she was his dearest, sweetest little Mayflower . . . to remember that she would always be loved.

"I remember now, Papa," she said as she wiped away a sheen of tears. "I remember you telling me that no matter what happens, this forever kind of love is always worth the risk." She kissed his cheek and stepped back. Her gaze met Radford's. "Please excuse me a moment. I need to speak with the viscount in private. It is truly something that shouldn't wait."

Radford stammered and blushed as she led him out the room, down the stairs, and into the Newburys' meticulously groomed flower garden. A heavy perfume traveled on the gentle autumn breeze and tickled her nose. May was about to comment on the scent when Radford pressed a finger against her lips.

"I need to explain something to you. And no, it cannot wait for you to go first," he said. "I was a fool. I was so wrapped up in pride and fear I made unreasonable demands on what I wanted and ended up pushing you away. I would have chased after you immediately, but the duke asked me to wait and give you time."

He ducked his head and stole a quick kiss. That brief brush of their lips sent May's beautifully practiced speech flying.

"May, you are very important to me. I would like to court you properly. I will go to your father and beg his permission, if need be. I don't want this to be a burden to you, what with your parents' sudden return, but I have to speak my mind."

He took a step back and sucked in a deep breath. "Miss Margaret Sheffers, I am utterly, completely, and hopelessly in love with you. You are the only woman I would even consider asking to be my wife."

"Oh, Radford," May said with a sigh, "I brought you out here to tell you the very same thing. I shouldn't have let fear and pride keep me from telling you the truth about my feelings. I shouldn't have pushed you away. I love you, too." A great warmth filled her as she spoke the words she'd held hidden for far too long. "How quickly can we get married? We've wasted enough time already; I certainly don't have the patience to wait any longer."

"Nor do I, sweeting," he said with a shout of joy. "If we could manage it, I'd say let's get married today."

Epilogue

The wedding didn't happen right away. Both Radford's mother and May's parents demanded the wedding be a grand affair. Six agonizing months passed before they finally were able to say their vows. Radford penned long romantic letters to May and sent enough flowers to fill several rooms. May wrote him equally romantic letters and embroidered all sorts of handkerchiefs, nightshirts, and linens with his initials and figures of dancing horses.

The extra time gave her a chance to reacquaint herself with her parents and to grow to love her nearly wild brother, Perseus. But still, she lived for the day her life with Radford could finally begin.

"Are you sure you're safe up there?" Aunt Winnie called a year after the blessed wedding day. She was cradling the future viscount in her arms while watching with a twisted grimace as May sat atop a gentle old mare Radford had promised was the kindest of souls.

"She's as safe as if she were in my arms," Radford answered and gave May a look that made her blush from the top of her head to the tips of her toes. Never had she imagined marriage to be so pleasing.

A year had passed since the wedding night and he could still make her legs turn watery with just one heated glance.

Radford's mother reached over Aunt Winnie and fussed with the baby blanket. May watched as the two stubborn women argued over the most beautiful baby she'd ever beheld. He was the very image of Radford.

Thankfully, the dowager Lady Evers had welcomed May into the family, telling her how grateful she was that May had made her son happy again.

"Shall we trot toward the hill?" Radford asked. "I promise we won't stay away from little Henry for long. I can't bear to leave him yet either. But I want you to resume your practice so you will feel comfortable riding."

"As long as I'm by your side, I'm comfortable, Radford."

She watched as he and Princess trotted on ahead of them. Both man and horse moved as gracefully as the wind. May tossed back her head and laughed. She prodded the dappled gray horse into a full run, blasting past Radford. Her bonnet flew off as the wind sailed through her hair.

Within no time, Radford caught up to her. They flew across the field, side-by-side on two wondrous creatures. May had never felt so happy or so wildly free.